I0588279

DANGEROUS ASSUMPTIONS

DANGEROUS ASSUMPTIONS

A MIKE O'SHEA NOVEL

DESMOND P. RYAN

LEVEL
BEST BOOKS

First published by Level Best Books 2025

Copyright © 2025 by Desmond P. Ryan

All rights reserved. No part of this publication may be reproduced, stored or transmitted in any form or by any means, electronic, mechanical, photocopying, recording, scanning, or otherwise without written permission from the publisher. It is illegal to copy this book, post it to a website, or distribute it by any other means without permission.

This novel is entirely a work of fiction. The names, characters and incidents portrayed in it are the work of the author's imagination. Any resemblance to actual persons, living or dead, events or localities is entirely coincidental.

Desmond P. Ryan asserts the moral right to be identified as the author of this work.

Author Photo Credit: Desmond P. Ryan

First edition

ISBN: 978-1-68512-964-4

Cover art by Level Best Designs

This book was professionally typeset on Reedsy.
Find out more at reedsy.com

To those who dare greatly.

Praise for Dangerous Assumptions

"*Dangerous Assumptions* is a terrific addition to Desmond P. Ryan's compelling series. A toxic and amusing mixture of Ryan's knowledge of the way cops talk and think and the humour always at the ready. Mike O'Shea is the kind of cop who readers will cling to and want to follow book after book as he navigates the complex, and very human terrain of crime and justice. A terrific read. "—Robert Rotenberg, bestselling author of *One Minute More*.

Chapter One

11:47 a.m., Monday, April 8, 2019

"How was court?" Carla Hageneur asked, looking over her shoulder at her partner as he walked into the dingy detective office. Her hair, dyed black and cut in a sleek bob, swayed slightly with the movement, brushing against her cheek.

"I wasn't in court. Had a doctor's appointment," Mike O'Shea said.

He set the tray of coffees he'd picked up on the way in on his desk and then took off his trench coat. His lip instinctively curled as the unmistakable odor of body sweat, crack cocaine, and despair—trapped in the office by the permanently sealed windows—assaulted his nostrils. He hooked his coat on the rack in the corner near an unoccupied desk cluttered with half-empty coffee cups, expired property receipts, pocket lint, and god knows what else, forgoing the formality of the wire hanger. Carla's coat, on the other hand, was carefully hung up on the bamboo hanger that she had received when she ordered the coat online.

"Everything okay?" she asked, looking up from the memo book she had been flipping through.

"Yeah," he grunted, grabbing his coffee from the tray before settling into his desk opposite Carla.

The detective office in the Six District station was likely adequate when it was designated as such about fifty years ago, but it was far too small now. There were twelve desks—thirteen including the junker in the corner—set up in two groups of six, two desks facing two, with one desk on either end. One wall was lined with pigeonhole mailboxes and filing cabinets overflowing with case paperwork, while another was stacked with old Crown briefs. A clunky radiator stretched beneath the dirty windows overlooking a pointless courtyard on one side, and the doorway into the office was on the other, surrounded by cluttered filing cabinets full of ancient, unclaimed documents. The running joke was that if a fire broke out, it would take weeks for the firefighters to extinguish it.

"Richard Wajowitz called. He wants to have a case conference with you," Carla said. "Needs to get up to speed."

Mike sighed.

"I know he's not the same, Michael, but he's what they gave us."

"Christ," Mike muttered. Every time he thought of her now, his mind immediately went back to when he first met Bridget Calloway. She had just graduated from law school and turned more than a few heads when she joined the Crown Attorney's Office. Razor-sharp, she quickly became known as one of their brightest prosecutors. Over the next decade or so, Mike and Bridget handled numerous cases together, spending significant time both on and off duty, sharing a mutual spark, energy, and passion for the law. "Like Tracy and Hepburn," Mike's mother often remarked about them. Then, just before she was murdered, something shifted—something Mike couldn't comprehend, and Bridget never had the chance to explain.

"I'm going to look at a place tonight. If it's any good, I'm going to take it," Carla said.

"Great," Mike replied, cracking the lid on his coffee.

"Yes. It's time. More than time. I can't live with you forever, although I do appreciate your hospitality." The only thing still missing in her new life—aside from finding a supply of cute shoes in a women's size fourteen—was a place of her own. "And really, no woman over fifty should be living in her partner's basement."

"Uh-huh," Mike said, taking a sip of his coffee. "Just to be clear: it wasn't exactly my idea, you know."

"Oh, the spirit of Ron Roberts lives on," she said with a wink, recalling

Mike's previous partner, known as much for his curmudgeonly ways as for his eye for detail. "How is he, by the way? I haven't seen him since Marie's funeral, have you?"

"I've talked to him on the phone a couple of times. Been trying to pick a date to go for a beer. He's okay, I guess."

Mike hammered out the alphanumeric sequence of his password on the keyboard, his fingers moving with a mix of irritation and focus. It was a routine he could do without thinking—which was fine by him. After a lifetime of relentless shifts, questionable takeout, and chronic sleep deprivation, he had one last arrest he wanted to make. Then he'd be done. As far as cops went, he wasn't particularly tall or muscular, and the bits of gray in his hair were a subtle reminder of his age. His blue eyes remained sharp, and the fact that he still had all his teeth—remarkable, considering the number of scrapes he'd been in—was a testament to his resilience. But even so, it was time to go.

"Michael, how hard can it be?" Carla said, glaring at him over her half-moon glasses. "He's retired and, from what you've told me, has no outside interests or hobbies. And, from what I've seen, neither do you."

"Whatever."

Carla glanced back at the memo book she'd been leafing through, noticing a crack in the blood-red nail polish on one of her fingers. It had been just over four months since she'd completed her gender affirmation surgery, and this was the first time she'd let her nails slip.

"Thanks for the coffee," she said, wondering what else would start slipping if she wasn't careful.

"No problem."

"Amanda Black has taken over Bridget's case."

"I thought she'd recused herself," Mike said, scrolling through the long list of emails that had been sent to him within the last twelve hours.

"She did, but they...I don't know...un-recused her?"

"This might be one of the few she never solves." He gave up on the emails and opened another window, quickly typing in a name.

Oakes, Malcolm, DOB: December 12, 1968

He waited a minute and then smiled at what he saw on the screen.

Wanted. First Degree Murder

Times two, Mike thought, taking a very satisfying sip of his coffee.

"Hey, boys," the heavy-set uniformed station duty officer called out from the hallway, his voice echoing slightly off the dingy walls. He paused, a flicker of realization crossing his face, then quickly amended, "I mean...boy and girl..." He offered an awkward smile, as if doing so would somehow make a difference.

Mike looked up, his eyes shooting from Carla to the officer and back again.

"It's okay," Carla mouthed to Mike before turning to look at the officer.

"Sorry," the officer said, placing his hand on the door frame. "I'm just not used to having a chick back here."

"We are in the twenty-first century, aren't we?" Carla said with a smile as she looked back across her desk at Mike. "I'm beginning to understand how Julia Vendramini must feel."

"Huh?" the officer said, his face screwing up.

"Never mind," Mike said. "What do you want?"

"There's a call on the board for a suspicious death. Two of them. In a place at the back of a dog groomer's over on Roncey. Uniforms have just been dispatched. Thought you'd want the heads up before the Staff sends you out."

"Looks like we're having drinks to go," Carla said, snapping the plastic lid back on her coffee cup.

"Which is why you never take the lid off a coffee," Mike said, signing off his computer.

"Thanks for the pro tip. Duly noted."

"I'm thinking carbon monoxide," Mike said, snatching both of their coats from the rack.

"Sorry?" Carla asked.

"Likely an illegal apartment, poor ventilation, even worse furnace. Couple of warm days, furnace turned off, pilot light goes out, and here we are."

"Oh, right," Carla replied. "Of course."

Chapter Two

12:01 p.m., Monday, April 8, 2019

"Just to advise all units attending to use extreme caution when entering the location."

"10-4. And who am I speaking with, please?" the dispatcher asked, the dulcet tones of her voice slightly tinged with an affected Southern drawl.

"Detective O'Shea, 3115," Mike said into the radio, having just signed it out from behind the front desk at Six District station. "I'll be heading to the scene as IV2, accompanied by my partner, Detective Hageneur 2305, as soon as we clear the station."

"Wonderful. Thank you for that, Detective. Just a reminder to all attending units from Detective 3115: Use extreme caution when entering the premises."

"Better yet, Dispatcher—have Fire attend with carbon monoxide meters before anyone goes in, please," Mike added.

"Detective 3115 advising all units to use extreme caution," the dispatcher repeated, her voice smooth and almost silky. "Fire on the way."

Mike could feel the muscles in his back tightening as he returned to the D office to get Carla. His back was always tighter after an appointment with Dr Shimner-Lewis.

* * *

As the two detectives pulled up to the address, they saw a couple of firefighters standing by the pumper truck. Mike parked behind their vehicle, and he and Carla walked past the uniformed officer in the back alley leading to the apartment entrance. A second uniformed officer stood in the alley, a third by the door. Two firefighters were inside the tiny apartment.

"You in charge?" one of them asked Mike before the two detectives could enter the scene.

"My partner and I are, yes," Mike replied, his tone clipped but polite. He had quickly grown accustomed to the routine: Carla was either given a once-over from those who couldn't quite place her or was completely overlooked.

"Captain Ansty. All clear. No signs of carbon monoxide. Ambulance has already come and gone, took one of them to the General, I think. One of your officers was in the back with the crew."

"Thank you, sir," Carla replied, extending her hand to shake.

The fire captain hesitated for a moment, eyeing her outstretched hand before shifting his helmet from his right hand to his left and shaking hers. There had been words—along with more than a few unsavory comments—passed around the Hall about the six-foot-four transgender detective, but the captain chose to take the high road.

"Would you mind leaving your names and truck numbers with that officer over there, please?" Carla said with a smile, pointing to one of the uniforms.

"Certainly," he said.

"What do you think?" Mike asked as he and Carla walked into the apartment.

"I have no idea," she said deliberately. She sighed, shaking her head slowly as she took in the scene before her.

Mike stepped through the entrance after her. It was a tiny place. A dump. Filthy. He noticed some stairs along the right-hand wall and assumed they led up to the bedrooms. To the left, a small opening led into the living room.

"I'm going to take a look around," he said, walking past the couch and the decomposing body sprawled across it, careful not to knock the coffee table as he veered closer to the TV perched on a milk carton against the wall. A table—presumably where the occupants ate—partially blocked the doorway to the small kitchen nook. He wasn't surprised by the filth on the electric stove. Out of habit, he opened the fridge. The stench of decay hit him instantly, sharp and sour. He closed it quickly. Everything inside was rotten.

"What's on the other side of this wall?" Carla asked.

"Dog groomers," Mike said. *Must stink like wet dog in here.*

Right now, the air was thick with something worse, and it was almost suffocating. Mike returned to the couch to take a closer look at the deceased. The rotting body was bloated and darkened, bodily fluids dripping from the fingertips, suggesting that the body had been there for a few days. The face, discolored and decomposed, was no longer recognizable. The pulsating sound of the breathing apparatus still attached to it, pushing oxygen into the long-dead lungs, was eerie.

"Ron would have had a field day with this one," Mike muttered, stumbling towards the door.

"Everything okay?" Carla asked, taking a closer look at the body.

"Just need some air."

"Oh. Okay. Well, I'm going to see if I can find any bullet holes or anything like that." She pulled a pair of latex gloves out of her pocket as she crouched very close to the body.

"Watch behind you, eh?" Mike said. "Looks like the remains of the other guy there on the floor."

"Right. Thanks," Carla replied, shuffling a little closer to the corpse on the couch. "Looks kind of slippery, too."

"I'd imagine so," Mike said, standing just outside the door, gulping the outside air. "Are all you former traffic cops like this?"

"Like what?" Carla said, all but poking the bloated body with her finger.

"Never mind," Mike said, his face contorted in disgust.

"I wonder," Carla mused. "Why would the paramedics transport the other body?"

"I'm assuming because he was still alive when they got here, if that's possible."

Carla shifted her attention from the corpse to the coffee table in front of it.

"Hmm."

"What?" Mike asked, returning to the room.

"Lot of meds here."

"Well, I don't suppose you have an oxygen mask strapped to your head if you're healthy," Mike stated.

"True enough. Says these pills are for a Eureka Samuels," Carla said, reading one of the pill bottle labels.

"Then chances are that this is Eureka. Question is, who was here with her?"

Mike began to rummage through some of the papers on the coffee table, hoping to find another name on an envelope or magazine label.

"I don't know, but I'm going to assume that it's the same person who was taken to the hospital," Carla replied, snapping her latex gloves off like a surgeon before stepping away from the couch. "Watch your step, Mike. It seems that you've gotten yourself in the thick of it."

"Shit," Mike said with a grimace, noticing that he was standing almost exactly in the middle of the pool of bodily fluids he'd warned Carla about.

"Well, as long as you can explain it to forensics, not an issue."

"Yes," Mike said. "Remind me to leave my shoes outside when I go home tonight, will you? Don't want to be tracking any of this in the house."

"Right? And Phil will lose his mind licking the—"

"Okay. Enough," Mike said, a wave of disgust washing over him as the image of the Jack Russell his mother had brought with her salivating over his shoes flashed in his mind.

"Sorry. I didn't realize you were so sensitive."

"I'm not sensit—"

"Oh, Christ," the uniformed sergeant muttered from the doorway, stepping back rather than into the apartment as the stench hit him. "What the hell happened here?"

"Your guess is as good as mine," Mike said.

"Do you know who went to the hospital with the body?" Carla asked.

"Singh. Kazaks followed in the scout car."

Mike and Carla looked at one another.

"What?" the sergeant asked.

"Larry Singh? MaryAnn Kazaks?" Mike asked with a smirk.

"Yeah. Why?"

"You've got them as partners?"

"Why not?"

"Aren't they dating?"

"It's a young platoon. They all date each other sooner or later."

"Hrmph," Mike said. "Do we have a name yet on the body that went to the hospital?"

"No, but he's male and they're putting him at between twenty-five and forty."

"That's quite the age spread," Mike said, furrowing his brow.

"He's quite the mess. I've got an officer canvassing the neighbours to see if they know of anyone in that age range who might live here."

"How's he doing?" Carla asked.

"I dunno. He looked pretty dead to me, but the monitor they put on him showed that he had a pulse when they threw him in the back of the ambulance, so...?"

"Do you know if the door was like this when Singh and Kazaks got here?" Mike asked, looking at the popped deadbolt and destroyed framing around it. "I'm assuming they were the first ones on scene?"

"Yeah. They were. Door was secure when they got here, so they waited until Fire arrived and then Fire rammed it open," the sergeant said.

"By the looks of all of these footprints, I'm assuming the entire crew didn't waste any time getting inside," Mike said. "They couldn't have just stood outside and let Singh and Kazaks in, could they?"

"You told them to wait," the sergeant replied.

"I told them to use caution," Mike corrected.

"Well, at least they were more careful than you've been," the sergeant said with a smirk, looking over at the footprint in the bodily fluids.

"Has Homicide been notified?" Carla asked, looking over at Mike but saying nothing.

"Nope. We were waiting for you," the sergeant said, popping a piece of bubble gum in his mouth and then tossing the wrapper into the alleyway.

"I don't think you should be doing that," Carla said.

"What?"

"That wrapper you dropped. Would you pick it up, please? And would you have one of your officers tape off the area about twenty feet to the right of the doorway there where we all came in and secure the area to the left, all the way to the wall on the other side? That's our crime scene until further notice."

"Suit yourself," the sergeant said, bending down awkwardly to retrieve the wrapper before walking back to his scout car.

"I hope you don't mind me being so bossy, Michael," Carla said. "Taking over like that, I mean. I know I'm new to this detective stuff, but really…is it just me or has quality assurance gone out the window?"

"Huh?"

"What part did you miss?"

"All of it," he said absently.

Carla looked a little closer at her partner.

"Are you okay?" Carla asked.

"Yeah. I'm good," he said, shoving his hand into his pants pocket.

"You're not back on those pills, are you?" Carla asked, recalling the Oxycodone Mike had been using to self-medicate when they first became partners a few months ago.

He didn't answer.

"You deserve better," Carla said, biting her lip.

Mike stepped over to the couch.

"How do you turn this thing off?" he asked, staring at the oxygen machine as its rhythmic hum and the clunk of the plunger initiating the next cycle continued.

"Like this." Carla reached over to push the button.

The scene fell silent, as if the woman on the couch had just died, though it was clear that wasn't the case. The two detectives stood motionless, frozen by the weight of the stillness.

"I'll call the Staff at the station and then call Homicide," Carla said, clearing her throat. "Hopefully, they'll be here quickly and we can go to the hospital to see our survivor. Sound like a plan?"

"Sounds like a plan," Mike replied, turning towards the door.

Chapter Three

The General occupied an impressive building for its time and had been extensively renovated over the years. Now, its capacity was strained to its breaking point. Many of the urgent care services had been relocated to neighboring hospitals, but had been brought back due to increased demand. As a result, most funding was allocated to supporting these services rather than maintaining the aging building, and it showed.

"Where's your partner?" Mike asked when he and Carla walked into the emergency room.

"Oh, he just had to go to the washroom," Police Constable MaryAnn Kazak answered. "He'll be right back."

Everyone around the bed knew that Larry Singh was probably retching his guts out, hopefully in a washroom, assuming he had been able to make it that far. Given the circumstances, it could just as likely have been any of them down on their knees, emptying their stomach into the toilet. The scene had been horrendous: two bodies decomposing, the stench from both belching through the front door, and then the shock of one of the bodies being alive. It was enough to make anyone vomit, never mind someone with the constitution of Larry Singh.

"So what do we know?" Mike asked.

"Um," the young officer began, pulling out her memo book, "not much. No positive ID, and, as you can see, not much to go on."

She was right. What both detectives saw before them was a body with a series of tubes stuck into both arms and an oxygen mask on a bloated purply-black face hooked up to a machine that made the same noise as the one Carla had recently turned off. It was evident that this man had lain motionless on the floor, undisturbed, likely for as long as the body on the couch had been there. A clear line of lividity marked where it had set in, crossing his face and visible parts of his body. If Mike hadn't heard the faint blip of the heart monitor and seen a slight rise in an otherwise flat line on the screen, he would have believed this man was as lifeless as the body they had left at the scene.

"Sorry about that, detectives," Larry Singh said as he approached the bed. "Just had to—"

"We understand, don't we, Michael?" Carla said with a warm smile. "Not everyone is good with dead bodies."

"Oh, it's not that," Singh began, blushing slightly. "I just had to—"

"Excuse me. Are you related?" a forty-something woman in grey scrubs, her blue-black hair pulled tight against her head and her arms covered with tattoos, asked, striding towards them.

"No. I'm Detective—" Mike began.

"Then you'll have to leave. Only one visitor at a time, and we're already making an exception," she cut in, looking over at the two uniformed officers.

"We're not visitors," Mike stated.

"In which case," the nurse said, not backing down, "you'll all have to—"

"I'm sorry," Carla began. "I'm Detective Carla Hageneur from Six District. And you are…?"

"Gwen, the nurse in charge of this unit. I'll give you my last name as well if you want to write it down."

"Assuming your patient doesn't die, I don't think we'll need it," Mike said.

"Ron Roberts lives on," Carla mumbled.

"Your choice, Detectives," the nurse said, pursing her lips as she looked from Carla to Mike. "You can leave now, or I can call Security."

"If anything changes, give us a call. And, if he wakes up, we'll be back to talk to him," Mike said to the officers before looking at the nurse and adding sarcastically, "Assuming that's okay with you?"

"That's fine," she said with a sniff. "Provided the patient wants to speak with you, and there's just one of you."

"Good luck with Nurse Ratched," Mike said to the two uniforms. He watched her turn abruptly and walk back to the nursing station, and then looked over at Carla. "Let's go, shall we?"

* * *

"Well, that was unpleasant," Carla said once she and Mike were back in their car.

"What was?" Mike asked, starting up the engine.

"The charge nurse. Or is this how people usually respond to you? Candy?" Carla reached into her purse to pull out a package of Werthers.

"Sure," Mike said, taking one before putting the car in gear. "If our boy comes to in the next few hours, assuming he wakes up at all, I'm thinking it'll be Russ McLean talking to him."

"Oh no."

"Yeah," Mike said with a laugh. "Seeing the charge nurse handle him would be worth the price of admission alone."

Mike navigated the narrow streets towards the station while Carla gazed out her side window. The SUVs and pickup trucks parked along the curbs had replaced the smaller cars these roads were originally built for, making the streets even tighter. As pleasant as the candy was, Mike wished he'd popped one of the oxys he had in his pocket. He wasn't in any immediate pain, but he craved something to dull his senses. He couldn't quite pinpoint what was bothering him; he just knew he wanted to numb out.

"Do you want to grab a coffee before we go back?"

"Hmm?"

"A coffee," Carla replied. "Do you want to get one before we go back?"

"Sure. I suppose you'll want one of those fancy ones?" Mike asked, noticing an upscale coffee shop just ahead.

"Absolutely. You have to seize life's simple pleasures when and where you can."

"If you say so," Mike said as he parallel parked the car in front of the shop.

"Simple pleasures," Carla said, getting out of the car.

Although they had only driven a couple of blocks, this coffee shop was in a distinctly different neighbourhood from the one near the hospital. Mike held the door open for a young woman pushing a stroller that likely cost her more than his truck was worth as she exited the shop. Inside, he noticed a small group of men and women lounging on a couple of couches near the back, one of whom had a newborn swaddled against his chest in a sling. Carla moved past Mike, placing their order before motioning for Mike to take a seat on a stool overlooking the street.

"So, what do you think?" Carla asked as she joined Mike, drinks in hand.

"About what?"

"Are you even here today, Michael?" Carla asked, sipping her latte.

"Sorry. I'm a bit...I don't know. Sorry." He rubbed his neck before taking a sip of his Americano.

"How was your appointment with Shimner-Lewis?"

"Fabulous," Mike said sarcastically. Although it was meant to be confidential, it was common knowledge that he had been directed to see the service's psychologist a few months ago. His outward objections barely concealed his awareness that he wasn't handling things as well as he should have, even before Bridget's murder. He suspected that Lisa Clayton's death had pushed him over, though if he took Rachel's word—he and the doctor were on a first-name basis—he had likely been struggling long before that.

"Does she know about the pills?" Carla asked, watching a woman juggling a tray of coffees and a bag of pastries with one hand while holding her coffee in the other, while her husband stood outside on the sidewalk.

"Huh?"

"The oxys, Michael. Does she know you still use them?"

"Oh." Mike looked down at his coffee. "No."

"So you are?"

"You got me there, partner," he said with a laugh.

"I can't imagine what it's been like for you, Michael."

"Having both you and my mother crash at my place has been a challenge."

"Seriously, Michael. I don't know of anybody else on the job who's had their partner die in their arms."

Mike felt as if he'd been dropped into an ice bath.

"So nobody would blame you, but she should know you're using again."

Mike could suddenly feel the weight of Sal's body sagging against his own as clearly as if it were happening right now. He could feel Sal's head—what was left of it—on his shoulder. He could smell the gunpowder, and his ears began to ring. He could—

"Michael?" Carla's voice cut in.

"Huh?" he said, giving himself a mental shake.

"Let's just get ourselves back to the station, okay?"

"Yeah," he said, wiping the sweat from his forehead. "Sure."

Chapter Four

"It's a homicide, folks," Detective Ralph Crowley advised, ducking his head as he walked into the detective office.

"Holy shit, Ralph. How tall are you?" Mike asked, looking up from his computer screen.

"Six-eight. Just a little guy," he said with a grin. "Anyway, Mama was definitely murdered."

"Mama?" Carla asked, turning slightly to see him as she closed the bottom right-hand drawer of her desk while wiping the last bit of hand cream in.

"Eureka Samuels, although she was known as 'Mama'. Actually, she wasn't really known at all because she was fundamentally housebound and had no one except her son, Seth, who took care of her. Hence the moniker."

"And Seth is the guy—" Mike said, moving his mouse to click the SAVE icon on the Crown Request form he had just opened. "You'd think they'd have autosave on these forms by now, wouldn't you?"

"Yep. He lived with her and was her primary...only...caregiver. He's still in a coma, though."

"How do you know it was murder?" Carla asked, reaching for the coffee on her desk and snapping the little piece of plastic that covered the sip hole. "You see, Michael? Just in case." She took a sip. "Sorry, Ralph. If I'd known you were going to be here...."

"Oh, no, I'm fine," he said. "I've got one on the way."

"So, murder," Carla continued, taking a sip of coffee. "How do you know? We looked at the body, or what was left of it, and didn't see anything out of the ordinary."

Ralph shifted back into a serious demeanor as he stated, "It wasn't the body that was out of the ordinary. It was her oxygen tank. Seems someone has tampered with it."

"That may have been," Mike slowly began, "us."

"Huh?" Ralph said, inadvertently looming over Mike just by virtue of standing close to his desk.

"It was actually me who turned it off," Carla confessed, reaching down and opening the drawer she'd just closed to pull a pair of half-moon glasses out of her purse.

"I asked her to," Mike added.

"Good to know," Ralph said as his lips tightened, looking at the two detectives more like petulant children. "But we kind of assumed that somebody had, and now we can eliminate at least one set of prints we should find on that valve. The real problem, though, is the bit of cheesecloth we found over the line at the nipple adapter by the flow regulator."

"Of course," Carla said, rolling her eyes as she put the glasses on. "Why didn't we see that?"

"I know, right?" Ralph said with a self-deprecating grin. "You'd have to look pretty close. "My guess is that the cheesecloth not only slowed the air, but that it had been soaked in something used to poison her."

"Why?" Mike asked, rolling his chair away from Ralph.

"When the forensics officer removed the cloth, it was pink in the middle."

"Which means...?" Mike asked.

"Dunno. We'll have to wait for Tox, but I don't imagine it's a good thing," Ralph said, stepping back towards the door.

"But you do think she was murdered," Mike said.

"No other explanation for that cloth being in the tube where it was, unless Sonny-Boy can tell us something to the contrary."

"If he wakes up," Carla said, glancing over at Ralph.

"Well, yeah," Ralph said. "Blood work shows that he's chock-o-block full of cocaine and a cocktail of other drugs. They've got Mama's list of meds now and will be doing a quick scan to see if any of those are in the mix."

"Is it possible," Mike said, "that he killed his mother and tried to kill himself?"

"Anything's possible, Mike. It's early days, although the one thing we do know is that there was at least one other person in that apartment prior to her death."

"The place has been printed already? Wow," Mike exclaimed, looking at his watch as he considered how long it took district detectives to get results back from forensics. "Must be nice."

"No. The woman who has the dog grooming place on the other side saw Sonny-Boy come home with a woman a couple of nights ago."

"She was watching?" Carla asked, checking the lid on her coffee cup before taking another sip. "That's not creepy."

"Well, no. At least, I didn't get that impression from her. It was more that she wasn't used to seeing him with anyone, let alone a woman, that made her take note. And that they were both fairly lit."

"And so...?" Mike asked.

"Don't know, but that was the last time the dog groomer saw anyone coming or going from the laneway. I'm thinking we should find this mystery woman's prints in the apartment, and we can go from there. Whether or not they're on the oxygen tank is another story."

"That's assuming her prints are on file," Mike said, stating the obvious.

"Well, at least that gives you a bit of a timeline," Carla said.

"Gotta start somewhere," Ralph said, reaching into his jacket pocket. He pulled out a cell phone that looked like a child's toy in his huge hand. "Excuse me. It's the boss. Hello, Amanda."

Ralph ducked as he stepped around the corner into the hallway.

"Ugh," Carla said as she took the plastic lid off the cup. "I don't trust this thing to stay put, and the last thing I need is to dump hot coffee all over myself this morning. I sure hope Amanda's the lead on this."

Detective Sergeant Amanda Black was one of, if not *the* best, investigators in the Homicide Unit. Known in equal parts for her tenacity, no-bullshit approach, and towering stiletto heels, she alternately intimidated new officers and suspects alike while impressing the hell out of both prosecutors and defense attorneys. She also had quite a history with Mike and, by association, now Carla.

"Given that he was likely her only caregiver, the kid's prints will be all over the tank," Mike said as he returned to filling out the form on his computer. "Pretty hard to prove he tampered with it."

"That's why we call in the Big Guns," Carla said, opening an email on her computer. "Oh, for goodness sake! You'd think someone could have told me that this officer was off on parental leave the first four times I requested his notes!"

"Amanda's at the scene now," Ralph said, coming back into the office. "Says she's on her way to the station. Can you get your notes done up and put a photocopy of them in the box at the front desk sooner than later, please?"

"I thought this new system we're using was supposed to get rid of all of this paper," Carla said.

"It does," Ralph said. "Some dinosaurs just haven't acclimatized themselves to the new way of doing things and like a hard copy to refer to."

"I hope Amanda doesn't hear you say that," Mike said with a laugh.

"I was referring to you, Mike," Ralph said. "Oh, and Amanda told me to tell you that she's going to bring you two in on the investigation if the autopsy shows no natural cause of death."

"Sure," Mike said with a nod.

"So why would the son OD?" Carla asked, clicking on the next email in the dozen or so that had accumulated since yesterday afternoon.

"I'm not saying he did," Ralph said. "Maybe it was the woman he brought home."

"Tried to kill them both?" Mike asked. "Sounds like a longshot to me."

"Your guess is as good as mine at this point and, as Amanda Black says, we don't get paid to guess in Homicide," Ralph said.

"What if," Carla began, "this woman was someone Seth was actually involved with?"

"So she tried to kill them both because…?" Mike let his words hang.

"I don't know. Life insurance policy?" Carla offered.

"I don't think people like them have life insurance policies," Mike muttered.

"Maybe not, but you never know. We're not making any assumptions, so that's certainly something we'll be looking into," Ralph assured them.

"What if," Make said, "the kid tried to kill himself *after* the mother was murdered?"

"Dunno. I gotta say, though: things were a lot more straightforward in Hold-Up," Ralph said. "Ah, well. Career move. How are you feeling these days, Mike? Heard you got into quite a tussle with our Mr. Blackmore a while back."

"Yeah. For a burned-out politician, he was pretty feisty," Mike said. He stretched his neck, letting out a little grunt. "Head is getting better. Still not one hundred percent, but you know…. Thanks for asking."

Carla looked over her monitor. She gave Mike a sharp look. It was not lost on Ralph.

"You two still living together?" Ralph asked, playing into what had become a joke among their colleagues. After returning to work following gender affirmation surgery, Carla ended up living in her car. Though it was Ron Roberts' suggestion, it was Mike's mother, Mary-Margaret, who had insisted that Carla move into Mike's big old house. And so she did. And every cop in the city seemed to know it.

"Jesus," Mike said. "Does nobody on this job have a life?"

"I'm looking for my own place," Carla said.

"Shouldn't be that hard," Ralph said.

"Renting While Trans," Carla said with a forced smile. "It's a thing."

"Oh," Ralph said. He shifted his weight from one foot to the other and then cleared his throat. "Well, I'll go see if Amanda's here yet. She's got both your cell numbers, right? Just in case she wants you?"

"We'll be right here," Mike said.

"Great. I'll give you Amanda's cell…"

"Same as last time?" Carla interrupted.

"Yep."

"Then we've got it. Thanks."

Chapter Five

7:25 a.m., Tuesday, April 9, 2019

"Oh poo!" Carla exclaimed.

"Everything alright?" Mike asked, a feeling of fatigue starting to creep over him. He had not slept well the night before. After her comment yesterday, he had tossed out the oxys in his pocket on the way home and, to calm his nerves after dinner, had made his way to the pub around the corner for a pint. Or two. Or, as it turned out last night, five or maybe six.

"Yes," she sighed, reaching into the bottom right-hand drawer of her desk for her purse. "I almost forgot that I have Court today, so I better get going."

"You've got matters up in Court already?" he said with a yawn, leaning back in his chair to stretch. "I thought it would take a while before—"

"It's one of Ron's," she said, referring to a case that she had taken over from her predecessor. "I just hope it's not a trial. I'm not sure I'm ready to handle that yet."

"You'll be fine, but I'm sure the Crown would have given you the heads-up if it was going to be."

"Well, I'll have my cell phone with me and keep you updated," Carla said, gathering up her things.

"I'll be okay," Mike said, though he wasn't sure he believed it. Just as he had come to depend on the pills and booze, he'd begun leaning on her to get through the day-to-day.

"Wish me luck," she said, grabbing her coat from the rack in the corner.

"Upstairs for Parade, you two," Detective Sergeant Black said, poking her head in the doorway.

"Sorry, Amanda," Carla said as she brushed by her. "I'm off to court."

"You better hurry," Amanda said, looking at her watch. "Traffic this time of day is brutal."

"I know!" Carla said as she rushed out the back door.

"Well, I guess it'll just be you, then, Crumply Pants," Amanda said. She stopped and sniffed. "Is that you or me? Smells like stale booze, so it must be you. Go brush your teeth or douse yourself with aftershave or something before you join us, okay?"

Mike stopped into the men's changeroom before heading to the lunchroom, where the uniform platoon officers were preparing to receive their details for the day. Gone were the days of stand-up parades, when the staff sergeant and parading sergeant would scrutinize each officer, ensuring they had all their equipment—and checking for signs of alcohol. Mike figured it was for the best.

Now, the uniformed officers who looked like kids sat at the lunch tables, designer coffees in hand, as if it were a social gathering. Roll call was no longer bellowed out by last name, but gently spoken using first names. The only thing that stayed the same were the assigned details: guard an overnight crime scene, go to another division to help with a victim translation, or quickly clear the station to start responding to the backlog of radio-calls in pending.

This morning, Detective Sergeant Amanda Black was sitting beside the parading sergeant, ready to update the officers on the Samuels homicide, known internally as Homicide 95 for 2019.

"Good morning, boys. And girl," Amanda looked pointedly at MaryAnn Kazak, the only woman on the platoon. "I'd like to first thank you for doing an excellent job securing the scene at yesterday's homicide. For those of you who weren't here, officers were alerted to the scene by a neighbour who noticed a bad smell. A very bad smell. Upon entering the unit, officers found what appeared to be two dead bodies in a state of decomposition.

Your Detectives, O'Shea and Hageneur, attended the scene. Thank you for joining us this morning, Detective O'Shea."

Mike nodded.

"As you likely already know," Amanda continued, "one body, belonging to a sixty-eight-year-old woman named Eureka Samuels, was quite deceased. It also appears that she was murdered. The other body, if you will, was— is—still alive. This body belongs to a twenty-eight-year-old male named Seth Samuels, whom we believe to be the son of Eureka Samuels. Mr. Samuels remains in critical condition at the General. Now, I know that a couple of you guarded him at the hospital yesterday, and we've had officers on him all night, but we are going to discontinue that detail as of today."

A collective sigh of relief passed through the room.

"However," Amanda added, "we are going to be detailing someone to check in at the hospital to see how Mr. Samuels is doing every four hours or so. Because you are available, Detective O'Shea, the Staff has suggested that you do that for today. He's been moved to the fourth-floor ICU."

"What?" Mike objected.

"Fourth floor. ICU," Amanda repeated. She gave him a look that made it clear that she was not prepared to discuss the matter any further.

"Pfff," Mike said.

"At this point," Amanda said, turning her attention back to the uniformed officers, "we do not know the cause of death for Eureka Samuels. We have reason to believe that it was a drug overdose of some kind, intentionally caused by a person or persons unknown. We do not know what happened to Mr. Samuels, although we do know that he has a high level of cocaine in his blood stream, as well as a shitload of other drugs, the origins of which we are trying to determine as I speak. We don't know why or how these drugs got into his bloodstream, but we're looking for at least one other individual—a woman—who may have been in the apartment. I don't have details on her yet, but when I do, you'll all be notified. That's all I've got for now."

Amanda looked up at the officers, some of whom looked back at her, others checked their phones, or looked down at the table in front of them.

"I'm sure there is nothing more important at…7:46 am than the details

24

surrounding my homicide, officer," Amanda said, looking pointedly at one of the officers on his phone. "You're on company time now and, if you ever want to get into my unit or any other sexy unit, you won't be looking at your phone during a briefing. Understood?"

"Uh, yes," the officer stammered, his face crimson.

"Good. And one more thing," she said, addressing the room. "We found an inhaler at the scene that does not appear to be a part of the many medications Eureka Samuels was taking, nor prescribed to Seth Samuels. The name has been scratched off the dispenser, but we need to find out whose it was."

"Could be any crack whore's pipe," a voice interjected, referring to the practice among street-level sex workers of using discarded plastic inhalers as crack pipes.

"That's exactly what we're thinking. Some of you will be detailed to canvas the neighbours."

There was a collective groan.

"It is my belief," Amanda continued, "that, after you've completed this task today, I will have a better picture of who the deceased was in life. I also hope to discover what young Seth's life looked like and who he knew. For the purposes of my investigation, I will need to know both Eureka and Seth Samuels as well as if they were my best friends. It's your canvassing that's going to help me paint that picture. I'm telling you this to impress upon you how vitally important your efforts are."

Amanda paused and looked at each officer.

"Thank you, Officers. And I'm glad to see that, while they've changed the times for morning parades, not much else has changed since I was the Parading Sergeant doing them."

Amanda got up and walked out of the room, motioning for Mike to follow her as she went.

"What's up?" he asked in the hallway.

"I just want you to know that it was the Staff's idea to have you check in at the hospital every few hours today, not mine. He said that you are kind of on light duties still and thought it would give you something to do."

"I *have* something to do. Carla's in Court all day today, so any bodies that come in under arrest will be mine to process. I don't have time to run out to the hospital three times today."

"Sorry, Mike. I'm just following the Staff's lead on this one. And I still need your notes on the Blackmore case. Oh, and have you spoken to the union lawyer yet?"

"No. Why should I?"

The best defense is a good offense, and given his nature and status, Mr. Blackmore is likely to become very offensive. The arrest seemed pretty clean to me, but I wouldn't be surprised if he spins it into a full-blown Donnybrook—excessive force, assault, you name it. You'd be wise to be proactive here. Blackmore has a lot of powerful friends with deep pockets. Do yourself a favor and make the call."

"Yeah. Okay." Mike's head throbbed. He couldn't tell if it was from the injuries sustained during that arrest, the pints from last night, or the lack of Oxy. Either way, it wasn't a good feeling.

"Anyway, look in on Seth Samuels. Try to sweet-talk the nurses so we can trust them to give us a call if he wakes up. None of us have the time for this kind of babysitting. It's so much easier when they're under arrest...it's like pulling teeth to get the uniform staff sergeants to send a couple of guys to watch a victim. Anyway, I have an 8 o'clock with the unit commander, so you might as well make your first trip now. Good luck on your day, and call me if our boy wakes up."

"Sure," Mike muttered, wandering back downstairs to the office.

"And Mike?" Amanda called down the stairwell.

"Yeah?"

"Pick up some breath mints before you go to the hospital."

* * *

"You still here?" Mike said, seeing Carla walking up the hallway from the back doors, a key attached to a miniature hockey stick in her hand.

"Car needed gas," she said. "Can you be a doll and take this up to the front for me? I don't have time."

"Why didn't you just take one of the other cars?" Mike said, taking the stick and key from her.

"Keys were nowhere to be found," she called as she barged through the back door.

"That's not good," Mike muttered to himself, hooking the key ring on the hook by the front desk. On paper, the detective office had four unmarked cars available to them but, on any given day, at least one was in the shop and another was loaned out to another divisional squad who needed cars for something. That should have left two, which would be fine. If one of them was missing…?

He returned to the detective office and went immediately to Russ McLean's unlocked desk drawer, where he found the keys to 02, a dark burgundy four-door Ford Taurus.

Bastard.

The first thing Mike did when he started the car was open the windows to release the smell of cigarette smoke and, quite likely, Russ McLean's body odor. Smoking in police vehicles was forbidden, but maintaining one's personal hygiene wasn't. Clearly, Russ McLean had the rules mixed up. Fortunately, the General wasn't far from the station because the morning rush hour, which went from about 6:30–10:00, was already in full swing.

He's not going anywhere soon anyway, Mike thought as he made his way to the hospital, parked the car in the 'Police Only' spot, pulled out the portable police light, and placed it on the inside front dash.

Without even thinking, Mike wandered in through the emergency doors, reached around the nursing station to buzz himself into the emergency room, walked through, and ended up at a set of staff-only elevators. He paused while he waited for the elevator, recalling Amanda's suggestion to pick up some mints. Watching the numbers decrease above the elevator, he chose to disregard it, getting into the elevator along with a couple of people wearing scrubs. No one challenged him. He waited until the elevator stopped on the fourth floor and got off, making his way to the intensive care unit. From there, he proceeded through the automatic doors to bed seventeen, where Mr. Seth Samuels lay, ventilator pumping air into him.

Mike's mind shot back to the sound in the apartment yesterday.

He blinked a couple of times and then sat down in the chair beside the bed, a seat typically reserved for the most immediate family members. Mike was used to occupying that position. In his years of policing, he had often been the only one who seemed to care about his victims—at least the kinds of people who typically found themselves in his case files. Somehow, caring had become part of the job.

He looked around the unit. It was eerily silent. All twenty-four beds were full, some with people who, like Seth Samuels, looked dead, others appearing slightly more alive and sleeping soundly, most likely as a result of being heavily medicated. Most patients had someone sitting beside the bed, the majority of whom looked as bad, if not worse, than the people they were keeping a vigil over. How quickly life changes, he thought.

Mike looked over at the body on the bed beside him. His face was still discolored in the way a rotting body gets discolored.

Lying face-down for over forty-eight hours would cause blood to pool, whether you were alive or dead, Mike thought. *Especially if your heart's not beating that fast.*

He had never seen anything like that before and could see how the first officers on scene would think he was dead. And now, the kid was being pumped full of god-knows-what that was rehydrating him, stabilizing his heartbeat, and, hopefully, bringing him back to life, whatever that life might look like.

But not any time soon.

Mike took another look at the kid's face before getting up and heading back to the elevator. He'd initially hoped the kid would regain consciousness, sparing him from having to babysit, but seeing the state he was in, Mike resigned himself to making a few more trips today.

He left the hospital, the cool air of the late morning a sharp contrast to the sterile quiet of the ICU. He picked up a coffee and drove back to the station, where he slipped into autopilot mode. He processed a couple of arrests that were more of an inconvenience than anything else, made a couple of trips back to the hospital to check on Seth Samuels, and plowed through the backlog of paperwork.

No word from Carla.

Mike signed out when his relief arrived, drove home, and parked his old truck in front of his house. He didn't bother going in. Instead, he walked down the street to the pub.

He liked it there. He liked sitting at the bar, talking to the bartender, the other regulars.

Everyone likely knew he was a cop, but nobody asked any questions. He liked that.

Nobody asked about his time in the Juvenile Prostitution Task Force, about the girls they never saved, or his final case with the unit—the one that should have been a slam dunk.

Except his partner got himself killed. And the fucker who shot him got away with it. And Chelsea Hendricks, the girl who sparked the investigation, was never found. And Mike had been chasing shadows ever since.

Nobody asked anything about that. He liked that.

Five quick pints and no dinner later, Mike weaved home, dragged himself up the stairs, and passed out in his bed. It was 8 o'clock at night.

Chapter Six

9:00 a.m., Wednesday, April 10, 2019

"Good morning, everyone," Detective Sergeant Amanda Black said, looking at the half a dozen uniformed officers, eight men in old clothes, and Mike and Carla. She then looked at the walls of the Major Crime office. She paused before taking a breath, partly due to the pervasive stench of unwashed bodies and various unidentifiable odors lingering in the air, and partly because she was annoyed to be confronted by what she saw. She knew that this was not a hill she was willing to die on, but she couldn't let it go. "If I'm going to be spending this much time here, I shudder to think that I may have to take on an operational supervisory role. Please save me the trouble of documenting you MCU boys by either stopping people from getting murdered in this division or cleaning up the offensive materials on the walls. Since you have no control, I'm assuming, over the former, I'd suggest you manage the latter."

"Yeah, Nerdster," Billy-Bob, a burly officer who could easily pass as a member of ZZ Top, said. "Get yer smut off our walls."

Nerdster, or Theodore Weinstock, a youthful-looking officer known for his button-down shirts and tasselled loafers, rolled his eyes, having grown accustomed to his partner's teasing.

"And I know the windows are painted shut, but could you at least leave the door open once in a while or learn to manage your flatulence a bit better, please?" Amanda added.

"That's all on you," Nerdster said to Billy-Bob.

Pending the return from mat leave of the lone female officer in the unit, the MCU was an all-male domain, just as it always had been prior to her arrival. Given the self-generated mystique of the unit and the cloak-and-dagger nature of the investigations the officers often embarked on, the physical space of the office itself seemed always to be off-limits to the usual levels of supervision at the station as well as, more often than not, the janitorial staff. As such, the room looked and smelled more like a cross between a pubescent boy's bedroom and a by-the-hour motel room than an investigative office within a police facility.

"And now for the business part of this meeting," Amanda said. She opened her daytimer. "As you may know, a sixty-eight-year-old woman now known to be Eureka Samuels was found dead in her apartment. Seth Samuels, her twenty-eight-year-old son, who resided with her and, we have since discovered, was her primary caregiver, is currently in critical condition in the ICU at the General. We have reason to believe that the woman's death was a homicide. We also have reason to believe that the son overdosed on drugs, but we don't know if it was intentional or not, or if the overdose is tied to her death or not. We also don't know if he will regain consciousness. What we do know is that there was an unknown woman in the apartment prior to the time of the death of our victim. I want you to find out who she is and bring her in."

Amanda looked at Ricky Jergensen, who was standing by the side wall with the five other foot patrol officers.

"Yes, Constable, you heard me correctly," Amanda stated.

All eyes shifted towards him. The then-D/C Jergensen's hasty and arguably unlawful arrest of one of Amanda's former homicide suspects had become almost legendary throughout the city. Equally renowned was Mike O'Shea's decisive knockout of Jergensen in the station's cell area. Jergensen's being back in uniform was his punishment for his part in the debacle. Had Mike not been brutally beaten shortly thereafter by the same suspect, he would likely also be back in uniform, but as a patrol sergeant.

"Bring. Her. In. And, if I'm not here, call Homicide and have them page me. I need to talk to this woman sooner than later. In the meantime, I need someone from this office to sit by Seth Samuel's bed until he wakes up or I tell you otherwise. Theodore—"

"We're practically family now, Amanda. You might as well call him Nerdster," Billy-Bob said.

"While this isn't the family I'd have chosen, I'll take that as a compliment. Okay, Nerdster, you look the least scary of everyone here, so you'll take the first shift. The rest of you: sort it out, but please clean up a bit before taking over. In the meantime, find my mystery woman."

Amanda got up and left the office.

"That was quick," Mike said, hurrying after her.

"Not much to say," she said, not slowing her stride. "And I honestly don't know how much longer I could take the stench in there. Do they not have bathroom privileges here?"

"Detective Sergeant?" the front desk uniformed officer called to her. "Someone here to see you."

Amanda turned and saw the local news truck parked in front of the station through the glass doors at the front of the station.

"No. Just...no. Mike, I want you or Carla, I don't care which one of you, to go speak to Janelle Austin and tell her that we've got nothing for her yet, please. On second thought," Amanda said, looking at Mike, "get Carla to do it."

"Do what?" Carla said from a few steps behind.

"Talk to Janelle Austin. She's waiting out front."

"She's still after me to talk about—"

"I know," Amanda said. "And the more she sees you in a professional capacity as a police detective, the less she'll see you as—"

"Amanda?" the front desk officer called back to her.

"Detective Hageneur will be right up," she called back, unclipping her iPhone from her belt to check a message.

"Go get 'em, Tiger," Mike said as he and Amanda continued into the detective office.

"I want you to speak to the woman at the dog groomers," Amanda said as she sat down at the desk she'd commandeered beside Mike's. "They own the building and have a key to the apartment. I need you to go in and find whatever you can for next-of-kin."

"The scene's been released?"

"Just," she said, responding to a message on her iPhone. "If I'd known they were going to be this quick, I would have had one of you there while they were finishing up. Doesn't matter. The dog groomers are friendlies."

"Okay," Mike said, getting his coat from the rack in the corner. "Do you want me to wait for Carla?"

"No," Amanda said. "Your Staff is already pissed because I'm stripping him of all of his officers. He'll want her to stay back and look after anything that comes in."

"Fair enough," Mike said, looking down at is watch. "Shop's likely open, so I'll see what I can find out. Any updates on the Calloway murder?"

Amanda stared at Mike.

"I take that as a no?" he said.

"Take that as an I-couldn't-tell-you-if-I-wanted-to. You know that, so don't ask me again."

"We all know it was Malcolm Oakes," Mike said.

"Mike, I know—"

"You know fuck all," he snapped.

For the second time in less than an hour, Amanda paused before speaking.

"I've known you for too long and too dearly to react to that," Amanda said, her voice slow and steady. "And we're in private. But don't ever speak to me like that again, private or not."

She turned on her heels and walked out of the room, leaving Mike behind. He stood there for a moment, then reached into his pocket, his fingers skimming the fabric. He came up with only some loose change and his car keys.

My sweetest friend, what have I become?

Chapter Seven

10:05 a.m., Wednesday, April 10, 2019

"Hang on," a woman's voice called out from the back of the dog groomers. "I'll be with you in a minute."

"No rush," Mike called back.

"How can I help you?" a thirty-ish pink-haired woman with numerous facial piercings said as she came around the front.

"Detective O'Shea," Mike said, pulling out his badge and holding it up for her to see. "I'm here about your tenants."

"Oh. Just a sec. I'll get Susan. She's just in the office downstairs." Without moving, the woman simply hollered, "Suze!"

"Thanks," he said, looking at all the dog toys, treats, collars, and leashes that hung on the walls.

"You have a dog? You look like a dog person."

"No," he said, and then thought about Phil. "I mean, yes. I suppose I do."

"Dog share?"

"Pardon?"

"With your ex. Week with Mommy, week with Daddy?"

"No," Mike said, wishing he'd picked up those mints. "It's my mother's neighbor's dog."

"Now that's a share. What kind?"

"Jack Russell."

"Busy dogs," she said, directing Mike to a group of toys lining one wall.

"You're going to want to get…him? Her?"

"Him."

"Something like this. Especially if he's a chewer. Is he a chewer?"

"Not that I'm aware of," Mike said, now considering whether Phil was a chewer and this was yet another thing his mother was keeping from him.

"And one of these travel bags is great," she continued, motioning towards another wall. "Especially if he's going from your mother's to your place a lot. Dogs, especially small dogs, like to feel secure in the car."

Mike looked at the price tag.

"It's a little pricy, but it's worth it," she said, noticing the look on Mike's face. "You don't want your best friend to be anxious."

"A bit late for that, I think." Mike started to feel the muscles in his neck tightening.

"Can you check to make sure we've got lots of dry towels in the back, please, Menga. We've got Anthony and Cleo coming in shortly, and I know their owner'll want to pick them up just after noon. I tell her that they won't be completely dry, but you know how she is. Oh, hello," a heavy-set woman who had just entered the room said, holding her hand out to Mike. "I'm Susan Stang. Most people just call me Suze."

"Detective O'Shea," Mike said, showing his badge again. "Is there some place where we can talk?"

"Sure. I'm assuming this is about Eureka and Seth? My god, if I'd only known. Follow me." Not waiting for a response, Suze turned and walked into the back. She stopped at a staircase. "Mind your head."

Mike ducked slightly as he followed her down the steep stairs into an unfinished basement, its walls lined with boxes of dog supplies.

"Have a seat, Detective," Suze said as she sat down, pointing to a wooden chair beside a desk that was cluttered with papers and old coffee cups from the shop around the corner. "And don't mind the mess. I'm usually much more organized, but it's been crazy-busy these last few weeks with everyone wanting to get their dogs ready for the warmer weather. Always is this time of year. Now I'm thinking you probably want to see the lease agreement for that back apartment. It's just in this drawer here."

Mike sat down while Suze pulled out a file folder from the drawer and produced the document. She handed it to him.

"They've been here a while," Mike said as he glanced at it. "Must have been good tenants."

"Lovely people," Suze said. "Which is why it makes what happened even worse."

"How well did you know them?"

"Pretty well, I'd say. I live above the shop, so I'd see them often."

"Them?"

"Mostly Seth. He's the one I saw mostly. Eureka was housebound, as I'm sure you figured out."

"Why was she housebound?" Mike asked.

"Well, I know she had emphysema, which is why she had the oxygen, and I think there were a few other things going on with her. When they first moved in, I didn't expect that they'd be here more than a couple of years, to be honest."

"Did the son work?"

"No, he was unemployed. Well, no, that's not fair to say. He looked after his mother."

"Nobody else looked after the deceas—Eureka Samuels?"

"No, not at least from…" she said, leaning towards him to point out the date on the lease, "2013, so…."

"He was young," Mike said, counting back in his mind, his thoughts drifting back to what he himself was doing at twenty-two.

"Young to be a full-time caregiver to such a sick mom, yeah." Suze sat back in her chair.

"So where did they get their money? I'm assuming you wanted some sort of guarantee that they could cover rent."

"You bet I did. I'm nice, but not that nice." She smiled at Mike, who smiled back. "Eureka's daughter gave me a year's worth of rent up front with the agreement that she'd continue to cover it for however long her mother needed it."

"And did she?"

"Sure did."

"A year in advance, or did she go month to month?" he asked.

"Year in advance. And she included a five percent increase every year."

"That must have suited you."

"Sure did. I'm divorced and on my own. When my ex and I split seven years ago, I took everything I had, mortgaged myself up to my eyeballs, and bought this building. It was a disaster. Just a long room with a crappy apartment above it. I built the apartment in the back, put my dog grooming business in the front, and fixed up the place upstairs. All in less than twelve months. Getting that much rent in one lump sum was a godsend. Having it every year all at once like that has been a game-changer. Thanks to Eureka Samuels's daughter and the loyal dog owners in the area, Detective, I now own this building outright. Everything else is gravy."

"Sounds like it," Mike said.

"Yep," she said, leaning back in her chair. "And the people in this neighbourhood sure love spending money on their dogs. Do you have one, Detective?"

"Yeah," he said, wondering if he was starting to believe it. "A Jack Russell."

"Funny, I pictured you more as a big dog kind of guy," she said. "What else do you want to know? I don't mean to rush you, but I've got a lot of dogs coming in to get groomed today."

"I'm curious about Seth," Mike said.

"That boy was devoted to his mother, let me tell you. He cooked for her, cleaned the apartment–"

"I'm sure that didn't take up all of his time, though?" Mike said, mentally reviewing what the apartment had looked like.

"I'm thinking most of his time was spent taking care of his mother. He took her to all of her appointments, picked up her meds, did everything for her. And I mean," Suze said with a nod, "everything."

"That must have been difficult for him," Mike said.

"I've never seen anyone more devoted to another person, Detective."

"Do you think he resented—"

"Not at all. In fact, if people were as loyal as that boy was to his mother,

37

I'm sure we wouldn't need dogs. But then I'd be out of business, wouldn't I?" Suze said. She smiled, her expression softening. "So maybe it's a good thing most people are jerks."

"I guess I'd be out of a job, too," Mike said with a chuckle as he made a notation in his steno pad.

"I am so sorry, Detective." Suze placed her hand lightly on Mike's arm, as if suddenly remembering something important. "I never offered you a coffee. Would you like one?"

"No, I'm good, thanks. And you can call me Mike."

"Mike," she repeated. "As in Michael?"

"Yes, although only my mother and my partner call me that."

"Nice. How long have you and your partner been together?" she asked, her expression brightened with genuine interest. "Sorry if I'm being too nosy—it's just—"

"Oh, it's not like that," Mike said with a smile. "She's my work partner, and we've been working together for a few months. My old partner retired."

"Gotcha," Suze said. A faint flush coloured her cheeks as she glanced away. "So about Seth. Did he have any visitors or...?"

"Not really. I don't know if he had any friends. She had so many needs, especially over the past couple of years. I'd see him take her out once in a while, likely to medical appointments. It was just the two of them, really. He and Eureka. Such a wonderful name, isn't it? Eureka. Imagine a baby arriving and saying 'Eureka!'"

Mike did not respond.

"But in answer to your question," Suze continued, another flush of colour on her cheeks, "Seth pretty much spent all of his time with his mother."

"Did that strike you at all as a bit...odd?"

"I might not be the best person to ask, Detec—Mike. When you spend as much time with animals as I do, you start to see the world through puppy dog eyes, I guess, so I kind of see the world a little more fairy-tale-ish than everyone else does. But, honestly, I thought they were sweet together."

"Hmm," Mike said, looking down at his steno pad.

"I don't suppose your world is very fairy-tale-ish, is it?"

"No." He took a deep breath. "Not a lot of happy endings."

"I'm sorry," she said, and he felt as if she meant it.

Before either of them could say anything more, they could hear several dogs barking upstairs.

"Sorry, Mike," Suze said. She began to give his arm a rub and then stopped abruptly, as if she'd just realized that he was not a dog. "I've got to get upstairs. We've got a lot of drop-offs around this time, and it can get a bit chaotic. Not everyone plays well together, as I'm sure you know."

"Right," Mike said. "Can I take this lease with me?"

"Can I make you a copy instead?"

Before Mike could respond, she had placed the lease on the photocopier behind her, made a copy, and was handing it to him.

"If you ever want to give your dog—what's his name?"

"Phil."

"If you ever want to give Phil a treat, I'd be more than happy to give him the spa treatment sometime. On the house."

"I'll keep that in mind," Mike said, taking the copy of the lease from Suze and following her upstairs.

Chapter Eight

2:15 p.m., Wednesday, April 10, 2019

"**A**re you going out for a drink after work?" Carla asked.

"Probably. You?"

"If you are, sure. Otherwise, I was just going to head home."

"Hot date?" Mike said with a wink.

"Yes. With Netflix. It's been a long shift, hasn't it?"

"I suppose."

"Hello and goodbye, my gorgeous people," Detective Julia Vendramini said as she came into the detective office, a coffee in one hand, an enormous black Prada handbag slung over the shoulder of her other arm.

Mike looked up at the clock on the wall.

"You're here early," he said.

"Last day for you guys," she said, looking for the cleanest corner on her desk before setting her coffee down. "I figured you'd want to get out of here early. Anything I should know about? Any updates on the homicide?"

"The son is still in a coma," Carla added. "They've got the MCU watching him."

"They must just love that!" Julia said, taking her coat off and carefully hanging it on the rack. She then returned to her desk, opened the bottom right-hand drawer, and pulled out a box of wet wipes, replacing it with her purse before closing the drawer.

"Don't ever put your purse anywhere but in the bottom drawer, Carla,"

Julia said as she tore off several wipes and began to vigorously wipe the desk down. "And make sure you wipe down every surface. Every surface, you hear what I'm saying? God only knows who or what comes through here."

Julia came on the job about the same time as Mike did, and the two of them had worked together on the Juvenile Prostitution Task Force in 2005. She was the one who had come down the stairs to find Mike holding Sal's dead body, and she was the one who wrapped him in her jacket until the paramedics arrived. Unlike Mike, however, she seemed to have made it through the years unscathed and unchanged, although she never wore Armani again.

"I hear they're going to put a job call out for the detective position. You going to apply, Carla?"

"Oh goodness me, no," Carla said. "I barely know what I'm doing, and without Michael, well…I couldn't imagine running an office like that."

"Ugh," Julia said, looking at the blackened wipe before tossing it in an overflowing garbage can and pulling out another. "How does it get this filthy in less than twenty-four hours? This place ought to be condemned."

"If he wakes up," Mike said, shutting down his computer, "they're to call Amanda Black."

"My God," Julia said, nodding approvingly at the relatively clean wipe she had just used on the second go-round on the desk. "That woman is everywhere, isn't she?"

"What time's Russ coming in?" Mike asked.

"Thanks be to God, he's not. I cannot tell you how much I wish Dave hadn't gotten promoted. He was such a lovely man. But Russ? Don't even get me started. No. I'm sorry," Julia said, looking up and crossing herself, "I shouldn't have said that. We are all God's children. Even Russ. But, in answer to your question, he took tonight off. Mental health, he said. Speaking of which, how are you feeling these days, Mikey?"

"Been better," he said.

Carla looked over at him.

"Any luck finding a place?" Julia asked Carla.

"I saw a good place on Monday night, and I've called back a few times and left messages, but…."

"Not like when *we* were looking for apartments, is it, Mikey? Landlords used to be calling *us* back, right?" Julia said with a sigh. "Okay, you two. Get outta here before something comes in and I need you to stay. Hey, did you hear about Fred?"

Mike cocked his head.

"You remember. Hoagy? My partner in the JPTF? Sheesh! Anyway, he died last week. Heart attack. So young."

"You stayed in touch?" Mike asked. After Sal was shot, Hoagy had resigned, and Mike hadn't really thought of him since.

"We did for a bit. Met up for coffee a few times after, and then, well…you know how it goes. Anyway, I just saw something on Facebook and thought you'd like to know."

Mike got up and put on his coat just as the phone on his desk rang.

"Don't answer it," Julia said. "Let it go to voicemail. You're on days off."

Mike let the call ring through. Minutes later, his cell phone began to vibrate. Call display showed that it was from an unlisted number.

"God, you're lucky to have Julia as your relief, Crumply Pants," Amanda Black said when Mike answered the phone. "But don't get too drunk tonight. I need you and Carla to come in tomorrow."

"I can't speak for Carla, but I've got nothing going, as long as it's been cleared by the boss."

Carla looked over at Mike.

Amanda, he mouthed.

Carla nodded.

"All good. Just be in for 7, okay? And can you let Carla know if you see her? Save me a call."

"Will do," he said, nodding to Carla.

"Thanks. See you in a few hours," Amanda said, ending the call.

"Are we staying?" Carla asked.

"No, but we're going to be back at 7 a.m. tomorrow. Let's go over to The Blind Pig for a quick one."

"You buying?" Carla said.

"No."

"Always the charmer, aren't you, Mikey?" Julia said with a smile.

"I'm just going to freshen up," Carla said. "I'll see you there."

* * *

The Blind Pig was an unassuming two-storey place at the bottom end of the district. Rather than going for a trendy patio, the owners opted to cement the front and leave it empty, giving the place a look that didn't stand out. The Pig, as it was known, used to be Mike and Ron Roberts' haunt after they discovered it while responding to a call about a man in the deep fryer who had ended up with third-degree burns over most of his body. No indication of foul play or employer neglect was determined, just drunken misfortune on the part of the cook. The owner had invited Mike and Ron to come back for a drink after shift, and for no good reason, they did. Once Ron retired, Mike introduced Carla to the place. Unimpressed by the drab exterior and equally dingy interior, Carla wasn't overly keen on it, but she perked up considerably when no one gave her a second glance. And it was a good place to go for a quiet drink to talk shop.

"How are you really doing, Michael?" Carla asked after the server had placed a flute of prosecco and a pint glass of Guinness on the table.

"What kind of question is that?" Mike said, his voice defensive, almost like a reflex.

"A question a friend would ask."

Mike wanted to come back with a smart-ass response but refrained, lifting his pint glass instead.

"Sláinte," he said.

Carla lifted her flute.

"Since you're asking, I have to say I miss Bridget more than I thought I would."

"How much did you think you'd miss her?" Carla asked, taking a sip of her prosecco.

"Fair enough," Mike said after a gulp of beer. "I still can't believe it."

"I'm sure Amanda Black will make an arrest soon."

"I'm not."

"Michael, this has nothing to do with Malcolm Oakes."

"Yeah, it does," he said. "Amanda told me that Bridget was working on it."

"On what? Your conspiracy theory?"

"It's not a theory. It just hasn't been proven." Mike took another gulp of beer. "Yet."

"Brian Salvatore's death was a long time ago, Michael."

"Murder. And yeah, it was. What's your point?"

"I'm sure they're doing everything they can, even after all these years, to find whoever murdered him."

"That fucker murdered him. We know that. We've known that since Day One. And now we know that he's been hiding in plain view, likely for years. Someone dropped the ball, and now at least one other person has been murdered because of it."

"If you're talking about Lisa—"

"Who the hell else would I be talking about? Aside from the girls he's probably killed—or had killed—that we don't even know about yet. Because they're still dropping the ball. That's why a cop-killer's still out there—walking free, probably with some nice little income and a legit place to stay—fifteen years later."

"Michael," Carla said, her voice as calm as his was agitated, grateful that no one else was within earshot. "I understand why you'd think that, but—"

"*Think that?*" Mike spat. "Lisa Clayton was *dating* him before she was murdered!"

"Michael, please," Carla said, her voice barely above a whisper. "This isn't the time or the place."

"Bridget Calloway was helping Amanda Black look into my so-called conspiracy theory when she was murdered," Mike whispered back, his words sharp, like they were being spat out.

"We don't know who shot Bridget Calloway or why," Carla pointed out.

"If it wasn't Malcolm Oakes, it was someone close to him," Mike said. He looked over at the server and caught her eye. "Another, please?"

The server came to the table. "And you?" she asked Carla.

"No, thanks. I'm fine," Carla replied, looking at her nearly full flute.

"Sal was murdered by Malcolm Oakes, who got away because someone wanted him to. When Lisa Clayton got murdered, we found Malcolm Oakes, and it should have been just a matter of time before we caught him. But we didn't catch him, did we, because…you tell me. That's how deep the corruption goes. Some of our people are looking after him and have been for a long time. That's what Bridget and Amanda Black were working on. Now Bridget's full of formaldehyde six feet under. Either it's an amazing coincidence, or…."

Mike let the words hang in the air as the server replaced his empty glass with a full one.

"So why isn't Amanda Black dead?" Carla asked.

"Give it time," Mike said, raising his glass. "Sláinte."

"Do you really believe that?"

"If she knows what Bridget knew, then yes. Unless, of course, she's in on it, too."

The two sat silently, each taking a sip of their drink.

"Well," Mike finally said with a heavy sigh, "we've both got an early start. Unless you really don't want another, let's settle up and I'll see you tomorrow at 7."

"I'll get it," Carla said, reaching for her purse.

"No. I invited you. I've got it." Mike pulled his wallet out of his jacket pocket. "Just don't let word get around."

He felt his cell phone vibrate. Pulling it out, he saw that it was an unknown number.

"What's up?" he answered, assuming it was Amanda Black calling.

"Detective?" a young man's voice asked.

"Yeah. Nerdster?"

"Yes. I called Homicide, and they're going to let Detective Sergeant Black know, but I thought I should call you. Seth Samuels has regained consciousness."

"We'll be right there," Mike said, ending the call and shoving the phone back in his pocket. He turned to Carla, his voice flat. "Our boy is awake."

Chapter Nine

11:07 p.m., Wednesday, April 10, 2019

To those unaware of the serious business involved in keeping people alive in an ICU, the unit can seem almost serene, especially late at night. Once all but the essential family members sitting vigil over their loved one have gone home and the lights have been dimmed, it can appear that the place is run by a skeletal nursing staff who sit and monitor machines that beep and blip in response to the bodies attached to them. This was the sight that greeted Mike and Carla when they arrived in the ICU at the General.

"Over there," the nurse said, motioning to the old clothes officer and his charge, seeming to intuitively know that the two off-duty detectives were, in fact, detectives. "I don't know how long he'll stay awake. He's been through a lot."

"Thanks," Mike said, nodding to her.

"Hi, Detective," Nerdster said. "I mean, Detectives."

"How's he doing?" Mike asked, looking at the scrawny man tucked in the bed in front of him.

"He's just fallen back asleep."

"But not unconscious?" Mike asked.

"I, uh, don't really know," Nerdster said.

"No," the nurse said, coming up behind them. "He's just asleep. And likely will be until the morning." She gently squeezed her patient's hand, checking his circulation. "You're more than welcome to stay, but I don't think he'll be saying much before morning, providing the RT takes the breathing tube out then."

"No point us sticking around," Mike said as the nurse continued on to the next patient. "Are you on all night?"

"No. Billy-Bob is going to relieve me..." Nerdster looked at his watch, "about now."

As if on cue, Nerdster's partner walked in carrying a tray of coffees, a box of donuts, and an iPad. He set the coffees and donuts down at the nursing station, taking one of each for himself, and proceeded towards his colleagues.

"Don't tell me he's awake and I can go home," Billy-Bob said.

"He's sleeping," Nerdster said.

"Smart boy," Billy-Bob said, looking at his watch. "Is he under arrest?"

"No, not yet," Mike said.

"So can I leave?"

"No," Mike said. "Let's keep things as they are until we hear differently."

"Thank you," the nurse said to Billy-Bob when she returned to her station and saw the coffee and donuts.

"Well done," Carla commented, acknowledging Billy-Bob's adherence to the age-old tradition of bringing treats for the nursing staff.

"Not my first rodeo," Billy-Bob said. "Now get the hell outta here, Nerdster. I'm sure your mother is wondering where you are."

"Am I good to go?" Nerdster asked, looking at the detectives.

"I don't see why not," Mike said with a shrug.

"We might as well go, too," Carla said.

"Sure. I'll just give Amanda a call and give her a quick update," Mike said, turning away to use his cell phone.

"Sorry, officer," the nurse said, looking up from behind the desk. "No cell phones allowed."

"Oh," Mike said. "I thought that was an old rule."

"Still in place," she said, shaking her head.

Mike went into the main hall with Nerdster following quickly behind, one of Billy-Bob's donuts in hand.

"Amanda, it's Mike," he said. "Carla Hageneur and I are at the hospital with Samuels. He's just asleep now. Give me a call."

Mike clicked off his phone just as Nerdster stepped into the elevator. Mike watched as the doors closed before heading back to the ICU.

"Good to go?" Carla asked.

"I think so," Mike said.

"Good," Billy-Bob said, putting his feet up on a chair he had pulled around from another patient's bedside. "I got a whole series downloaded here, and you're kinda eating into my viewing time."

Mike instinctively wanted to remind his subordinate that he was there to watch Seth Samuels, not whatever it was on his iPad, but held back as Billy-Bob put an earbud in one of his ears while logging into the device.

"Don't worry, Boss," Billy-Bob said, pointing to the ear without the earbud. "I'll hear his confession if he talks in his sleep."

Mike sighed as he looked at the slight lump under the blanket, wondering how much of it was the result of lying prone for several days without food or water, or if that was Seth Samuels' normal state. The sound of the young man's breathing apparatus was reminding Mike of the sound of the rhythmic push of what should have been life-infusing oxygen into Eureka Samuels' dead body. He shuddered before taking another deep breath.

"Time to go, partner," Carla said, walking towards the elevators in the main hallway.

They didn't speak as they waited for the elevator or as the elevator ascended to the main floor. They walked through the emergency room and out onto the side street where they'd parked their cars, neither one saying anything.

"Meet you at home?" Mike asked after walking Carla to her car.

"Sure," Carla said. "Should I put the kettle on?"

"You've been hanging around my mother too long," he said with a smile as he turned towards his old truck, waving her off.

Mike's cell phone rang as he hoisted himself up into his truck.

"Don't you ever sleep?" he asked.

"I could say the same about you, Crumply Pants. I thought you were off-duty."

"I was. I am. Carla and I were just out for a drink when Nerdster called to say our boy was awake, so we figured we'd just drop by to see what was happening."

"And?"

"He's asleep now. Not likely to say too much until he gets that breathing tube yanked."

"Okay. Well, I want you and Carla in tomorrow anyway. I still need to find next-of-kin."

"No problem," Mike said, turning the ignition on his truck. "Talk tomorrow."

"'Night."

Mike shifted his truck into drive and was checking his rearview mirror when he saw a car slow down long enough for someone to jump or get thrown out. He reached for the dashboard where the police radio would have been, had he been in a police vehicle, and then realized that he was not. In the second or so it took for the car to speed past him, Mike tried to catch the license plate number and see who was driving. Because of the dim lighting, he was unable to do either. Turning off the ignition, he jumped out of his truck and ran to where he'd seen the person dumped from the car.

No one was there.

For a minute, he wondered if he'd just imagined the whole thing. The neurologist had said that there was a very small chance that he might have hallucinations at some point during his recovery. Shimner-Lewis had warned him about the effects of constant stress and PTSD and fatigue and all sorts of shit.

Fuck me, he thought as he looked around the empty street.

"Fuck! Me!" he shouted.

"Help," he heard a tiny voice say.

Mike stood in the middle of the side street, looking wildly around him.

"Where are you?" he demanded.

"Help," he heard again.

Mike dropped to his hands and knees and peered underneath the cars parked along the side of the road. He didn't see anything.

"Help."

He looked towards where he had heard the voice and crawled beside the parked cars until he found her, glistening with fresh blood, clothes practically torn off, curled up underneath a Honda Civic.

As soon as she saw him, she drew herself back further beneath the car.

"I'm a police detective," he said, looking at her. "I won't hurt you. Give me your hand."

Mike reached his hand out under the car and waited. A slender hand grasped his, and he felt her fingers tighten around his own. Later, when asked, Mike couldn't recall how he managed to get the young woman out from under the car and into the emergency room, nor could he explain her condition. Despite the cool spring evening, the moment she took his hand, the faintest echo of heat prickled at his skin. Memories flooded back to him of that night with Ron Roberts, rescuing those girls from the burning factory. He felt the heat of the fire around him, heard its roar instead of the silence of the empty street, felt the fresh pain of Sal's death.

He had no recollection of what had just happened—only that something had, and now he was back in the driver's seat of his truck, turning the ignition key.

Mike sat motionless as the engine revved. He looked from side to side. He looked down at his hands. He saw blood on his coat. He looked at himself in the rearview mirror and saw blood on his shirt. He looked out the passenger window and saw that he was parked outside the emergency entrance of the hospital. He held his breath as he patted himself down.

No. It's not my blood... It can't be. Is it...Sal's?

For a moment, Mike was back in the underground, Sal's warm body slumped against his. Neither Mike's nor Sal's heart registers that Sal is already dead as Mike gently lowers him to the ground. Sal's heart beats once, maybe twice more, pumping most of his blood out of the exit wound in the back of his head, spilling onto Mike and the cement floor before stopping forever. Mike looks up and sees the shooter—the man with the Glasgow smile. The man he would come to know as Malcolm Oakes.

Mike felt a sharp pain in his chest. He gave it a rub. He felt something wet and looked down at his hand. He saw the blood again and looked around him.

No. Blood's not his, either.

Realizing that something was terribly wrong, Mike turned off the engine and got out of the truck. He walked back into the hospital and stood in the middle of the emergency room, bustling paramedics maneuvering gurneys around him. Those waiting to be seen glanced up at him from their plastic seats until a passing attendant guided him to an open seat, assuring him someone would attend to him soon.

Mike didn't respond. He just sat where he was told and looked down at his blood-covered shirt.

"Mikey, what are you doing—?" Julia Vendramini stopped short. "Are you okay?"

"Yeah," he said, still in a daze. "I'm good."

"What happened to you?"

"I-I-I…"

"Just give me a minute," Julia said, flashing her badge at the nurse behind the bulletproof glass.

"She's in here, Detective," a nurse said as she clicked the door open. "And if it wasn't for that man over there, she'd have likely died of shock under that car."

"Oh," Julia said, turning away from the unlocked door and returning to Mike. "That explains the blood. Good. For a minute there, Mikey, I thought maybe something had happened to you."

"No," he mumbled. "I'm…good."

"I'm going to talk to the victim for a few minutes. You going to be out here for a while?"

"No," he said, weaving as he got to his feet. "I think I'd just rather go home."

"You sure you're okay to drive?" Julia asked.

"Yeah. I'm fine. Just…tired."

"Okay. Well, say hello to your mother for me," Julia said as she turned back towards the locked door. "Sorry. Buzz me in again, please?"

Mike didn't remember driving home, but he did recall parking his truck on the street. He recalled walking down the laneway leading to the back of his house, taking off his jacket, shirt, and t-shirt, tossing them into the trash bin, and then letting himself in through the back door before heading upstairs to bed.

Chapter Ten

5:35 a.m., Thursday, April 11, 2019

Mike woke up without a hangover, something he hadn't felt in a while. As he dragged the razor across his face, he looked at his reflection in the bathroom mirror and briefly considered grabbing his suit jacket from the garbage bin behind the house. He remembered it was covered in blood. The thought of facing the dry cleaner, owned by the Korean woman, and offering awkward apologies was more than he could handle. Besides, he wasn't ready to admit that Shimner-Lewis might be right about him being more fucked up than he'd realized. Instead, he spent the next thirty minutes getting ready for work, avoiding his mother, who had taken to running both his home and his life.

Finally, Mike walked into the kitchen, where she stood by the sink with her back to him, to get his coffee.

"Ye'll not make old bones livin' the life ye are," his mother said without turning towards him.

"Okay," he said, as casually as he could manage, walking directly to the coffee maker on the counter.

"Okay for ye, me son, but what about Max?" his mother asked, neither looking at him nor moving from the sink.

"I'm sure I've got a few more years in me," Mike said as lightly as he could, reaching up to get the tin of coffee from the cupboard by the stove.

"Well, I'm glad ye know when yer time is comin'. It must be nice to be so special in the eyes of our Lord."

"Yep," he said, scooping out some coffee and dumping it into the plastic filter basket before pouring some water into the machine's reservoir.

"Would have been nice if God had let me know when yer Da, God rest his soul, would be passin'. Could have saved up a bit more, maybe left off having Katie. Don't tell her I said that, luv. She'd be shattered, not like she was planned, but just the same. Regardless, it's ye who God has revealed His plans to. And here's me, workin' at the Church and all...."

Mike didn't hear most of what his mother was saying, having had years of experience blocking out the sound of her voice. Instead, he watched the coffee drip into the decanter and was just about to pull it out to fill his travel mug when his mother turned and placed her hand over his.

"Michael, somethin's goin' to give, and I don't want it to be ye."

He looked at her briefly, acknowledging the concern in her face before shrugging her away.

"I can't leave you alone for a minute, can I?" Carla said, coming up from her suite downstairs into the kitchen. She cocked her head to one side and then the other as she slid an earring into each ear. "One minute, you're right behind me; the next, you're not. What happened to you last—Oh, good morning, Mary-Margaret."

Mary-Margaret shot Carla a look, as if her fears about Mike had been confirmed. Carla bit her lip, glancing between Mary-Margaret and Mike.

"I might as well pack me bag and go if yer intent on killin' yerself."

"I'm not, Mom," Mike muttered. He yanked the decanter out with a sharp tug.

For reasons known only to a Jack Russell, Phil came bounding into the room at that moment and began scratching at the back door.

"If you do go, Mom, make sure you take that dog with you," Mike said, pouring the coffee into his travel mug and then turning to Carla. "Want some?"

"Only if you've made enough," Carla said, realizing she'd walked into something she wasn't prepared for.

"Unlikely," Mary-Margaret said. "Michael only thinks of himself these days, unless God's told him his partner would be comin' up the stairs wantin' coffee as well. Direct line, has our Michael."

Mike reached up into the cupboard and took down another travel mug.

"I'll be packed when ye get home this evenin'," Mary-Margaret said, snatching the leash from the back door and snapping it on Phil's collar. "I won't be able to haul all of me gear home in Daphne, so ye'll be givin' me a lift in that environmental disaster of a truck of yers."

Before Mike could respond, Mary-Margaret was down the few steps from the back door leading into the parking space where her car was parked and away into the laneway, Phil dancing wildly around her legs.

"Do you want to talk about it?" Carla asked, looking past Mike through the open door.

"No, I don't," he said, handing her a travel mug.

* * *

"I'm not sure who looks worse," Amanda Black said when she saw Mike walk into the detective office. "You or Seth Samuels."

"Don't you have your own office somewhere?" Mike replied.

"I do, but I have to pop into court and wanted to speak to you and Carla on my way over. Where is she?"

"Who? Carla? I don't know. I'm not her keeper."

"Sounds like Crumply Pants has turned into Grumpy Pants," Amanda said.

"I can't wait until we get to the new station," Carla said as she came into the office and dumped her Michael Kors bag on her desk. She stopped. "What are you two looking at? Oh, shoot. I should probably wipe this down first, shouldn't I?"

"Wouldn't want any germs to get on that overpriced bag of yours," Mike muttered.

"I have no idea how you work with him," Amanda said. "Let alone live at his house."

"It's been a challenging morning, Amanda," Carla said, pulling a couple of antibacterial wipes from the container in the corner. She paused, noticing the paperwork on Julia Vendramini's desk. "Julia hasn't signed out yet? Must have been a busy night."

"I imagine it was," Mike said.

"When do you see Dr. Shimner-Lewis again?" Amanda asked.

"Dunno, and it's probably none of your business," Mike snapped.

"I beg to disagree," Amanda said, her posture straightening so quickly that her head jerked back.

"You going to pull rank on me now?" Mike said with a huff.

"I think I'll go freshen up," Carla said, tossing the used wipe into the garbage bin before slipping out of the office.

"No. I'm deciding whether or not you'll have time to interview my prime suspect—or witness. I haven't decided which yet. And, okay, yes—I care about you and want to make sure you're getting the support you need."

"I feel the love," Mike said, hammering away on the keyboard in front of him.

"I also want you to talk to Seth Samuels. I honestly wasn't expecting that he'd come out of this, so the plan has changed."

"Whatever."

"Mike," Amanda said, her voice softening, "I don't know what the hell's wrong with you, but I need you to sort it out."

"Nothing's *wrong* with me," he said.

"Then you've just become a…a…an…asshole all of a sudden?"

"Mikey," Julia said, coming into the detective office through the door attached to the holding cells. "That girl last night? Lucky to be alive."

"What? Are you a volunteer firefighter now?" Amanda asked Mike.

"Just in the right place at the right time," Mike said to Julia, ignoring Amanda.

"Anybody see a record of arrest lying around?" Julia said, glancing at her desk for the missing paper. "They're looking for the original in the booking hall. I could have sworn I put it in the dope sheet, but—"

"So what happened?" he asked.

"Here it is," Julia said, looking at a piece of paper right beside her keyboard. "I don't know about you, Amanda, but once I hit menopause, my brain—"

"Is she okay?" Mike asked.

"Hopefully. God, the life these girls live. Let me just run this back to the booking hall and then I'll—"

"Here," Amanda said, holding her hand out. "Give it to me. I'll run it back while you update Crumply Pants. And then I need you to focus. Okay, Mike?"

"Thanks," Julia said. Amanda took the paper and left the office by the door Julia had just come through. "I have to say, that girl has never let her rank go to her head. Wish more of them were like that. Anyway, after I left the hospital, I decided to drive by the stroll and talk to some of the girls. You know how it is, Mikey: we can never turn it off, can we? Anyway, one of them got the plate number of the car and handed it over."

"Anything come of it?" Mike asked.

"Yep. Uniforms went to the registered owner's address, and while she wasn't too happy about it, she gave up her boyfriend. It's his paperwork I'm just finishing up now so that he can get to court this morning."

"A john or a pimp?" Mike asked.

"Just a john. Reminded me of the old days." Julia logged off of her computer. "But is it me, or have they gotten more violent over the years?"

"Safe to come back?" Carla asked, poking her head into the office.

"Why not?" Julia said. "I was just telling Mikey about the john who nearly beat a girl to death on the stroll last night—who's now sitting in our cells. Thanks to Mikey."

"I thought you'd dropped in on a secret girlfriend or something," Carla said.

"As if," Mike said.

"I tell you, she's lucky you were there, Mikey. Doctors said she would have—"

"But she didn't, did she," Mike said.

"Did you put in for a call-back?" Julia asked.

"No."

"You should," Julia said. "You were there until well past three."

"Was I?"

"Did I just hear," Amanda said, coming back into the office, "that you were at the hospital most of the night?"

"Mikey probably saved my victim's life, Amanda," Julia said. "I'm going to see if the boss'll write him up."

"I'm thinking maybe I'll have someone else go with Carla this morning," Amanda said.

"Why?" Mike said, looking over at Amanda.

"Because I don't think you're up to it."

"Fuck you," he muttered. Amanda bristled.

"Michael's an experienced detective," Carla began. "I'm sure he would know if he was incapable of doing a statement, wouldn't you, Michael?"

"That's right. I am and I would. Do you want us to talk to this guy or not?"

Amanda looked at her watch.

"I've got to talk to…what's his name? The new Crown?"

"Richard Wajowitz," Carla said.

"Yes. Him. In about twenty minutes, and it's likely going to take me twenty-five to get there." Amanda gathered up her belongings. "Looks like you're all I've got, Grumpy Pants."

"I feel so special," he said.

"Let Carla be the lead," Amanda said as she strode out of the office. "Keep me posted, Carla."

"Who's the dayshift relief?" Carla asked, taking a sip from the travel mug.

"They're just out grabbing a coffee. Should be back soon. In the meantime, I hate to do this to you guys," Julia said, "but I'm signing out."

"Sure," Mike said. "Your work here is done."

"Hardly," Julia said, squinting as she filled in the boxes on the self-reporting screen that would account for her time.

"I've got a spare pair of readers if you want them," Carla said, reaching into her purse.

"No, I'm just tired," Julia said.

"Careful on the drive home then," Mike said.

"Oh, I'm not going home yet," Julia said, pulling her purse out of the bottom drawer. "I'm going to grab a cappuccino and some biscotti at the Dip and then head over to court. I want to make sure this *sbalzo* doesn't get bail."

"Just like the old days," Mike said with his first grin of the day.

"Except I'm too old for those days now," Julia said. She grabbed her coat from the rack as she slung her purse over her shoulder. "I don't need to put this on, do I?"

"I would. Now," Carla said. "Used to run like a furnace, and now I'm cold all the time."

"I used to be the same way, but not now. Menopause."

Mike closed his eyes and let out a huge sigh.

Chapter Eleven

9:17 a.m., Thursday, April 11, 2019

T he first thing Mike noticed when he and Carla walked into the ICU was a young officer he didn't recognize sitting beside Seth Samuels' bed. Her bulletproof vest was undone at the sides, and her clip-on tie was dangling from the neck of the vest. Her hair was no longer tightly pulled back, and wisps of it hung down around her drooping head. Had he not seen the iPhone in her hand and the earbuds in her ears, Mike would have thought she was asleep. Before he had a chance to say anything, her head jerked up and she pulled one of the earbuds out.

"Am I getting relieved or what?" she demanded, her voice sharp.

Mike nodded slightly, taken aback. "Good morning."

"Sorry," she said, rubbing her eyes. "Long night."

"Nobody's come to relieve you?" he asked.

"Nope. I hope they haven't forgotten about me."

"I'll make a call," Carla said, spotting the same nurse who'd lectured Mike a few nights ago. She walked toward the hall, phone already to her ear.

"You might as well go," Mike said to the officer. "No reason for you to wait. We'll be here a while, and your relief should be here before we're done."

"Good," the officer said, checking her watch as she tightened her vest and clipped her tie back into place. She gave a curt nod. "See ya."

"They're sending the next available solo unit over," Carla said, narrowly avoiding being run over by the officer as she made her exit.

"Have a good sleep," Mike called after her.

The young officer turned to glance at him. Mike couldn't decipher the look she gave him, but he thought he saw her shake her head as the elevator doors closed.

"Batting a thousand today, Michael?" Carla quipped as she returned.

"Apparently," Mike muttered.

"Only one visitor allowed," the nurse said.

"We know," Mike said. "We're not visiting. We're here to interview him."

The nurse looked down at the man sleeping in the bed and then back at Mike.

"Good luck with that," she said, giving Mike a dirty look.

"Perhaps we could," Carla began timidly, "bring another chair around and wait until your patient wakes up to speak with him."

The nurse glanced at Carla and shot Mike another dirty look.

"Suit yourself, but if I get any complaints, one of you is out."

Looking around the room at the mostly comatose patients, Mike was about to respond.

"Thank you," Carla said before he could before pulling up a chair from the bed next to them as the nurse walked away. "Little victories, Michael. Little victories. And at least they've taken the breathing tube out."

Mike nodded. "I'm surprised. I thought they'd wait until morning."

"Maybe it was bothering him," Carla offered.

"I guess he's not as sedated as I thought," Mike said, glancing at the nurse now stationed at the desk, eyes down, writing up her notes.

"I don't suppose Nurse Ratched would give us a peek at his chart, do you?" Carla asked with a smile.

"I don't know, but I'm sure as hell not going to ask."

Carla stood up, straightened her shoulders, and walked over to the nursing station.

"It's a man's world, isn't it?" Carla said to the nurse.

"Pardon?"

"You know. We do all the work, and they get all the credit," she continued. "I'm just going downstairs to pick something up to nibble on. Can I get you anything? My name is Carla, by the way. Gwen, isn't it?"

The nurse looked blankly at Carla.

"I've got a horrible sweet tooth and was looking at that banana bread. I can just as easily pick up two slices," Carla continued, looking the nurse up and down. "But with a figure like yours, I bet you don't eat that sort of thing."

"Don't count on it," Gwen said, her tone flat but not unkind.

"I don't mean to pry, but I found that, after...uh...a certain age, between the shiftwork and all of the changes my body's gone through, I just can't keep the pounds off. What's your secret?"

The nurse looked up at Carla.

"Or not." Carla turned towards the lobby. "By the way, if my partner gives you any trouble, just let me know. I know how to handle him."

"Wait," the nurse said. She stood up and pulled some change from the pocket of her scrubs. "I'd love one of those chocolate muffins."

"A girl after my own heart," Carla said with a smile. "And it's on me. The least I can do for you."

"Thanks. And yes, I'm Gwen. Good memory."

Gwen smiled as Carla headed towards the elevators. Then her face relaxed into its resting scowl as she looked over at Seth Samuels, who was beginning to cough.

"Nurse?" Mike called out.

"He's fine."

"He's choking."

"He's fine." ·

Mike stood up and put his hand behind Seth Samuels' back to help him sit up. The young man continued to cough.

"You okay?" Mike asked.

"Yeah," Seth said, his voice raspy. "Water."

Mike looked around him and saw none.

"Nurse," he called out without taking his eyes off Seth. "Can I get a cup of water over—"

Before he could finish his sentence, she was on the other side of her patient, holding an ice cube in a paper towel.

"Here," she said, placing the paper towel in Seth's hand while guiding his arm up to his mouth. "Suck on this for a minute."

Mike watched the nurse, surprised by her tenderness.

"Give yourself a minute," she said, gently pulling Seth's hand away from his mouth. Without moving his body, he looked over at her.

"Okay. Suck on this again." The nurse stood by until the ice cube was gone. "How's that?" she asked.

"Better," he croaked.

"You had a breathing tube down your throat for a few days. Do you remember that?"

He shook his head.

"You were pulling at it, so the RT took it out a few hours ago. That's why your throat is so irritated. Do you remember the tube coming out?"

He shook his head again.

"Your throat is going to feel irritated for a while. I'll bring you a bowl of ice cubes. I want you to suck on the ice cubes when your throat feels dry, okay?"

He nodded.

"No water until the doctor does his rounds," she said, looking over at Mike. "And try not to talk too much."

The nurse did a cursory check of the other patients on the floor before returning to her station. Mike was just about to get up to talk to her when he saw Carla coming into the unit carrying a paper bag and a tray with three coffees on it.

"For you, Gwen," she said, setting the tray down on the nursing station counter before carefully pulling out a chocolate muffin and handing it to her. She looked over at the tray. "Take whichever coffee you want. I'll bring the bag back with the fixings in it in a minute."

She made her way to where Mike was sitting, handed him the bag, and removed both coffees from the tray before tossing it into the overflowing garbage can next to the bed.

"Sorry, Seth," Carla said as she placed both coffees on the table by his bed.

"You weren't awake when I was taking my orders; otherwise, I would have picked you up something. I did get an extra cookie if you're interested?"

"Thanks," Seth squeaked, shaking his head, then looking at Mike.

"Nurse said he can't have anything until the doctor sees him," Mike said, pulling the tightly wrapped slice of banana bread out of the bag.

"Oh. Well then," Carla said, snatching both the bag and the banana bread from Mike's hand and placing the slice back in the bag. "We'll have to wait as well, Michael. Don't want to be rude."

"It's okay," Seth whispered.

"She seems a lot happier," Mike said, motioning towards the nurse. "I owe you one."

"You're welcome," Carla said, handing the banana bread back to him. "Honey is always better than vinegar. Here. Take your coffee. And some milk. Gwen, how do you take yours?"

Mike took the plastic lid off the coffee cup and added the milk as Carla went over to the nursing station. He looked at Seth, who had shut his eyes.

"How's your snack?" Carla asked, sitting down in the chair beside Mike's.

"Haven't touched it yet," Mike said, setting his coffee down on the floor beside him before trying to unwrap the tightly wrapped banana bread. "Who the hell wrapped this? One of the surgeons?"

"Here," Carla said, taking it from him and quickly finding the loose end that would open the packaging. "Try this."

"Thanks," Mike said, looking over at Seth again. "I don't think he's going to be saying too much this morning. We might as well leave once the uniform gets here."

"Where's my mother?" Seth suddenly whispered; his eyes still closed.

Mike and Carla looked at each other. Mike cleared his throat.

"What is your mother's name?" Mike asked.

Seth's eyes fluttered open. "Eureka Samuels."

Mike took a deep breath. "Seth, I need you to listen to me. Your mother… she's gone. She died."

Seth blinked at him, a flicker of confusion crossing his face. "She's dead?" he whispered, disbelief thick in his voice.

"I'm sorry," Mike said quietly. "She died...sometime before Monday."

"What day is it today?" Seth whispered.

"It's Thursday."

Seth's face went pale. He looked at his arms, which were still connected to IVs, and shook his head slowly. "No. No..."

"When the officers arrived, they found you unconscious and your mother, deceased, on the couch."

Mike waited. When there was no response, he continued. "Judging by the scene, it would appear that both of you had been there for a few days. Do you have any idea what might have happened?"

"She's dead?" Seth said, looking straight ahead.

"Yes," Mike said. "I'm very sorry."

"No," Seth began, shaking his head, slowly at first but quicker as he repeated the word, his voice rising.

"I know it must be a shock—" Mike began.

"NO!" Seth screamed and began pulling the tubes from his arms.

"Sedative!" the nurse called out.

Almost immediately, the nurse and a man with a syringe appeared on the far side of the bed, facing Mike and Carla. Within moments, the syringe's contents were administered into Seth's veins, and he lost consciousness. The man muttered something to the nurse, who was busy adjusting the tubes in Seth's arms.

"Which one of you is leaving?" the nurse said.

"Both of us," Carla said, looking behind her and noticing the uniformed officer exiting the elevator.

"Good," the nurse said, heading back to her station.

As Mike updated the officer, Carla stepped towards Gwen, taking her coffee and banana bread with her.

"He doesn't have much of a bedside," Carla offered.

"Clearly," Gwen replied flatly, her gaze never leaving the desk.

Carla paused for a moment, then pulled a business card from her purse and handed it to the nurse. "I don't suppose we'll be back today," she said, "but if Seth has any questions or wants to talk, here's my card."

Gwen took the card wordlessly, offering only a brief nod in acknowledgment before returning her attention to her work.

The two detectives walked toward the elevator. As they reached the doors, Carla spoke again, her voice softer now. "It doesn't get easier, does it?"

Mike glanced over at her but said nothing for a moment. His jaw tightened, a faint trace of weariness in his eyes. "What doesn't?"

Carla shook her head slowly. "You know…this. *All* of this." She motioned vaguely to the sterile hospital corridors, to the chaos of the world around them, the grief, the lies, and the truth that never quite seemed to make it into the light.

Mike sighed, his shoulders sinking a little as the elevator doors opened. "No," he said quietly, his voice rough. "No, it doesn't."

They stepped inside, the doors sliding shut with a soft hum, leaving the sterile hallway behind them as the elevator descended in silence.

Chapter Twelve

12:45 p.m., Thursday, April 11, 2019

As usual, the tapping sound of her high heels on the linoleum tiles preceded Amanda.

"Well?" she demanded as she stormed into the detective office. "Where's my statement? And where's everybody else?"

Mike looked up over his monitor.

"Nurse Ratched shut us down," he said.

"That's not exactly true, Michael," Carla began, looking across at her partner, her half-moon glasses perched low on her nose. "And they're on a call. Robbery. Shouldn't be too long."

"And he could barely speak because he just had the breathing tube taken out," Mike added.

"Barely speak is good enough. What did he say?"

"Still not exactly true, Michael," Carla said.

"For the love of God!" Amanda said, exasperated.

"I told him his mother was dead and he was in the hospital, and he lost it."

"And?"

"They sedated him," Carla added. "As in: out cold."

"Tell me we've still got a uniform with him, then."

"We've still got a uniform with him," Mike said.

Carla sighed and briefly closed her eyes.

"I'm glad you're finding this so amusing, Crumply Pants," Amanda snapped.

"In the meantime, we located next-of-kin. A brother and sister, both in Chicago. They're on their way and will be staying at the Delta across from Headquarters. They should be getting in shortly. I want you and Carla to go and pick them up. Get a feel for them."

"Okay," Mike said slowly. "Anything in particular you want to know?"

"Really, Mike? If I thought I'd have to spoon-feed you, I'd go talk to them myself. And don't even ask how court went. Wajowitz is no Bridget. Luckily, the judge called in sick, so we're adjourned for a few days."

"Speaking of which, how's *that* investigation going?" Carla asked.

"I don't know," Amanda said. "I recused myself. Again. Billy Gill is the OIC now."

"No, you backed out because you know Malcolm Oakes is responsible," Mike said.

"No. I identified my conflict of interest because I realized that I'm too emotionally close to the situation to be effective," Amanda corrected.

"I thought you did that the first time around, and they said no," Mike countered. "But now, looking at how you're on your way up the corporate la—"

"Well," Carla said. "I'm sure we'll find out who killed Bridget."

"Oh, we know, but we'll never make an arrest," Mike muttered.

"Pardon?" Amanda said.

"You heard me."

Carla looked at Mike and then Amanda before focusing on the monitor in front of her.

"If there's something you want to say," Amanda said to Mike, "I'm all ears."

"Okay," Mike said with a nod. "We all know that Malcolm Oakes is involved in the Calloway murder, even if he's not the shooter. It fits his MO."

"Shooting someone at close range isn't exactly a unique identifier."

"In a parking lot."

"Happens."

"Cut the bullshit, will you? We all know that Malcolm Oakes shot my partner fourteen years ago and got away, despite having a remarkably obvious scar on his face and police agencies all over the world allegedly looking for him. We also all know that he's been here in the city for at least the past few years and is likely still in the pimping business."

"Not my investigation," Amanda said.

"But you are—were—looking into it on the down low."

Amanda stared at Mike.

"Don't play dumb with me. You told me you were, and that Bridget Calloway was helping you."

"If you two will excuse me," Carla said, getting up from her desk. "I'm just going to powder my nose."

"Good idea," Mike said. "The less you know about all of this, the better."

Mike and Amanda watched Carla scurry out of the office.

"Mike, you're making some pretty strong—"

"Oh, I'm not finished," he spat through his clenched jaw, his eyes blazing.

"Yes, you are," Amanda replied, barely able to conceal her own anger.

"Just because you're on the list for promotion doesn't mean that I'll stop looking for Malcolm," Mike stated.

"What did you just say?"

"You heard me. You're on the list to become a white shirt, and we both know that it's those pricks that have been protecting Malcolm Oakes."

Amanda paused before slowly walking towards the office door and gently closed it. She then turned and locked eyes with Mike.

"I am, and will always be, a cop, Mike. Whether I'm in an investigative capacity or an administrative—"

"Save it for the promotion panel," he said, looking back at the monitor in front of him.

Amanda's jaw dropped.

"And talk to me in five years when Gill has shuffled Bridget's murder investigation over to the Cold Case Unit, unless he's done it already because he's been told to."

In one of the rare moments in her life, Amanda found herself completely lost for words.

"And yes, you were a cop. A damned good one. Once." Mike looked up at her. "But now you're just like the rest of them, looking for your next bump, your next plum assignment. Within a year of putting on that white shirt every day, you'll be so far away from the good cop you were that you won't even recognize yourself."

"Fuck. You."

"Tell me I'm wrong," Mike continued, his voice getting louder. "Tell me nobody was getting kickbacks from that prostitution ring we were following when Sal got shot. Tell me nobody made a phone call or two to make sure Malcolm Oakes got away. Tell me that filth isn't still somewhere in the offices of the 'Ivory Tower.'"

Amanda held her tongue.

"You can't, can you?" he said menacingly. With a derisive exhale, he looked away.

"I can tell you that I don't disbelieve some of what you've said," Amanda began, her words measured. "I don't think I need to tell you that there's been a lot of change since 2005, but I agree that some of what you've said is still true. And I can tell you that I will take my last breath rooting out whatever corruption, cronyism, or other unsavory practices I find that may still exist if and when I find them."

Mike smirked and shook his head.

"And I can tell you that Billy Gill is well aware of the issues you've identified."

"And...?"

"I believe you, Mike. Bridget believed you. But neither of us could prove it, and both she and I believed that whoever is behind all of this was—is—very dangerous."

"So you agree that Bridget's death is related—"

"Whether I agree or not is immaterial. I'm staying as far away from that investigation as possible so that if Gill determines that Malcolm Oakes is responsible, I know that the investigation was done thoroughly, which means that he's ruled out every other possibility. At this point, I don't think I could."

"And then what?"

"Once we have him, I'm going to charge him for Lisa's death. And Sal's.

And take a run at him for Chelsea Hendricks'—"

"We don't know that Chelsea Hendricks is dead," Mike cut in sharply.

"Mike," she said, taking a deep breath. "It's been years, and—"

"And what? Do we have a body? Remains? Anything?"

"Please...."

"Until we have something, there's still a chance that she's alive."

"Sure," Amanda said, nodding slowly.

Mike's stomach churned as he heard Brenda Hendricks' voice again, the same fragile, desperate tone she always used on Chelsea's birthday, a call that had come every August 23rd without fail. Her words hit him like a cold wave: *"Have you found my baby yet?"* He pressed his lips together, the weight of it sinking in. Every year, it was the same question, the same raw, unrelenting hope clinging to each syllable, drowning in booze and desperation. He could almost see her, slurring through a haze of alcohol, as if, somehow, Chelsea might still be out there. Mike always told her that they—he—hadn't stopped looking and never would.

"In the meantime," Amanda continued, "I need you to stay in your lane. I need you to do your job and do it well. And that includes taking care of yourself. I want you to be there with me at the finish line. You're a good man, Mike," Amanda said softly. "Don't let this fuck you up."

Mike heard the click of the back door as a uniformed officer came in from the back parking lot. She came into the detective office and stopped before pulling her memobook out of her cargo pants.

"Oh. Is it okay if I sit here to update an occurrence?"

Mike smelled something. Something sweet, like roses mixed with...? The scent of Armani perfume. The perfume that was on the coat Julia Vendramini wrapped around him in the underground that afternoon, just after Sal had been shot.

"Too late," he said to Amanda, ignoring the officer as he rubbed his cheek. He glanced at his hand, almost surprised to see that there was no blood on it.

"Stay in your lane, Mike," Amanda repeated softly. "And we'll get there. I promise. In the meantime, find your partner and go pick up my family members."

Chapter Thirteen

3:15 p.m., Thursday, April 11, 2019

Mike and Carla made their way through the crowded Arrivals Hall of Terminal 1 at the airport, with Mike grumbling about being given a hard time for parking in the short-term lot, even after he'd flashed his tin.

"He's just doing his job, Michael," Carla said. She scanned the crowd for a young-ish woman and a man not much older, matching the photos emailed to them.

"If that car is gone when we get back—"

"Over there," Carla said, having spotted the woman amidst a sea of faces. "Although I don't see him. Never mind. I'll do the talking, okay?"

"Sure," Mike said as a mob of teenagers pushed past him. "Hey!"

"Ms Samuels?" Carla said as she extended her hand.

"Yes," the woman replied through tight lips, her eyes wide.

"I'm Detective Hageneur, and this is Detective O'Shea."

Mike held out his hand. She took it, her eyes still on Carla.

"Is your brother getting your luggage?" Carla asked, noticing that the woman was holding a carry-on bag and her purse, and wanting to scream *Yes, I'm trans. Let's move on.*

"He…he couldn't come. Last-minute thing. They have kids and…" she stammered, and then paused. "I've just brought a carry-on. Didn't think I'd need many—"

"Yes, of course. Why don't you come with us, then? We're just parked over there," Carla said, pointing towards the main glass doors of the airport. "Michael, why don't you carry Ms—"

"Ruth," the woman said.

"Yes. Ruth. Well, Michael, why don't you carry Ruth's bag for her?"

"No," Ruth said as Mike reached for it. "I'm...I'm fine."

The three moved through the crowds to the unmarked police car parked exactly where Mike had left it. He reached again for her carry-on, intending to put it in the trunk, but Ruth held on to it.

"I'd rather—"

"Michael, slide it in the backseat with Ruth, will you?" Carla directed.

"Sorry," Ruth said once they'd all gotten settled in the car. "It's just...I'm feeling...I don't want to lose...I need to hang on..."

"We understand, don't we, Michael?" Carla said. "Now, would you like to have a few minutes to freshen up at the hotel, or are you okay to come straight to police headquarters to talk to Detective Sergeant—"

"I'm good. Let's just get this over with."

Mike felt something vibrate against his chest. He pulled his cell phone out of his jacket pocket. Unknown number. He pressed a button to answer.

"Crumply Pants," Amanda Black said. "Change of plan. Do you have them with you?"

"Just the sister. Brother's not coming," Mike said, looking over at Carla.

"Fair enough. Okay. I need you to take her to Six District for the interview."

"Really?" Mike said, reflecting on how professional HQ appeared in comparison.

"Really. And I might just get you to do it on your own with Carla."

"Okay. Do I want to know why?"

"I've been told that there's a demo out front of HQ. No need to subject our family member to that. And I'm at a scene at the other end of the city, and I don't think I'll be able to make it back downtown in this lifetime."

"What are you doing there? I thought you were on the promotion list and they'd want to keep you out of harm's way."

"I am, but even Homicide's short-staffed, and I offered to help. Just a secondary this time. I'll head out in a while, but you do the interview, and I'll see you when I see you."

Mike clicked off the phone and put it back in his pocket. Carla looked over at him.

"Change of plan. We're going to Six District instead."

"Is that a bad thing?" Rush asked from the backseat.

"No," Mike said. "Just not as nice a building."

"It's quite close to the hospital where Seth is, though," Carla added. "I'm sure you're anxious to see him, and we can drive you over after, can't we, Michael. Unless you'd rather we take you to your hotel?"

"Did he kill my mother?" Ruth asked.

Mike looked at her in the rearview mirror.

"Do you think he did?" Mike asked.

"We don't know what happened yet," Carla replied, glaring at her partner. "The investigation is in its infancy."

"No," Ruth said, responding to Mike's question. "I don't think so."

"So why did you—"

"Let's wait until we get settled in at the station, shall we?" Carla said.

The ten-mile drive took almost as long as the flight from Chicago to Toronto. Between the gridlock on southbound 427, the relentless red lights on Burnhamthorpe, and the chaotic mash-up of buses, cars, and kamikaze cyclists, they were fortunate to reach Six District in less than an hour. And, aside from their initial conversation, no one spoke for the entire drive.

Mike found a parking spot in front of the station and quickly pulled in.

"Well, here we are," Carla said. "Now, are you sure you don't want Michael to—"

"No. I'm fine," Ruth said, pulling the carry-on across the seat as she got out. "Thank you."

"Okay, then," Carla said, leading the way.

The first glimpse inside Six District never failed to underwhelm. Most of the linoleum tiles on the floor were cracked and had lost their luster years ago. The bile-colored walls were permanently filthy and, despite being immediately replaced after being regularly smashed by angry protesters and cowardly lone wolves, very little light came through the front windows, a gloominess always seemed to cling to them. And to the people who worked behind them. *Once they were in the new station....*

"We might as well go right downstairs," Mike said.

"Unless you want to freshen up first?" Carla offered.

"Yes, I'd like that," Ruth said.

While Carla took Ruth to the bathroom, Mike got the recording equipment set up in the interview room.

"And here we are," Carla said, leading Ruth in.

"What can you tell me about the relationship between your mother, Eureka Samuels, and your brother, Seth Samuels?" Mike asked after giving Ruth the standard cautions.

"We should never have put that much responsibility on him," Ruth blurted out. "I told Simon that Seth was too young to look after our mother, but Simon disagreed, and I went along with it. Is Seth going to be okay?"

"We don't know," Mike said.

"Which is to say, it's early days for him," Carla cut in.

"Did Seth harbour any resentments towards looking after your mother?"

"Not that I was aware of."

"And how often did you speak to Seth? Or your mother?"

"Not often enough, so I'm seeing."

"So, once a month? Once in a while?" Mike asked.

"Once a week."

"A phone call or—?"

"Zoom call."

"And your brother? Simon? How often did he—?" Mike continued at a rapid-fire pace seldom used with grieving relatives.

"Seldom."

"Meaning...?"

"I don't know. Once every few months? But he's busy. They have kids—"

"It doesn't take much time to call your mother, does it?" Carla said softly, looking at Mike.

"Maybe busy isn't the right word. He...he was...fed up with her. Had enough, I think. Glad to dump her on Seth."

Ruth took a deep breath the moment the words left her lips, bringing an abrupt stop to the rapid-fire Q&A. Mike leaned back in his chair.

"But she was sick," Carla said after a minute, taking charge of the interview.

"That's not how Simon saw it," Ruth said. "He blamed her for her emphysema. Said she brought it on herself with years of heavy smoking."

"What about your father? Is he still in the picture?"

"Never was," Ruth said with a harsh laugh.

"So—"

"He left when Mom was pregnant with Seth. Nice, eh? And then he quit his job so that he didn't have to pay child support. His legitimate job, anyway. I'm sure he made money somehow."

Ruth paused.

"Must have been difficult for your mother," Carla said.

"No kidding. Simon was seven and I was five when he left. And, of course, Seth was just a newborn. We moved in with Mom's parents for a minute. That didn't last. So then she found a room above a donut shop and we lived there for a while."

"What did your mother do for money?" Carla asked.

"She worked in the shop downstairs. Mostly at night when we were in bed."

Mike glanced over at Carla.

"I know, but you do what you gotta do, right?"

"She mustn't have made much money—" Carla said.

"She also worked during the day when we were at school. And we ate a lot of donuts. Like, I mean a *LOT* of donuts," Ruth said, patting her flat stomach.

"But this whole time, you and your brothers were—"

"Doing what kids do. We didn't really know how badly off we were. I mean, we knew we were badly off, but not *badly* off, if you know what I mean."

"And it looks like both you and Simon did well for yourselves…?"

"One thing we both figured out pretty quickly was that money makes the world go 'round, and Mom told us that the only way to make good money was with a profession, so we studied our asses off and both got scholarships for school."

"And Seth...?"

"He was the baby. And...I don't know. By the time he was old enough to know what was going on, our lives had kind of normalized, you know?"

"So he didn't...?"

"He also wasn't that bright, to be honest."

Mike looked over at Carla again.

"But he was bright enough to look after your mother?" Mike asked.

"*Is*," Carla corrected. "Seth is still alive."

Ruth paused.

"He was dumb enough to let us dump her on him."

No one said anything for a few minutes.

"That's the truth of it, Detective," Ruth said. "Neither Simon, or I wanted to take her on. We both figured we'd suffered more because of her poor choices, and now it was Seth's turn."

"What poor choices?"

"Marrying our father, getting pregnant again with Seth, moving us into that stupid room above a donut shop."

"I'm sure she never—" Carla began.

"So you resented her?" Mike cut in. "You and Simon?"

"I guess we did, yes," Ruth said. "And now she's dead, and Seth's...he's going to be okay, though, right?"

"I don't know," Mike said. "I've spoken to him, but I don't know what the long-term—"

"Simon'll love this."

"Love what?"

"Well, someone's got to look after Seth now, don't they?"

"I...I don't know," Mike said. "But let's focus on your mother for a bit, okay?"

"Really, there's not much more I can say. We set them up in that apartment behind the dog groomers—"

"Any particular reason why there?"

"Access. And price point. Most cheap places have stairs, and, as I'm sure you can imagine, Mom couldn't do them, so we were looking for a ground-floor place, and this is all we could find. I suppose they got used to the smell of wet dog."

"Why didn't either of you take your mother in?" Carla asked. Mike shot a quick look at her that suggested she'd misspoken.

"Are you kidding?" Ruth laughed. "Simon was a hard no, and I...I...there was no way I could afford—"

"The reasons why are immaterial," Mike said.

"She was better off here," Ruth answered.

"Did she have any enemies?" Mike asked, clicking his pen.

"No."

"Did Seth?"

"I have no idea."

"Is there anyone that you can think of who might want—"

"I did a ten-minute Zoom call with my mother once a week. I don't really know her at all."

"I see," Mike said.

"Do you?" Ruth said with a little laugh. "I don't think you have any idea how hard it's been for us. All of us."

No one in the room spoke. Mike cleared his throat.

"Is there anything else you'd like to tell us?" he finally said.

Ruth shook her head.

"In that case," Mike looked down at his watch before looking back at the camera behind him. "I'm concluding this interview at 5:07 p.m."

Chapter Fourteen

5:12 p.m., Thursday, April 11, 2019

"Hey, Mike," the booker said as Mike passed by the front desk. "We got an O'Shea in the cells. Looks a lot like you."

"Well, it isn't. I can't be everywhere," Mike called back as he walked towards the D office, a knot starting to form in his stomach. A familiar, unsettling feeling crept over him, and he couldn't shake the dread that had settled deep in his gut. He hadn't heard from Petey in years. It couldn't be him, could it?

"I'm just going to get my purse, and then Michael and I can take you to see Seth, if that's still what you'd like?" Carla asked Ruth.

"Yes. Please," Ruth said.

"It's not much, but it's all we've got," Carla said, pointing to the radiator cover that ran along the front window of the station and doubled as a bench. "Give us a minute."

By the time Carla had turned back towards their office, Mike was already at his computer, logging the interview they'd just completed. While he knew she'd be notified automatically of the submission, he also sent a quick text message to Amanda.

Interesting family dynamics

"I'm just going to freshen up, and then we'll take Ruth to the General?" Carla asked. "I'll drive, if you don't mind."

"Sure," Mike said, logging off. "I'm just going to check the cells."

81

"Expecting someone?"

"No, just...curious," he replied, disappearing through the back hallway that led to the cell area.

Rather than leading a prisoner from the booking hall into one big bull pen as was done decades before, the cell area at Six District station had been reconfigured sometime around 1960 so that the booking officer had his choice of twelve individual holding cells to place the accused. Each cell was outfitted with a metal toilet and tiny sink and a metal bed bolted securely to the floor. To avoid co-accused talking to one another, or—as was more often the case—threatening each other, the twelve cells were divided into two blocks of six, each block having its own hallway. From those cells, the occupant stared across at a puke-green cement wall. On the other side of one of those cement walls lay another hallway leading to the cramped interview rooms and the detective office. Mike stepped out from this passage, glancing down the first corridor to find six empty cells.

He continued toward the booking hall and glanced down the second hallway. The first cell door was open, but the second one was shut. When Mike looked inside, a deep sense of dread settled in his chest. An emaciated, filthy man slumped on the metal bed, hunched against the corner of the cell, his head bowed, tangled hair covering his face. The stench of years of living rough hit Mike with a force, and suddenly, he was back in their childhood home, hearing his mother's hopeful voice calling for the little boy Petey once was.

"Petey?" Mike called, his voice hollow.

His brother's head lifted briefly, vacant eyes unable to focus, before his chin dropped

again. Mike's stomach twisted. Memories of Petey flooded his mind—his brother's interference with Katie, the violent confrontation, and then his sudden disappearance.

To their mother, Petey had been the lost soul she still hoped would return—still believing, no matter what, that he could be the little boy she had loved so deeply. But here he was—neither that little boy nor the younger brother Mike had run off.

"Any relation?" the booker said, stepping into the cell area.

"No," Mike said, quickly turning away from the cell.

"Didn't think so," the booker said. "I don't know how these guys stay alive."

"Yeah," Mike mumbled as he hurried past him.

"All set?" Carla asked, popping her head into the office just as Mike was returning to his desk.

Had he had the wherewithal, Mike would have been glad that Carla was driving. As it was, however, he was lost in a swirl of memories and emotions, none of them good.

When they got to the floor Seth had been on two days prior, Carla led them over to what was now an empty bed.

"Oh," she said.

"Over there," the nurse said, pointing to the end of the hall. One of the hospital security guards was sitting on a chair outside a glass-walled room.

"Oh," Carla repeated, her voice markedly lower. "Well, let's go have a look, shall we?"

"He can't have visitors," the nurse said.

"We're not visitors, we're—" Mike began.

"This is Seth's sister," Carla said, giving Mike a disparaging look before motioning towards Ruth. "She's just flown in from Chicago and was hoping to—"

"Why don't I get someone from psych to speak to you, then," she said, looking at Ruth. "I'll just page them and I'm sure they'll send someone up as soon as they can."

"Can I at least see him?" Ruth asked. "Through the glass?"

"Sure," the nurse said. "But don't wake him up."

The security guard looked up dismissively as Ruth and the two detectives approached the cubicle.

"We're the police," Carla said, stepping closer to him while rummaging through her purse to find her badge. "And this is Seth's sister."

"Okay," the guard said, unmoved.

"Ruth, here, just came from Chicago and wants to see her brother," Carla continued, holding up her shiny new detective badge.

"Well, there he is," the guard said, motioning with his chin towards the man passed out on the bed.

Ruth stood frozen, her hands pressed against the glass as she stared at her brother, lying on his back, his hospital gown up around his midriff such that his genitals were clearly visible, the front of his gown covered in blood, his arms and legs strapped to the bed. The sight of him like that made her knees buckle.

"What—what happened?" she asked with a gasp.

"I can't really say," the guard said coolly. "All I know is that he's on suicide watch."

"He's obviously sedated," Ruth said. "Did you have to tie him down like that? And can someone get him a clean gown or at least go in there and pull that one down?"

"We had to restrain him until we could get him sedated," the guard answered. "And no one is—"

"But—"

"Sorry," the guard said unconvincingly. "The restraints stay on. I have no idea how long the sedation's gonna work, and I'm not going in there to wrestle with him if it wears off while I'm sitting here."

"But—"

"And you're the...?" a woman who looked no older than Ruth asked as she approached them.

"I'm Detective Hageneur, this is my partner, Detective O'Shea, and this is Ruth Samuels, Seth's sister."

"Good. So we've got a next of kin," she said, looking at the clipboard in the slot by the sliding door. "Good. Are you okay with me talking in front of the police or would you prefer to go somewhere quiet?"

"Here is fine," Ruth said.

"The pati—your brother is, as you can see, being monitored as a result of displaying extreme self-harming behaviour."

"You mean he's suicidal," Mike said.

"We don't like to use that—"

"He couldn't be suicidal. He'd never hurt a fly," Ruth said, giving the security guard a dirty look. "And how could he even—"

"Prior to our intervention, your brother was over there," the doctor said, motioning to the empty bed. "It was there that he got out of bed and began smashing his head on the floor. Hence the blood."

"Maybe he was just disoriented," Ruth said.

"Yes, well," the doctor continued, "after he was physically restrained, he tried to bite his tongue off. Likely the cause of more blood."

Ruth let out a sob as her legs buckled beneath her. Mike reached out quickly, steadying her as she collapsed against him. Without thinking, he ordered the security guard out of his chair, guiding Ruth into it with practiced care.

"I'm so sorry, Ms. Samuels," the doctor said.

"Why?" Ruth whispered, her voice thick with disbelief. "Why would he do this to
himself?"

"Your brother mentioned to one of the nurses that he felt responsible for your mother's death."

"No," Ruth gasped, shaking her head. "That can't be right. He's not—"

Her words caught, and Mike saw the weight of her guilt hit her like a physical blow. Her hands trembled as she gripped the chair's armrests, her breath coming in shallow gasps.

"I'm so sorry, Ms. Samuels," the doctor repeated softly, stepping back, giving Ruth some space.

Mike's phone vibrated in his pocket. He pulled it out and looked down at the screen.

What families aren't?

He grimaced and put the phone away without responding.

Chapter Fifteen

9:01 a.m., Friday, April 12, 2019

"Good morning, Gwen," Carla said as she and Mike walked into the ICU. She stopped and placed a coffee and a chocolate muffin down on the charge nurse's desk while Mike continued on and spoke to the uniform officer seated beside Seth Samuels' bed. "I see our boy's been moved back to a bed. I take it he's doing better?"

"Not really. We needed the space for someone sicker. Here," Gwen said, reaching into her pocket.

"No," Carla said. "Consider this my nod to all of the work you do over and above."

"What about you?"

"I'm guessing my paycheck's a bit bigger than yours," Carla replied, smiling. "It's a man's world, honey."

The two women gave each other a knowing look.

"You look all fluffy and new," Carla said to the hospital security guard as she joined Mike. "You must be the day shift."

"I am," he said.

Mike, Carla, and the security guard all turned toward the body lying on the bed. Many of the monitors seemed to have been reattached, including an intravenous tube taped to Seth's hand. His gown had been replaced, and now Seth lay covered by a blanket. The blood had been wiped off, leaving him almost peaceful-looking—except for the four-point restraints and the strap across his chest.

"Why don't you grab a coffee or something?" Mike said. "We want to have a word with Seth. Give me your cell number and I'll call you when we're done."

"I'm not allowed to leave—"

"I'll take responsibility for him if things go sideways. Go grab yourself a coffee."

"Uh, okay," the security guard said, briefly torn between hearing his wife's voice confirming her pregnancy— though he already knew from her text— and the possibility of the patient going off the rails.

"Shall I get my own chair again, Michael?" Carla said, looking around her.

"I'll get one for you, Detective," the security guard said, eyeing a chair by a vacant bed.

"Thank you," Carla said. "Surprised to see one empty."

"Guy died," the security guard said. "They just removed the body."

Carla grimaced.

"How's he doing?" Mike said, looking down at Seth.

"Dunno. You'll have to ask the nurse," the security guard said as he retrieved the chair for Carla. "I'm just here to watch him."

"And a fine job you've been doing," Carla said with a smile as he set the chair down by the bed. "Thank you."

"Looks pretty dead to the world now," Mike said.

"Dunno," the security guard said as he turned away. "I'll just be downstairs, okay?"

"Sure," Mike said, his attention on Seth. "Hey. Wake up."

When there was no response, Mike stood up as he closed his hand into a fist and began rubbing Seth's chest with his knuckles.

"Wake up."

"Detective," the nurse said as she swooped over to them. "I'm going to have to ask you to refrain from touching my patient. His skin is still very sensitive."

"Of course. Sorry about that, Gwen. My partner can get a little... overzealous," Carla said. "Michael, why don't you sit down for a moment and let me see what I can do. May I?"

The nurse tucked the sheet gently around Seth and smiled at Carla before stepping back.

"Seth?" Carla said softly. "Seth, I'm Detective Hageneur, and this is my partner, Detective O'Shea. We'd like to ask you a few questions."

Seth did not stir.

"Seth?" Carla said a bit louder. "We're the police and we're here to talk to you."

Seth grunted, but still didn't open his eyes.

"Seth," Carla said firmly. "Open your eyes. We need to ask you what happened with your mother."

There was a pause, and then Seth opened one eye, and then the other. He stared up at Carla for a few seconds before licking his lips.

"Well, that's an improvement," she said, noticing the Styrofoam cup with the curved plastic straw that had replaced the ice cubes from the day before. She brought it down to his mouth. "Here. Take a sip."

Seth took a sip and then tried to sit up.

"What the...?"

"Apparently you were trying to harm yourself yesterday," Carla said.

"Can you at least get this strap off my chest?"

"Nurse?" Carla said, deferring the decision.

The nurse came over to the side of the bed a few minutes later, having looked at his chart at the nursing station.

"I can take off this strap, and we'll loosen these. Would that help?" she said as she took off one strap and began loosening the four points.

"Ugh," Seth said, shaking himself out as much as he could. "Yes. Can you at least take the ones on my wrists off?"

"I'm sorry, no," she said. "You'll have to speak to the doctor about that." She walked away before he could respond.

"Can you help me get the back of the bed up?" he asked Carla.

Before she could respond, Mike noticed the remote that had fallen between the side rail and the mattress. He handed it to Seth, and the back of the bed lifted. Seth slid down, his arms still tethered to the top of the frame.

"Michael, hoist our friend here up, will you?" Carla said.

Mike grabbed the back of Seth's hospital gown and pulled, causing the neck of the gown to tighten around Seth's neck.

"Excuse me," the nurse said, appearing suddenly behind Mike. "Let me do it."

Mike stood back and watched the nurse help Seth up.

"Pfff," she said as she walked over to the next occupied bed.

"Not enough chocolate muffins?" Mike muttered once she was out of earshot.

"Michael…" Carla admonished.

"Clearly, I'm not a nurse," Mike said, sitting back down. "So, how are you doing, Seth?"

"Alright, I guess."

"Better than last night, I'd say," Mike continued.

"I don't really remember."

"Do you remember talking to your sister?" Carla asked.

"Ruth was here?"

Carla glanced over at Mike, who sighed.

"My partner, Detective Hageneur, and I would like to ask you a couple of questions. Is that okay with you?" he asked.

"Sure," Seth said hesitantly. "Is my mom okay?"

Mike looked over at Carla.

"Do you have any idea why you're here?" Mike asked.

"Not really," Seth answered. "Is my mom okay?"

Mike looked at Carla again.

"I'll tell him this time," Carla whispered.

"She's dead, isn't she?" Seth said before Carla could speak.

"Yes," Carla answered. "She is. Do you know what happened?"

"Shit!" he cried. "Shit. Shit. Shit."

Before either Carla or Mike had a chance to do anything, Seth began slamming his body on the bed and began to wail.

The nurse came rushing back.

"It wasn't me," Mike said, his hands held up after he moved his chair out of the way.

"My mom is dead, and it's all my fault!" Seth sobbed.

"What do you mean?" Carla asked, leaning forward.

"I'm sorry, Carla, but I'm going to have to ask you and your partner to leave," Gwen said, her tone firm.

"I should never have given it to her," Seth continued, struggling against his restraints.

"What, Seth? Given what?" Mike asked, his voice sharp.

"Detective, I'm asking you to leave," the nurse repeated.

"Just a minute," Mike said, not budging.

"Do I need to call security, Detective?" the nurse snapped.

"I told them it wouldn't work," Seth cried, his body jerking with each thud against the mattress.

Mike exchanged a look with Carla.

"Detectives, I'm going to have to—"

They all looked at Seth, curled up on the bed, his body crumpled as much as the four-point restraints would permit, his sobs shaking him.

"What if we just stood at the end of the bed?" Carla suggested.

Gwen looked over at Carla.

"Like this," she said, getting up from her chair and standing at the end of Seth's bed. "Come on, Michael. Over here."

Mike joined his partner, but the nurse remained unconvinced.

"I'd prefer not to sedate you again, Seth, so I'm going to have the detectives leave," Gwen said.

"He seems—" Mike began, but then stopped when Carla elbowed him in the ribs.

"Your blood pressure is pretty high right now, Seth, and we don't want to put any unnecessary strain on your heart," the nurse said to her patient, and then looked back at Mike. "You're going to have to—"

"We found it on the sidewalk and were going to use it to smoke crack," Seth cried out.

"Seth," the nurse said. "Just try to relax, okay? Detectives—"

"Did it still have that little canister in it?" Mike asked, thinking Seth meant the small metal cartridges that could be used with inhalers.

"Detective," the nurse cautioned.

"Yeah, it did," Seth said quietly. "When she started gasping, I thought maybe that stuff would help her."

"Did you use it on her?" Mike asked.

Seth began to thrash about on the bed again.

"Security!" the nurse called.

"Michael, please!" Carla said loudly.

Gwen went quickly over to her desk.

"Code Gray, fourth floor, ICU," she said, her voice sounding clearly over the loudspeaker. "Repeat. Code Gray, fourth floor, ICU."

"Seth?" Mike continued, his voice low and clear. "You know what happened. Tell me."

Seth became very still.

"It didn't work, so we doused a cloth with it and stuffed it in the humidifier bottle," he whispered.

"Humidifier bottle. Where's that?" Mike asked, his eyes narrowing.

"It's right where you attach the breathing tube."

Mike looked over at Carla.

"Detective, I'm not going to ask again, and security is on their way," the nurse said, returning to his bedside. "In the meantime, Seth, try not to speak, and let's get you sorted out here."

Seth's bed had shifted away from the wall, and the sheet that had covered him was now on the floor. His gown was twisted around him, and the pillow that had been under his head was now wedged beneath the bed and his lower back. Despite the one-man melee, none of the tubes or monitors had come loose, allowing the nurse to check his blood pressure just as a man in blue scrubs appeared. He glanced at Seth, then at Mike and Carla.

"I'm assuming you're not family," he said.

"No. I'm Detective—"

"Didn't think so. I'm Dr. Frimeth, the intensivist here, and from what I can see, this patient is in no frame of mind to speak to the police. You'd be better off to give it a few days before trying to make any sense out of what he has to say. Now, Mr. Samuels, I need you to lie very still for me."

Carla nudged Mike, and they both walked out of the ICU.

"What do you make of that?" Carla asked as they stood by the elevator doors.

"Promethazine overdose," Mike said. He pulled his cell phone out of his pocket and dialed the number he'd written down on his steno pad. "That's the stuff in the inhalers."

"I hope Forensics got samples of the water in that little bottle," Carla said as the light above the elevator door lit up.

"Might be the difference between murder and manslaughter."

"How so?"

"If Seth's story is true, that's the stuff on the cloth we found shoved in the respirator. Given what Seth's said, he or whoever he was with were just stupid and had no intention of killing the old girl."

"So...?"

"So he should have known better than to tamper with the breathing apparatus and it'll be up to the defense to prove that that he didn't. Given that he's been her primary caregiver for so long, good luck with that." Mike tilted his head slightly and spoke into his phone. "Hey, bud. It's O'Shea. We're done." He clicked the phone off and noticed an alert on the screen before he could put it back in his pocket. "Shit."

"What is it, Michael?"

"I've got an appointment with Shimner-Lewis in twenty minutes."

"Well, let's go. Do you want to drive or shall I?"

Chapter Sixteen

11:58 a.m., Friday, April 12, 2019

"I'll just be on the fourth in the cafeteria," Carla said. "Text me when you're done."

Mike gave her a brief nod as he stepped out of the elevator on the second floor.

"How's it going, Mike?" Dr. Shimner-Lewis asked, glancing up from her notepad.

"Depends who you ask," Mike replied.

"I'm asking you."

"I'd say I'm doing okay."

"So who says otherwise?"

"My partner. My boss. My mother," Mike paused. "All the women in my life."

"Does that bother you?"

"That everyone else thinks I'm fucked or that I'm surrounded by women?"

"Both. Either."

"I don't know."

"Any updates on Bridget Calloway's murder investigation?"

"What are you, a cop?" Mike laughed.

"The details don't matter, Mike. I'm just interested in how you're coping."

"Not that they're telling me."

"Do you think they're intentionally not telling you?"

"No. I don't think they know shit."

"Why's that?"

"Because they don't want to."

"Why not?"

"Because to name Malcolm Oakes as the shooter in the Calloway case would be admitting that I'm right."

"About what?"

"If I'm going to see you twice a week, you've got to stay on top of things," Mike said with a sardonic smile.

"How do you know it was Malcolm Oakes?"

"Because I do."

Rachel paused, looking at him intently.

"Any other reason, Mike?"

"Trust me, Rachel. It was him."

"Could it be that you're transferring your frustration with the lack of progress on your former partner's murder onto the investigation of your friend?"

"If that was the case, I'd be frustrated all the time."

"And are you?"

"Why, exactly, am I here again, please?" Mike asked, shifting in his chair. "Aside from having been sent?"

"You tell me, Mike. You were sent the first time, but you keep coming back. What's in it for you?"

Now it was Mike's turn to pause.

"You're good," he said with a half-smile and a slow nod.

"I try. Now, what's really going on with you?"

"I know this sounds crazy, but I know I'm right. I know there's a cover-up happening and that it's been happening for a long time, and I know that Bridget's just another piece of collateral damage."

"Collateral damage?"

"Yes. She got in the way."

"If that's so, then aren't you in the way, too?"

"Not like her. She has...had credibility. I'm just 'the Conspiracy Guy.'"

94

"How does that make you feel?"

"Doesn't matter."

"The people in your life seem to think it does," Rachel countered.

"All I want is to tell Janice Salvatore that we've caught her son's killer."

"Is that it? What about the rest of your life? And the people in it?"

"This *is* my life, Doc."

"Only if you want it to be, Mike and, if you do, do you think you're selling yourself short?"

Mike considered this.

"Okay," Rachel continued. "Let's say this Malcolm fellow is the murderer. Of both Sal and Bridget. And let's say that he ends up getting arrested and charged and convicted and is now rotting in jail. What does that change for you?"

"Nothing?"

"Really? Okay. So let's just say, for argument's sake, that everyone comes around and apologizes for stigmatizing you for all of these years, and you get the hero cookies. What happens next in the life of Mike O'Shea?"

"I retire, I guess."

"And then what?"

"I don't know."

"I see a couple of things here, Mike. First, you've pinned your hopes on catching Sal's killer. Then, even if they get him, you're still walking away with no more than a moment's relief. Does that sound right?"

"I hadn't really thought about it, I guess."

"In the meantime, what I'm hearing is that you're alienating not just," here she made air quotes with her fingers, "'the women' in your life, but your colleagues at work who, from what I've seen of the policing culture, make up a pretty significant social set. Does that sound reasonable?"

"I suppose."

"What about your last partner. Ron, wasn't it? You seemed pretty close to him."

"He retired."

"And?"

"I don't know. He's busy."

"Is he?"

"I don't know."

"Mike, if I may: one of the upsides of policing, from what I've observed and studied, is that it can be like a never-ending frat party. The downside is…that it can seem like a never-ending frat party. Except we all know that everything ends. And most frat parties don't end well."

Mike smiled. He had never been to a frat party, but he had been to enough shift parties to know the drill. Fistfights, confessions, and vomit.

"Maybe the issue isn't the corruption you suspect," Rachel continued. "Maybe it's your own sense of self-worth."

"I'm not following," Mike said.

"Well, could it be that the reason you're hanging on so tightly to that moment in time with Sal is because you were doing something that you felt was really meaningful and, when that got torn away—"

"Blown away is more like it," Mike muttered.

"Blown away, then, you didn't think you would ever do anything as impactful again, so you want to hold onto it as long as possible."

"That's bullshit."

"Why?"

"Because that," Mike began, making exaggerated air quotes, "'doing something that I felt was really meaningful' involved seeing my partner get his head blown off. Not exactly something I want to 'hold onto.'"

"So why do you?"

Mike looked away.

"Give me a minute before you completely shut down, Mike. I'm going to bring you back around. I promise."

"That's the second time I've been given a promise today," Mike said sarcastically. "By a woman."

"You can't stop people from doing bad things."

"I know that."

"And you can't stop good people from doing bad things."

"I know that, too," he said, annoyed.

"Do you?" Rachel asked softly.

The two of them sat in silence.

"Mike, they may never catch whoever it was who killed Sal."

"Malcolm Oakes," Mike said.

"Malcolm Oakes," Rachel repeated. "And they might never catch who killed Bridget Calloway."

Mike glanced up sharply.

"I mean," Rachel said, softening her approach, "they likely will, but there's a chance they won't. Regardless, we need to focus on helping you get to a place where you can function—"

"Function?" Mike repeated the word. "Isn't that what I've been doing?"

"Thrive," Rachel said. "Sorry. I misspoke. Thrive is what I mean. Because you've got a lot of life ahead of you, and I'm assuming you'd rather be happy than stuck."

"Is this where you give me the off-the-ledge talk?"

"You're a smart man, Mike. And very lucky. You've got people in your life who care about you. Enough to send you here. I know you care a lot about the people you've served, and you've changed a lot of lives for the better."

"Do I get a plaque when you're done, or am I dead and hearing my eulogy?"

"Which would you prefer, Mike?"

"If this is the part where you determine whether or not I'm a danger to myself or anyone else and should be sent off…"

"No," Rachel said with a smile. "This is the part where I help you to dig out of the hole you've been living in for too long. Still popping those pills and drinking too much?"

"How did you know?"

"Not all addicts roll around in the gutter with their pants around their ankles. Now," she said, reaching for her daytimer, "let's pick another time for an appointment. What works for you?"

Chapter Seventeen

1:01 p.m., Friday, April 12, 2019

"Here he is now," Carla remarked, looking up from her seat at the cafeteria table. Detective Sergeant Gill turned his head, his eyes tracking Mike as he navigated the busy lunchroom, weaving past the occupied tables, careful not to knock anyone or their steaming coffee.

"Ready to go, Carla?" Mike said without acknowledging the D/S. "Thanks for waiting, by the way."

"Mike," the D/S said, extending his hand. "Billy Gill."

"I know who you are," Mike said, offering a quick nod. "Ready?"

"Billy was just telling me that they have some good leads on the...on Bridget's case," Carla said.

"Yeah. Spoiler alert: it was Malcolm Oakes," Mike said, his tone flat. "Ready?"

"Listen, Mike," Billy said. "I know—"

"You know shit," Mike said.

Carla shot Mike a glance, her voice firm. "Michael, we're all on the same team, remember?"

"Sure," Mike said with a shrug.

"We know it was Oakes," Billy Gill affirmed. "We just don't have enough to arrest him yet."

"Yeah? Why not arrest him for killing Detective Constable Salvatore in 2005? Or don't you have enough for that, either?" Mike said, his voice cold.

Billy's face tightened. "Give me three days—"

"A lot can happen in three days," Mike said with a bitter laugh, recalling that it was about three days from the time they almost rescued those girls in the hold house until Sal lay dead in his arms. "Trust me."

"Is there anything you need from us?" Carla asked.

"No," the D/S said, shaking his head. "I just wanted to keep you posted."

"Great. Let's go," Mike said, walking away, Carla following quickly behind.

"What is wrong with you, Michael?" Carla asked as they waited for the elevator.

"Nothing."

"You wanted an update, and you got one. You wanted confirmation that it was Malcolm Oakes, and you got that, too. What else can the man do?"

"They won't catch him," Mike said as the elevator doors opened.

"Of course, they will," Carla said, stepping into the elevator behind Mike as a couple of clerks stepped off.

"Not until they get rid of Amanda Black."

Carla didn't respond. In the elevator, the hum of the doors closing was the only sound between them. When they reached the third floor, several suited figures stepped in, and the doors closed behind them. Mike glanced up at the flashing floor numbers, his jaw still set, while Carla shifted her weight from one foot to the other, trying to read Mike's mood. When they hit the main floor, they exited the elevator without a word. Neither of them spoke as they took another one down to the underground parking lot.

"What did you mean 'get rid of Amanda Black?'" Carla asked, breaking the silence once they reached the car.

Mike climbed into the driver's seat, starting the engine, his fingers tapping the wheel. "Do you think she's still at the station?"

"I have no idea," Carla said. "Why don't you just give her a call?"

"No, I need to tell her in person," Mike said as he drove up and out of the underground and into a heavy rainfall.

"Tell her what, Michael?"

"That she's next," he said, flicking on the windshield wipers.

Carla said nothing, just watched the rain bounce off the side window.

"You don't believe me, do you?" Mike said, the wipers struggling to keep up with the downpour.

Carla didn't look at him. "Believe what?" she asked, her eyes still on the water streaming down the window.

"Never mind," Mike said with an exhale. He flicked the wipers to high. "Fuck, I hate rain."

The drive was silent for a moment before Carla spoke again.

"What about Seth Samuels' statement?" she said.

"What about it?"

"Are we going to go back to the hospital and see if he's—"

"I'd rather talk a bit more to Seth's sister first," he interrupted. "I think there's a whole lot she hasn't told us."

Carla looked over at him, brows drawn.

"I don't think so," she said.

"What do you mean?" Mike said, glancing quickly over at her.

"Well, from what Ruth said, or what I thought she said, she and her brother just dumped our deceased on her youngest child. It sounds to me like either of them could have—"

"Maybe that's the best they could do."

"Really?" Carla replied, unconvinced.

"Well, at least here, her health care is covered."

"True, but still...."

"There's nothing saying she'd be living any differently in Chicago."

"I don't know, Michael. If his sister could get a plane ticket last minute, I'm thinking that at least she is probably living a whole lot better than Seth is."

"Let's not make any assumptions," Mike said, wheeling into the back parking lot. "Fuck. There's never anywhere to park back here."

"Well, once we're in the new station..." Carla said with a sigh as she recited what had become the District's mantra. "...things will be better."

"Yeah," Mike responded absently. He paused near the fence, glancing around. "You'd better get out here. I don't think there's enough room on your side if I park over there."

Carla reached for the door handle.

"We should have picked up a coffee," she said.

"You can have my spot," Amanda called from the back door of the station, spotting their car. She paused for a moment, then dashed to her own car. "I'm just on my way to court."

"Wait," Mike called, lowering his window.

"Can't," she said, unlocking her car door. "Got a meeting with NB."

"Who?"

"Not-Bridget...Richard Wajowitz," she replied as she slid into her car.

"Ouch," Carla said, raising an eyebrow.

They both watched as Amanda pulled out of the parking spot.

"Well, that worked out well," he muttered, eyeing the now-empty spot.

Amanda stopped when she got alongside them and rolled down her window. "But I do want to run a few things by you. The two of you can sign off once you've written up, and how about a drink when I'm done? I'll call you. Blind Pig work? Second floor? You're more than welcome to join us, Carla."

"I think I'll sit this one out, if it's all the same," Carla replied.

Chapter Eighteen

5:40 p.m., Friday, April 12, 2019

"Well, aren't ye just the picture of industry," Mike's mother commented as Carla brought a stack of folded storage boxes through the back door that opened directly into the kitchen. "I take it ye got the place, then?"

"I can move in on the fifteenth," Carla said as she dumped the pile down near the back stairs.

"Just because ye can doesn't mean ye have to, luv. I hope ye know that," Mary-Margaret said before turning and hollering towards the front of the house. "Michael, come down and help Carla carry these boxes down the stairs."

"I'm fine," Carla said, stepping backwards down a few stairs before assessing the load she had to carry. "And yes, both you and Michael have been more than welcoming. I don't know where I'd be if you didn't open up your home to me, Mary-Margaret."

"Don't let me Michael hear ye callin' it *my* home. Thinks it's his castle, he does. Doesn't seem to realize that even a castle is just a pile of stones if it's not lived in. Speaking of Himself…" Mary-Margaret took a breath, then shouted again, "Michael! Now!"

"What?" he instinctively replied from the second floor of the old three-story Victorian.

"Don't *what* me. Just get yer arse down here and carry these boxes down these stairs before Carla kills herself."

Mike huffed as he came downstairs.

"And keep yer huffing to yerself," his mother instructed. "Now take these downstairs, unless ye have another load in yer car that needs to come in, Carla?"

"I'm okay, Michael," Carla said apologetically. "Honestly, I can—"

"Far be it from me to give advice, luv," Mary-Margaret said, still standing over the stack of folded boxes, "but be sure to put these lads to work any time ye can. Idle hands are the devil's workshop. Michael, stop standin' there like yer waitin' for the dole and get to it."

"I think that's *idle minds*," Mike corrected.

"No, it's definitely hands, because otherwise it would presuppose that we all have minds, which, in yer case in particular, me son, I've come to highly doubt, as is further evidenced by this exchange. Now, enough chin waggin'. Get these boxes down the stairs and put them together."

"My car's just parked in the laneway. I'll go get the rest of them," Carla said, quickly skirting around Mike.

"Not likely," Mary-Margaret declared. "Michael will take care of it, won't ye, me son? Don't make me ask ye again. Now, I'm out for the evening shortly, but I'm not above having a cuppa before I go. Shall I put the kettle on for us, Carla?"

"What about me?" Mike asked, flattened boxes in hand.

"Yer busy," Mary-Margaret said and then turned to Carla. "And how about ye get us a few biscuits from the cupboard?"

No sooner had Carla reached up for the McVities than Mike was up the stairs heading towards the front door.

"Her car's parked out back, lad," Mary-Margaret said.

"What?"

"The car. Her car's in the back. Honestly, Michael, every time I think I can even consider returnin' to me own house, I get a look at the state of ye and see that I can't."

"Sorry, Mom, but I've got to go," he said, turning and giving her a kiss on the cheek before grabbing his keys from the hook by the front door.

"And leave us stranded like this?" Mary-Margaret objected.

"Amanda?" Carla asked.

"Yep."

"What could our Mandy possibly want that's more important than helpin' Carla out?"

"It's work, Mom. Not a social call."

"Well, off with ye then," Mary-Margaret replied. "It's not me place to be keepin' ye from savin' the world, Captain's Courageous. We'll just flounder along on our own here, won't we, luv?"

* * *

"I'll have a gin and tonic," Amanda said before the server got to their table and then glanced over at Mike. "Yes, it's been that kind of afternoon."

"And for you?" the young woman asked.

"A pint of Guinness, please," Mike said, his head starting to throb. His hand drifted down to his side and then over to his pant pocket before he remembered that he didn't have any oxys. He made a mental note to make a call on his way home and pick some up as he deliberately tried to push Dr. Shimner-Lewis' earlier comments out of his mind.

"Give me a second," Amanda said, her thumbs typing madly on her iPhone.

Mike looked over her shoulder at the muted flatscreen mounted in the corner of the bar, tuned to the 24-hour news channel. The bartender, his back to Mike, seemed to be watching it as well. Although Mike couldn't see the bartender's face, he recognized his posture and build, and something about him felt familiar, even though Mike didn't recall him being one of the regular bartenders, at least not from the times Mike frequented this pub. Still, Mike found himself staring at the back of the man's head, unable to place him.

Amanda dropped her iPhone into her purse just as the server was setting their drinks down in front of them.

"So?" Mike said, seeing Amanda on the flatscreen doing a stand-up, appealing for witnesses to the homicide they were working on.

"No 'sláinte' or 'bottoms' up' or…?"

Mike sighed, nodded, and raised his glass. "Sláinte."

"Sláinte," Amanda said, taking a gulp of her drink. She saw herself on the flatscreen. "God, I look old there, don't I? Maybe I should get some Botox or something."

"So?" he repeated, ignoring her comment. He leaned back and rubbed his temples as his headache flared up. He tried to focus on Amanda's words, but his mind kept slipping back to Dr. Shimner-Lewis' comments. He wished he could dull the pain.

"Have you seen Ron lately?" Amanda asked.

"No," Mike said, taking a swig of beer. "Is that what you called me here to talk about?"

"No." Amanda looked down at her glass for a moment before looking up at him again. "I need you to do something for me."

Mike could feel every muscle in his body tighten.

"Okay," he said slowly.

"He has that box that Robby Williams left for you, doesn't he?"

"Maybe."

"I need you to get it for me. I need to see what's in there, Mike."

Mike took a long pause, eyeing her.

"Why?"

"To confirm something. But I need to see it myself," she repeated. "Soon."

"Why do you need to see it yourself?"

Amanda paused and scanned the room. Aside from themselves, the only other occupants were the young server chatting with the bartender by the bar.

"I can't tell you."

"Oh, well then, by all means…," Mike said, taking another gulp of beer.

"I can't tell you," Amanda repeated, "because I need to look at what Williams left with fresh eyes to make sure that where my investigation is leading me and what Williams was telling us are the same thing."

"What? That there's been a decades-long corruption coverup that includes the trafficking of underaged girls and the murdering of anyone who gets in the way? Is that what you're finding?" Mike said, his voice rising.

The server looked over her shoulder at them.

"You know as well as I do, Mike," she said, lowering her voice to counter his increased volume, "that any good investigation has to be full, fair, and frank—"

"I thought that was just disclosure."

"You know what I mean."

"No, I don't. But what I do know is that any good investigation has to be thorough and can sometimes lead to unsavory outcomes."

"Thank you, Detective O'Shea," Amanda shot back.

"Sure." Mike took another gulp of beer.

"What I'm trying to tell you is that you might be right."

"Great," he replied sarcastically. "And...?"

"Jesus, Mike," Amanda said. "I've just confirmed that—"

"You haven't confirmed anything," he said, cutting her off.

"I'm doing the best I can."

"Do better," he said, finishing his pint. As he raised his hand to signal the server for the bill, he saw the bartender turn away. If he hadn't been so irritated with Amanda, he might have called out to the man or tried to remember where he knew him from. Instead, all he noted was the bartender's scruffy beard, which was in keeping with a pub like this.

"Will that be one bill or two?" the server asked as she approached the table.

"One. After another round," Amanda said, gulping down her drink.

The server returned to the bar.

"I called you here," Amanda said, "and I'll bloody well tell you when we're finished."

The server cautiously set the two glasses on the table, removing the empties with equal care.

"Sláinte," Mike said, the word dripping with sarcasm.

"Sláinte," Amanda said, raising her glass. She took a sip. "And reset. Deal?"

"Depends on who's buying," Mike said, a slight twinkle in his eye.

"I said I was."

"No, you said one bill. For all I know, you're trying to stick me with it."

"You're a classy guy, Crumply Pants."

"About that," Mike said. "When did this 'Not Bridget' thing start?"

"Oh, Christ." Amanda rolled her eyes. "I don't think they've got enough gin behind the bar for me to get into that."

"So we're agreed that Malcolm Oakes murdered Calloway?"

Amanda took a gulp of her drink. "That's an oddly unrelated assumption, but yes, I'm convinced of it."

"Why?"

"Because he had opportunity, means, and motive."

"Lots of people get murdered in parking lots, or so they say," Mike replied with a smirk, recalling her earlier comment.

"Sure, but it isn't very often that the victim is a crown attorney who has just put the finishing touches on an iron-clad case that would bring down a lot of important people."

"Stranger things have happened," Mike pointed out, casually taking a sip of his beer. "And who are these so-called 'important people' and how, exactly, do you know this?"

"I need you to confirm that we're talking about the same people by going through that box at Ron's, and I know Bridget had it all figured out because tech support found an email in her drafts that was to be sent to the AG's office, presumably the following day, requesting a face-to-face."

"Maybe she just wanted to hand in her resignation in person," Mike suggested weakly.

"To the Attorney General himself? *Highly* unlikely," Amanda said, taking another sip of her drink. "I think she wanted to present the material that she had."

"Where is it now?"

"I've got it."

"Where?"

"Not at work, if that's what you're asking."

"So much for evidence continuity."

"I'm not worried about that," Amanda said.

"Why?"

"Because this will never go to court. If I'm right—if what Williams left in that box confirms it—then most, if not all, of the players are long-retired or dead."

"So why is it still happening?"

"Habit," Amanda said, looking down at her glass.

"Because we've always done it that way?" Mike said, raising an eyebrow and making air quotes.

"You know as well as I do how things go around here."

"Or is it because someone still has to be benefiting?"

"No. I think it's just become a part of the organizational memory."

"As in, no one wants to be the whistleblower?"

"Something like that," Amanda said, reaching into her purse. "Excuse me. I've got to get this."

As Amanda turned away to take the call, Mike alternately felt as if the weight of the world had been lifted off his shoulders and that his chest was being squeezed so hard that his head was going to explode.

"I've to run," Amanda said, raising her hand for the bill. "But give Ron a call and get into that box as soon as you can."

The server came over to the table, mobile payment terminal in hand. Amanda passed the young woman her credit card without looking at the bill while Mike upended his pint glass and pushed himself away from the table.

"Thanks for picking that up," Mike commented as the two of them walked down the steep stairs to the front door of the tiny pub.

"Where are you parked?" Amanda, already a few feet in front of Mike, called over her shoulder.

"Just over—" Mike began, then noticed a dark car suddenly cut in front of another car, almost mounting the curb in front of them as it sped towards them.

Mike froze for a second. He saw something—metal glinting—sticking out of the passenger window. Then, the gunshots rang out, and instinct kicked in. Without thinking, he shoved Amanda to the ground, his body landing on top of hers. The car sped past, tires screeching, weaving in and out of the afternoon traffic. Mike barely heard anything over the pounding in his ears, his heart racing. But one thing was clear: someone inside that car had just tried to kill Detective Sergeant Amanda Black.

As the car disappeared into the chaos of traffic, Mike lifted his head, trying to catch a glimpse of the license plate. But the vehicle had already vanished, leaving only a trail of confusion in its wake. Pain suddenly surged through his arm, sharp and burning. He looked down at Amanda beneath him, blood pooling around her. His breath caught in his throat, his heart racing.

The sound of sirens began to pierce the air, but the scene around him felt surreal—chunks of cement scattered in the street, blood soaking into the asphalt beneath him. He couldn't focus, his mind spinning. It wasn't until the throb in his arm intensified that the realization hit him—he was the one who had been shot. Not Amanda.

Chapter Nineteen

8:45 p.m., Friday, April 12, 2019

Amanda straightened up as the doctor came into the cubicle.

"So who are you when you're not in my ER?" the doctor asked, first surveying Mike, who was seated on the gurney with the right side of his shirt covered in fresh blood, and then turning his attention to Amanda, standing next to him with disheveled hair, fresh scrapes on her face and hands, and torn knees in her pants.

"Michael O'Shea," Mike replied.

"And you are...?" the doctor asked, looking at Amanda.

"Detective Sergeant Amanda Black. Homicide," she replied.

"Interesting," the doctor said, looking at Mike's shoulder.

"That's not something you ever want to hear a doctor say when he's touching your arm," Mike grunted, his face contorting with pain.

"Are you a police officer, Mr. O'Shea?"

"Yes. A detective."

"I see," the doctor said. "That would explain why my emergency room is full of police officers. And you're in this cubicle rather than out there with everyone else. Can you remove your shirt and raise your arm? Yes? Good. Does it hurt when I do this?"

The doctor peeled off the bloodied gauze the paramedics had applied to Mike's upper arm and pressed Mike's shoulder.

"Jesus!" Mike cried.

"Sorry about that. Good thing is, though, doesn't appear to be any nerve damage. You're a lucky man, Mist—Detective O'Shea. Looks like the bullet just grazed your upper arm. Don't even need stitches. I'll put some clean gauze on that, and you'll be good to go."

"Good thing you're so fat and out of shape, Crumply Pants," Amanda said with an approving smile.

"Out of shape? Look at these pipes!" Mike said, then decided not to lift his arm when he saw the doctor's raised eyebrow.

"I'll be back in a minute," the doctor said. "Might not hurt to give you a tetanus shot while you're here. You're not squeamish about needles, are you, Detective?"

"I just got shot, Doc. I think I'll be good with a needle."

"Everyone's a tough guy until they're not," the doctor replied. "I'll be right back."

"What about painkillers?" Mike asked.

Amanda glanced over at him.

"I can prescribe some T3s if you'd like, but you should be—" the doctor began.

"Do you have anything stronger? It really hurts," Mike said, wincing as he lifted his shoulder.

"I suppose I could give you a few Percocets if you like."

"Thanks, Doc," Mike replied.

"Really?" Amanda said once the doctor had left.

"What? It hurts," Mike replied. "Any updates on the shooter?"

"Let's just get you sorted out first," Amanda said.

"It was targeted, wasn't it?"

"Let's just—"

"And the target was you."

* * *

"I'll be okay," Mike said as Amanda unlocked the front door of his house.

"I'd feel more comfortable if you'd at least let me help you up the stairs,"

Amanda replied, steadying him from his good arm side as Phil let out a bark and then came bounding down the stairs.

"Michael, is that ye?" Mary-Margaret called from the back bedroom. "If it is, will ye let Wee Phil out for a piddle, and if it's not, will whoever ye are still let the dog out?"

"You didn't call her, did you?" Amanda said, looking at Mike. Without waiting for an answer, she called up the stairs. "It's only us, Mary-Margaret. Mike and Ama—Mandy. And you might want to come down."

"Wha—?" Mike began, but it was too late. His mother stood at the top of the stairs, her bathrobe pulled tight around her. She froze, took a step toward them, gripped the railing with both hands, and let out a shriek. The doctor had cleaned and dressed the wound, but Mike was still wearing the bloodied shirt. And Amanda looked as if she'd been in a street fight.

"It's okay, Mary-Margaret," Amanda said, turning her attention from Mike and holding her hand out to the older woman. "Here. Give me your hand. Why don't you and I have a cup of tea after I get Mike into bed?"

Mary-Margaret cautiously made her way down the stairs and took the outstretched arm, allowing herself to be guided to one of the two wingback chairs near the front windows.

"What's happened to yiz?" she whispered as she eased herself slowly into the chair.

"He was shot after he tackled me to the ground on the street. But he's going to be fine," Amanda said matter-of-factly, then, looking over at Mike and smiling, added, "It's just a flesh wound."

"Why?" Mary-Margaret asked.

"We don't know at this time," Amanda said, adopting a too-familiar formal tone. "But we've got investigators at the scene."

"Ach, that's the end of it then, Michael," his mother said, regaining her composure. "Ye are to put in yer papers first thing Monday mornin'."

"Mom—" Mike began.

"No," Mary-Margaret said firmly. "I can put up with ye bein' beaten within an inch of yer life by that madman with the pipe, but this? No. Monday mornin', yer lettin' them know ye're retirin'. And not a moment later."

She got up and walked over to the china cabinet.

"While I'm waitin' for ye to get me son settled in, I'm havin' a wee dram. Shall I put a glass out for ye as well, Mandy?" she asked, not turning around.

"I think I'll pass, Mary-Margaret," Amanda replied as she began to follow Mike up the stairs. "But don't let me hold you back."

"That'll be the frosty Tuesday," Mary-Margaret said, reaching up to the top shelf for the bottle of Jameson.

"I don't need help getting into bed," Mike said as he trudged up the stairs.

"Leave him be, then, Mandy," Mary-Margaret said, her hand shaking as she poured the

whisky. "I'll check in on him before tuckin' meself in."

"I'm fine!" Mike called from the landing.

"So fine that ye nearly lost yer arm. Are ye sure ye don't want that dram, Mandy?"

"I hope I'm not intruding," Carla said, coming up from her downstairs bedroom, "but I heard voices and…"

"Not at all," Mary-Margaret said. "Just me Michael gettin' himself shot up."

"What?" Carla exclaimed, lowering herself back down on the last step. "Wait. Shot? Is he—?"

"He's okay," Amanda said. "Just grazed."

"And you?" Carla asked.

"I'm sure I'll be sore tomorrow," Amanda said, taking a closer look at the scratches on her arms. "Mike tackled me to the ground when the car drove by."

"A drive-by? So they had someone in mind? The lads with the guns, I mean?" Mary-Margaret asked. "What, in God's name, have we come to?"

"Shit," Carla said under her breath, uttering a word she had never used in her life. "Mike was right."

Chapter Twenty

1:05 a.m., Saturday, April 13, 2019

Amanda fumbled with her keys, struggling to retrieve them from her purse as Tony opened the front door.

"I just need a minute, Tony. Where are the girls?" Amanda said, not making any attempt to step inside.

"They're out with friends," Tony said, taking her gently by the arm. "They're fine."

"Sorry I didn't call earlier. By the time I got to Mike's—"

"Babe, it's okay," he said, helping her get her tattered jacket off. "What do you need?"

"A hug," she said.

She collapsed into his arms, her body rigid at first, then softening as she surrendered to the comfort of his embrace. Her hands shook slightly, clinging to him as if grounding herself in the only thing that felt stable. And then the tears began. And the trembling.

"It's okay, babe," Tony said, stroking her hair while holding her close. "You're safe."

"Fuck, Tony," she said.

"I know," he said, although he really didn't. His world as a plumber was very different from hers.

"Do you think the girls know? It was all over the news, apparently," Amanda said, pulling herself away from him.

"I doubt it," he said. "There is more to the world than police work, you know."

"Yes, but—"

"They're out with their friends. Doing whatever it is teenaged girls do, which probably doesn't include checking the news."

"You're right," Amanda said, trying to wipe her snot and tears off Tony's shirt.

"Can I get you a glass of anything? Wine? Water? Bourbon?"

"I don't know," she said, looking around her living room as if it was the first time she'd ever seen it.

"Why don't you sit down?" he said, guiding her gently to a seat, echoing the tender care she had shown Mary-Margaret a few hours earlier. "Do you want to talk about it, or do you just want to go upstairs to bed?"

"Yes? No? I don't know," she whispered.

"I'm going to get myself a bourbon. Can I get you one?"

She shook her head.

"You're safe," Tony said again.

Am I?

Tony reappeared in the living room a few minutes later, carrying his bourbon and a glass of water for Amanda. He settled next to her on the couch, his presence a steady comfort.

"If Mike hadn't seen the shooter—" she began.

"What was it you always said?" Tony gently interrupted. "'Doesn't matter what could have been or what might have happened...'?"

"I know, but still...."

"The main thing is, you're okay," Tony said as he snuggled next to her on the couch. "And I saw on the news that Mike's okay too?"

"Lucky bastard," Amanda said, taking a sip of Tony's bourbon. "Maybe I will have a drink."

Tony gave her a kiss on the forehead before going back into the kitchen. "Bourbon or...?"

"Wine, please," she called back.

"Here you go," he said, handing her the glass.

"Thanks, hun. You know, I should call and find out who the OIC of this investigation is and—"

"You should sit and let them do their work," Tony countered.

"You're right," Amanda said, settling herself against him. She took a slow sip of wine. "This is good."

"Hmmm," he said, pulling her closer. He could sense the familiar, subtle tension in her body—a silent cue that her thoughts were miles away. It was a tell he'd picked up early on in their relationship, as recognizable to him as her favorite sweater. He could almost hear the wheels turning in her head, fixating on the investigation. While he would have preferred to discuss nearly anything else, he knew it was wise to guide the conversation in that direction.

"They're saying it was a targeted shooting," he said, aiming to anchor her focus.

"Who *they*?" she asked, stiffening as she turned around to look at him.

"Janelle Aust—"

"Oh, Christ!" she said, her body flopping back against him before taking a gulp of wine. "I can't believe they haven't fired her yet."

"Why would they? People love her."

"Because she makes shit up," Amanda stated.

"I think she's the least of your concerns now," Tony said, taking a sip of his drink.

"You're right," she said with a sigh. "But if it was a targeted hit, I think I might have been the target."

"Why now?" he asked, attempting to sound as nonchalant as possible. "You've put away a lot of heavy hitters over the years."

Amanda took a deep breath before replying. "I think it has to do with Bridget Calloway's murder."

Tony's face remained impassive as he absorbed this. They both took a sip of their drinks, the quiet between them heavy with unspoken thoughts.

"And Sal's murder," Amanda continued.

"Whose murder?" Tony asked, momentarily puzzled.

Amanda turned to him, her expression one of disbelief.

116

"Oh, right. That murder," he said. He was about to say that he'd nearly forgotten about that one, but decided not to.

Instead, the two of them lapsed into an uneasy silence, both considering what it would mean if she was, in fact, the intended target.

"I don't follow," he finally admitted.

Amanda took a deep breath, her tone shifting to one of authoritative precision as if she were briefing a colleague rather than discussing matters with her husband. "You know that Bridget Calloway was investigating possible connections between Mike's old partner's murder and the possibility of internal police corruption, right?"

"Really?" he asked, feigning curiosity.

"Yes," Amanda continued, "I'm sure I've mentioned this before."

"Maybe," he said, although he wasn't entirely sure.

"And," Amanda added, her voice steady, "Sal's murderer, Malcolm Oakes, has been allowed to remain at large because he—or whatever organized crime group he's linked to—is or was somehow connected to our senior management."

"Do you really believe that?" he asked, his tone more skeptical than he intended.

"I'm just following the evidence, and it all seems to lead to the same place."

"I wonder if it's too late to call your parents," he said, anxious to change the subject.

"Shit. Right," Amanda said, looking at her watch. "Yes. Definitely too late now. If they haven't called either of us yet, maybe they don't know—"

"Might want to give them a heads up at Hope Care," Tony said, referring to the nursing home Amanda's sister had just been moved to. "Unless you want me to call?"

"Would you?" she asked. "Although I'm sure it can wait until morning."

"No problem," Tony said.

"This wasn't a random drive-by," she said, reaching over and taking a sip of Tony's bourbon.

"Well," he said, taking the glass from her and finishing it off, "whatever it was, I'm just glad you're safe. And that you'll be moving out of Homicide once your promotion comes through."

"Who said anything about promotions coming through any time soon?" Amanda asked. "Or moving out of Homicide?"

"I'd say making Inspector sooner than later is practically a certainty for you," Tony replied, settling back into his seat. "And if you're aiming to climb the ranks, moving out of Homicide might be a necessary step."

Amanda didn't reply.

"Another drink or are you ready for bed?" Tony asked.

"If I get this promotion and they move me out, is that because I've earned the promotion or because they want me to leave this whole Oakes thing behind?"

"Ooof. Dunno, babe," Tony said, getting up from the couch, "although I doubt there's anyone more qualified for a promotion than you. I'll see you upstairs, okay? And make sure you put in a call tomorrow to that psychologist lady. It's not every day that you get shot at."

"I'll be up in a bit," Amanda said, squeezing his hand.

"And don't wait up for the girls, okay," he said as he went upstairs. "Doing that would freak them out way more than knowing you'd been shot at."

Chapter Twenty-One

11:00 a.m., Saturday, April 13, 2019

Mike turned off the windshield wipers and eased his truck against the curb in front of Ron Roberts' house. From the street, everything seemed ordinary—too ordinary, perhaps. Nothing about the scene suggested that Ron's wife had died just a few months ago. The garden was ready for the season—though it was too early for anything to be blooming. The old rule of thumb used to be to wait until after May twenty-fourth for frost to pass, but these days, who could tell? The weather was unpredictable, just like everything else.

Whether or not a late frost would come, the front garden was neatly manicured. The heavy rainfall earlier that morning had nearly drained off of the parking pad—a pad Ron had been quick to remind everyone he'd installed *legally*. The walkway was level, and the railings leading up to the front door were sturdy and well-kept.

Of course they are, Mike thought as he pressed the doorbell.

The door opened almost immediately.

"What...were you standing behind the door waiting for me?" Mike asked.

"Good morning," Ron said, ignoring Mike's comment. Leaving his old partner where he was, Ron turned and walked towards the back of the house into the kitchen. "Coffee?"

"I'll never say no to that," Mike said.

Even in retirement, Ron Roberts was the epitome of discipline. His trim physique—more a gift of genetics than the result of any strenuous exercise routine—made him look more like an accountant or a tax lawyer than a retired police detective. His greying hair was flawlessly trimmed and combed, and his khaki pants and navy-blue shirt were impeccably pressed. Mike smiled in relief when he saw Ron's top button undone—it was the only sign he wasn't about to throw on a tie and come out of retirement. Though, if he were, it'd be a suit, not the casual attire he was wearing now.

Despite the recent loss of his wife, Ron's demeanor and the pristine state of his home gave no hint of mourning. In fact, if Mike didn't know any better, he would have assumed that Ron was just having a quiet day off—except Mike knew better. Ron Roberts didn't take days off. Not really.

Having been left standing on the porch, Mike stepped inside the house and casually looked around. He noticed that the inside matched the meticulous order of the outside. His eyes drifted to the right and followed the staircase to the second floor, where a cat lounged on the landing, its green eyes fixed on him with an unnerving intensity.

"Still have the cat, I see?" Mike said, his voice tinged with a wry amusement. He quickly looked away and walked into the kitchen.

"Hmm?" Ron responded absentmindedly, his back to Mike as he rummaged through the coffee cupboard.

"The cat. I thought you were going to give it back," Mike said, sitting on the wooden chair Ron had indicated.

"I tried," Ron replied, his voice carrying a touch of frustration. He glanced at the various bags of coffee beans.

"And...?"

"Wouldn't take it back. I'm assuming you don't have a preference?"

"Whatever you're having is fine with me," Mike said. "But when did you become a coffee—"

"Always was," Ron replied, his tone nonchalant as he selected a bag of beans and poured them into the grinder. The machine roared to life with a thunderous noise that filled the room, abruptly stopping with a jarring clatter. "There. That should do it. I heard you were involved in quite the one-sided shoot-out last night."

"News travels," Mike said, suddenly aware of the pain in his left arm.

"Hard to miss. It was all over the news. Not every day an off-duty cop gets shot," Ron said. "Amanda's lucky you were there. I heard she was the target."

"News travels," Mike muttered, suddenly aware of the dull throb in his left arm.

"Don't worry," Ron said, his back to Mike as he continued to make the coffee. "Janelle Austin was the only one to suggest that it might have been more than a random drive-by."

"Shit."

"Here," Ron said, passing Mike a steaming mug of coffee. "I'll bring the box up from downstairs."

"Got any milk?"

"No."

Mike sighed and stared down at his black coffee. Just perfect. The cat wandered into the kitchen, glanced up at him disdainfully, then proceeded to sit down in front of him and lift its leg over its ear to begin licking its ass.

Lovely, Mike thought, wondering if he should pop one of the percs the doctor had given him or wait until he and Ron were finished.

"I'm not surprised," Ron remarked as he came up the stairs, open box in his arms. He nearly tripped over the cat before setting the box down in the center of the kitchen table. He shot a look at the cat, whose leg was still held high above his head, although the licking had stopped. "Go on, get out of here."

"And this is why I don't have a cat," Mike said.

"You've still got that dog, though, don't you?"

"Not my dog," Mike grumbled.

"Not my cat," Ron shot back with a slight smile. "So. I've been going through your old boss's files—"

"I thought you were going to leave them for me," Mike said, his voice betraying more disappointment than he'd intended.

"I gave you how many months...?" Ron said with a touch of exasperation, though his eyes held a twinkle of amusement. "Anyway, you can peruse everything at your leisure if you'd like, but I'd strongly suggest you take a look at this index book I've put together if you want to save yourself some time."

Ron produced a dollar-store notebook, its flimsy cover showing signs of wear as he handed it over to Mike.

"I've gone through everything in that box," Ron said, gesturing towards the cluttered container in front of them. "Itemized and cross-referenced it all in here."

"Nice," Mike said, flipping through the alphabetized pages of the booklet. "Where did you learn to do this? We used to do something similar for major cases back in the day."

"Still waters run deep," Ron replied cryptically, casting a glance at the box. "How's your coffee?"

"I haven't had a chance to—"

"Are you going to Fred Hogan's Celebration of Life next Thursday?" Ron asked before Mike could finish.

"Why would I?" Mike asked suspiciously

"I'll take that as a no," Ron said dryly. "Not that I'm one for going to things, but it wouldn't hurt you to show up. You two were close, weren't you? I guess not."

"He bailed."

"And they say I'm a curmudgeon."

"So about this stuff…?" Mike prompted, looking at the box in front of them.

"Right. From what I've seen here," Ron said. He leaned in slightly, his tone becoming serious, "Your old boss was neck-deep in it."

"Shit," Mike muttered, his shoulders sagging as he dropped his chin to his chest.

"But," Ron continued, "and you'll never hear me say this again—it wasn't his fault."

"What do you mean?" Mike asked, looking up with a mix of confusion and curiosity.

"After that unsolved murder with the little girl," Ron said, his voice lowering, "he was a mess, and they knew it. They had him by the proverbial short and curlies."

"You've lost me," Mike said, his brows knitting together in frustration.

"It might be easier for me to show you," Ron suggested as he pulled a chair up beside Mike. "Give me the book."

"Good thing you're on our side," Mike said, passing the notebook to Ron. He watched him begin flipping through the pages. Each one was meticulously catalogued with names, dates, addresses, and phone numbers, forming an intricate web of connections and details.

"Who said I am?" Ron said with a wry smile. "Regardless, I'd suggest you leave the box here. I'll give you a key so you can come and look at it whenever you want."

"Are you that lonely?" Mike asked, a hint of teasing in his voice.

"No," Ron replied, shaking his head. "But you'll see that there's enough here to make anyone who gets in the way a target. If Bridget Calloway was involved in this investigation, then I wouldn't be surprised if whoever is behind all of this was the shooter or ordered the hit."

"So what about you?" Mike asked, raising an eyebrow.

"What about me?"

"Now you're involved. Aren't you worried that someone will—"

"I may have turned in my service revolver when I retired," Ron said, his tone matter-of-fact, "but I still have seventeen guns stored here. All legally registered, I might add."

"You're an odd little man, Ron Roberts," Mike said, wincing slightly as he took a sip of the milkless coffee. "This tastes like shit."

* * *

Amanda pushed open the heavy doors of O'Leary's Pub, the creak of the hinges almost as conspicuous as her entrance. After her eyes adjusted to the dim light, she noticed that, aside from a pair of middle-aged men watching soccer on the TV above the bar, Mike was the only person in the place. It was too late for the lunch crowd and too early for the evening patrons. She made her way over to his table, looking at the half-finished pint of Guinness in front of him.

"I see you've started without me, Crumply Pants," she said, eyebrow raised.

"This isn't a social call," Mike said flatly.

"Oh good," she said glibly, sitting down across from him with a dry smile. "I'd hate to think you'd started day-drinking."

"I just came from Ron Roberts," he said.

"And how *is* Ron?" Amanda asked, her intuition tingling as she began to notice something off about Mike.

"He's indexed the entire box," he stated.

Maeve O'Leary appeared at their table.

"What can I get ye?" she asked.

"I'm fine," Amanda began, and then paused. She looked over at Mike. "Actually, I'll have a glass of your house red."

"And yer okay fer now, are ye, Mike?" Maeve asked, eyeing him.

He nodded, barely looking up at her.

"Tell yer mam that she broke a few hearts last night with her singin' o'*Danny Boy*, will ye?" Maeve said. "Voice like an angel, that one. Not sayin' I was cryin', but me eyes were waterin', I'll admit. Haven't had singin' in this pub like that before. Reminded me of home. God, I miss it."

Mike nodded again, his disinterest in the conversation evident. Maeve caught the hint and turned to head back to the bar. Both Mike and Amanda watched her go.

"Everything we need to prove internal corruption is right there," he said, his voice barely above a whisper.

"And who, exactly," Amanda whispered back, leaning in towards him, "are our accused?"

Mike stared at her, incredulous.

"You're joking, right? I've just laid out a case of a decades-long cover-up, and you—"

"And I've just told you," Amanda interrupted, her tone firm but not unkind, "that I need a way to bring this to court. We're real cops, Mike. This isn't like on TV, remember?"

"Here ye go, luv," Maeve said, setting Amanda's wine down in front of her.

"And I saw on the telly that yiz were both shot at last night. Reminds me of The Troubles. Jaysus, Mike. The world's gone mad, hasn't it?"

"We're okay," Mike replied curtly, his tone ending the conversation.

"I guess this is another year you won't be getting the Mister Congeniality Award," Amanda said, once Maeve had returned to the bar.

"Are you not hearing me?" Mike spat, his frustration evident. "I've got—"

"The box, Mike," Amanda pressed, leaning in slightly. "Where is it?"

With an abrupt motion, Mike pushed his chair back from the table, causing the two drinks on it to teeter precariously. He glared at Amanda with a mixture of accusation and disbelief.

"You're on the list, aren't you?" he growled, his voice a low snarl, teeth clenched.

Amanda's eyes widened, and she cast a wary glance at the two men at the bar who had started to watch their exchange with keen interest.

"What are you talking about?" she asked, her voice barely more than a whisper. "And for god's sake, keep your voice down."

"The promotional list," Mike said, his voice dropping to a conspiratorial murmur. "You're on it. You're going to become one of them, aren't you?"

Amanda's expression hardened. She began to rise from her seat, but Mike's hand shot out to stop her.

"Mike, I think—"

"You want me to turn over the only remaining evidence so that you can shred it, don't you?" Mike snapped. "They sent you, didn't they?"

"Just to refresh your memory," Amanda corrected, her tone clipped, "you called me."

"And then you called them so that they could tell you what to do," Mike countered.

"And...we're done," Amanda said, reaching for her purse. "Don't worry. I'll cover your goddamn pint."

"Wait," Mike said, suddenly aware of the impact his words had on her.

"And if you don't get yourself off of those fucking pills," Amanda said sharply as she stood, her eyes flashing with a mix of frustration and concern, "I'm going to have to take disciplinary action against you."

"This has nothing to do with that," Mike stated.

"They're making you cra-cra, Mike," Amanda stated, softening a bit. "If you're going to help me put Malcolm Oakes away forever, I need you to be clean and sober, got it?"

"What about—"

"Let's go one step at a time," Amanda said, turning towards the bar. She paused and then turned back. "And when are you seeing Shimner-Lewis again, or are you too far gone now?"

Mike didn't answer as he watched Maeve push Amanda's credit card away.

"It's on the house today, luv," he heard Maeve say. He watched Amanda leave before upending his glass and heading towards the door himself.

"Don't forget to tell your mam," Maeve called after him. "Like an angel, she was."

Chapter Twenty-Two

6:17 p.m., Sunday, April 14, 2019

"Where is me Michael?" Mary-Margaret's voice cut through the chatter of her family. "We can't sit down until he gets here."

"Since when?" Allan muttered.

"Allan!" Teaszy hissed.

"It's not like we can't just sit down now. Like we've never started without him before," Allan whispered to his wife.

"I'm sure he's on his way," Katie said, trying to inject a note of calm into the situation. Her attempt was met with a skeptical frown from Mary-Margaret.

"On his way?" Mary-Margaret's eyebrows arched incredulously. "From where? He knows we eat at six sharp. The dinner's been on the table for…" she glanced at the clock, "ten minutes. The cabbage is getting soggy, and the corned beef isn't getting any warmer."

"Why don't we just sit down and—" Teaszy began.

"And what?" Mary-Margaret cut in, her tone suggesting to everyone that she was in no mood to be toyed with. "Pretend that everythin's just grand?"

"I'm sure…" Katie said, attempting to provide some reassurance, her voice faltering as Ahmed came to stand behind her.

"Are ye, now?" Mary-Margaret's gaze swung sharply to her younger daughter. "And since when did you and the Almighty start tradin' secrets?"

"What are you so concerned about, Mom?" Teaszy asked.

"Yer brother was shot at just the other night and yer askin' me—"

127

"I know, and I'm sorry," Teaszy said softly. "What I meant was—he can—" Mary-Margaret's stare shut Teaszy down.

"I think she's finally lost—" Allan started. He, too, was swiftly silenced by Mary-Margaret's fierce glare.

"You couldn't have just kept quiet, eh, Daddy-o?" Paulie said with a sigh.

"I've lost nothing," Mary-Margaret retorted, her voice brimming with defensive anger. "Except one son to the streets and judging by the looks of things now, another to his demons. Or the madman drivin' around out there shootin' at him."

"I think—" Ahmed began, but his words were overwhelmed by the weight of Mary-Margaret's rage.

"I don't care what ye think," she snapped. "Where is me Michael?"

The room seemed to hold its breath, as if everyone was bracing for what might come next.

"Gran," Max said, his voice calm and steady, the kind of tone that suggested he had been through this kind of thing before. "Dad's probably just running late."

Mary-Margaret's frantic gaze shifted toward her grandson, his words sinking into her like a soft anchor. If anyone should be frantic, it should be the one most affected if something happened to Mike—his own son. But he wasn't. Unlike his grandmother, Max hadn't forgotten that they'd been through this kind of thing before—late dinners, sudden changes in plans, and even injuries that made this latest one seem almost trivial. It was just part of life in a police family, where unpredictability was the norm and emergencies were never far behind. Mary-Margaret slowly exhaled, the tension in her shoulders easing slightly, and for a moment, the flood of worries in her mind seemed to slow. She blinked, as if snapping out of a trance, her eyes softening just a little.

"Ach, you're right, lad," she murmured, her voice losing some of its earlier sharpness. "Well then… shall we all just go ahead and sit down?"

They settled into their usual spots: Mary-Margaret at one end, Max to her right, and Paulie to her left. Allan was strategically seated at the top of the table, as far as possible from Mary-Margaret to avoid conflict. An empty seat was reserved for Mary-Margaret's late husband and another for her long-lost son, Petey, though it was sometimes taken by a guest. Katie sat beside Paulie, with Ahmed directly across from her. Teaszy was placed between Allan and Ahmed to prevent her from kicking her husband under the table after one of his snide remarks. Mike's spot next to his younger sister remained vacant.

No one said a word, a palpable tension still lingering in the air.

"Are you going to say grace, Gran?" Max prompted.

"Right," she said, bowing her head. "Bless us, O Lord, and these Thy gifts, which we are about to receive from Thy bounty, through Christ our Lord. Amen."

"Amen," everyone around the table echoed dutifully. Mary-Margaret made the sign of the cross, scanning the room to ensure everyone else had followed suit. The corned beef, cabbage, and mashed potatoes made their slow rounds around the table, the room filling with the rich scent of the meal. But still, no one spoke. The only sounds were the rustle of napkins and the quiet scurrying of Wee Phil under the table, hunting for scraps.

"'Tis no use, lads," Mary-Margaret said, getting up and tossing her napkin down on her chair. "Somethin' has happened to me Michael and I couldn't shove a bite down me throat if I tried with me stomach in knots like this."

"Well, when you put it like that..." Allan began, pushing his plate away.

"Which is no excuse for not eatin' me Sunday dinner," Mary-Margaret stated firmly as she strode into the kitchen. Teaszy and the tiny dog followed her, with Teaszy pausing to give her husband a swat on the back of his head.

"Do you think he's okay?" Max asked.

"I'm sure he is," Ahmed replied reassuringly.

"Has anyone tried to...oh, I don't know...phone him?" Paulie suggested with a shrug, rolling his eyes as he put a fork loaded with mashed potatoes into his mouth. "This shouldn't be rocket science, people."

"Right," Katie said, getting up to grab her purse from the coat rack by the front door. "I'll give him a call."

"You do know he's not actually missing, right?" Paulie said, scanning the table for some sign of agreement. Receiving none, he went on, carefully slicing a piece of corned beef and spearing it with a bit of cabbage. "Uncle Mike's a busy boy. Maybe he's finally actually taking some time for himself for a change. Who knows? He could be just about anywhere. Except missing, of course."

"Let's just…wait," Ahmed said, looking over at Max who, despite his mostly calm demeanor, was showing signs of concern.

"Mike. Katie. Call me as soon as you get this," Katie said into her cell phone. "It's Sunday night and Mom is frea—"

The front door opened as Mike stepped inside, nudging the door open further with his shoulder while juggling his keys in one hand and reaching into his coat pocket for his cell phone with the other.

"Where have you been?" Katie demanded as Wee Phil came bounding out of the kitchen towards him.

"Out?" Mike offered, stunned to see everyone sitting at his dining room table. "I suppose Mom's going to want me to take him out the back?"

"Do you not know what time it is?" Katie demanded. All eyes were on the two of them.

"Well, it's not dark out, so it can't be that late."

"It's after six, Mike. And it's Sunday. Mom's losing her mind!"

"Oh, shit," Mike said, his shoulders slumping as the dog danced around his feet. "I completely forgot."

"Forgot? Really? Since when do you forget Sunday dinner? Mom's practically—"

"Michael!" Mary-Margaret exclaimed, shoving past Katie and enveloping her son in a hug as if he were a long-lost treasure. "Oh, Michael!"

"Mom," Mike said, feeling the pressure of her grip. "Sorry. I forgot."

"Forgot, did ye? Ach, what in heaven's name has come over ye, Michael? It's not like ye to be forgettin' things. Are ye feelin' alright?" she asked, putting the back of her hand on his forehead. "It's that gettin' shot that's done ye—"

"Maybe we'd better just go home," Ahmed suggested as he stood up.

"She's losing her mind, Theresa," Allan said, using her full name for the first time in ages as she sat down beside him. "I told you—"

"There's nothing wrong with Mom," Teaszy said loudly. "It's Mike. He's the one—"

"Everybody just…just stay put. Sit down, Ahmed," Mike interrupted, gently extricating himself from his mother's embrace. "And you're right, Teaszy. It is me. And I'm sorry. Just give me a second to wash up and I'll be right back and we'll all have dinner. Does that work for you, Mom?"

"Why don't ye just wash up in here," she said, taking him by the shoulders and gently steering him past the table towards the kitchen.

"I also have to go to the bathroom, Mom," Mike said, pivoting towards the stairs.

"But—"

"Non-negotiable. And I'm alright. Just a bit late, that's all."

"But what if ye become unsteady on yer pins?" Mary-Margaret said. "Allan, go on upstairs with Michael and—"

"Stay where you are, Allan. I'm good."

Mary-Margaret watched Mike walk up the stairs, looking at him as if he might disappear after each step.

"See?" Paulie said, sitting back in his chair. "I told you he was fine."

Once Mike was out of view, Mary-Margaret took a deep breath and returned to the table, Wee Phil trotting at her heels.

"Since yer all for gettin' up, Allan, how about ye take the pup out to the jacks."

"I'll do it, Mary-Margaret," Ahmed said, noticing the scowl on Allan's face.

"Ach, such a gem," she said with a smile. "So, has everyone warm enough, or do I need to be shovin' plates into the microwave? Looks like you've already started, Paulie. Glad to see yer not slimmin' again."

Mike came down and took his seat, and everyone at the table lifted their forks almost in unison, as if to collectively bury the awkwardness of the few moments before.

"No, I'm done with men," Paulie said, reaching across the table for the bowl of mashed potatoes.

Allan leaned in towards Teaszy, his voice a low, knowing murmur. "I told you it was just a phase," he whispered to his wife.

Katie leaned across the table toward Allan and whispered, "I don't think it works quite that way."

"Well, however it works, I'm out," Paulie said dramatically.

"Girls are no better," Max chimed in before shoving a forkful of corned beef into his mouth.

"And you'd know this how?" Mary-Margaret asked. "And could someone pass the cabbage this way, please? Don't forget to have some cabbage, Paulie. It's very good for ye. Makes yer skin glow."

Allan looked as if he was going to say something, but Teaszy gave him a cautionary tap on his leg.

There was a knock on the door. Mike got up and answered it.

"Oh, shoot," Carla exclaimed, seeing the whole family seated at the table. "I'm sorry. It's just that I forgot my key. I didn't mean to—"

"Come in. Yer out," Mary-Margaret called to her. "There's a spot set for ye right beside Michael. Sitcheedoon."

"No, I'll just go downst—" Carla began, walking towards the back stairs.

"Sure and all, but ye'll have a bite of dinner first," Mary-Margaret stated firmly.

"Are there any more mashed, Gran?" Paulie asked as Carla and Mike sat down.

"There's plenty more in the kitchen," she replied with a wave.

Paulie got up, plate in hand.

"Are ye only servin' yerself, then, lad, or do ye want to take the servin' dish with ye and fill it up so that Carla can have a helpin' as well?"

"Oh, I'm—"

"Never let it be said that ye came to me table and there were no potatoes to be had," Mary-Margaret said. "Now, Paulie. Be a good lad and go fill the dish."

Paulie huffed but complied, bringing a full serving dish back to the table. The dish was passed to Carla, and as everyone started to talk again, the tension in the room seemed to lift slightly. Conversations picked up in fits and starts, a mix of light teasing and casual chatter. The atmosphere around the table, while still layered with some unease, began to soften. Mary-

Margaret smiled faintly as she watched her family, noting how the familiar rhythms of Sunday Dinner slowly started to take hold again.

She stood up to clear the plates in preparation for dessert, but before she could get far, Carla—who had been quietly sitting beside Mike—gently tapped her spoon against her water glass. The soft clink of metal on glass cut through the low murmur of conversation, drawing the attention of everyone at the table.

"I'd just like to make a toast, if I may?" she said, looking around the table. "To my friend, Michael, and his mother, Mary-Margaret, and all of you, who have made me feel so welcome since I showed up on the back doorstep a while back."

"Ach, 'tis us who should be raisin' a glass to ye, luv," Mary-Margaret said. "And speakin' of which, can ye pull down the whiskey on the top shelf there, Michael, and we'll have a proper toast?"

"I'll get it," Ahmed said, quickly rising from the table.

"Ach, yer a lamb," Mary-Margaret said.

As Ahmed poured a shot for everyone, Mary-Margaret lifted her glass with a flourish. "And let's not forget to toast Michael's retirement," she announced.

"I'm not—" Mike started to protest.

"Oh, but ye are," she interrupted with a decisive nod. "Sláinte!"

In unison, everyone downed their shots. Before Mike could get a word in edgewise, the plates were swiftly cleared away, replaced with generous bowls of bread pudding.

"Mom…" Mike tried again.

"Not a word more," she said firmly, her tone not allowing for argument. "Now, Carla, luv. Dig in. Not a calorie to be had in me bread puddin'."

Chapter Twenty-Three

9:03 a.m., Monday, April 15, 2019

The cell phone in Mike's pocket vibrated.

"Michael, 'tis yer mother."

Oh, shit, he thought. Carla looked over her reading glasses and, without being told who was calling, smiled. Mike responded with a dramatic roll of his eyes.

"It's after nine o'clock and I'm sure their offices are open now, so have ye sent them yer retirement papers?"

"No, I haven't," Mike answered truthfully.

"And why not?"

"Because I'm not retiring, Mom."

"I see."

There was a pause.

"So what I'm hearing is that—"

"What you're hearing is that I'm not retiring."

"I see."

There was another pause.

"Well, since yer intent on givin' St. Sebastian a run for his money, pick up some dog food for Wee Phil on yer way home tonight, will ye?"

"Sure, Mom."

"And not that cheap muck that ye picked up last time that had him havin' to run out the door faster than any of yer Aunt Celeste's boyfriends. Get the good stuff this time."

"Which would be...?"

"Ach, I don't know what it's called at this very moment, but I'm thinkin' it has a picture of a happy wee pup running in a field or some other such thing on the packaging."

"I'll be sure to pick up some Happy Pup Dog Food," Mike said, noticing that Carla was smirking.

"That is *not* what it's called, Michael," Mary-Margaret almost shouted into the phone.

"Good morning, Dream Team," Amanda Black said as she burst into the detective office. "Am I interfering with a personal call, Mike?"

"I have to go, Mom." Not waiting for a response, Mike clicked off the phone.

"And how is your mother this morning?" Amanda asked.

"Lonely," Mike said, then looked at Carla. "Are you sure you don't want to reconsider?"

"I'll always have time for your mother," Carla replied, "but it's time for me to put on my big girl panties and live on my own."

"Well, I'm glad we got that sorted out," Amanda said. "Seth Samuels is out of the ICU and onto a regular floor. We've had him moved into a private room. He needs to be interviewed this morning, and you two are doing it for me."

"Oh," Mike replied. "I thought we were back on regular—"

"As a favour," Amanda added.

"Oh."

"Unless you have anything more pressing?" Amanda asked. She looked towards the open door leading to the hallway that connected the office to the cell area. Along that hallway were two small interview rooms, typically used for questioning people under arrest, and the doors to both were empty.

"We'll just freshen up and be on our way, won't we, Michael?" Carla said with a smile intended to calm whatever storm Mike seemed intent on creating.

Mike gave a reluctant nod.

"Sure," he muttered, standing up and grabbing their coats from the coatrack.

"Great," Amanda said, turning to leave. "Keep me posted."

As Amanda left, Carla and Mike exchanged a look.

"That was awkward," Carla said, reaching for her purse in the bottom drawer.

"I guess."

"When did you become an insolent fourteen-year-old boy, Michael?"

"I didn't," Mike said. "I'm just tired of everyone sticking their noses in my business."

"Pardon me?"

"Never mind," Mike said. He tossed Carla her coat before shrugging his own on.

"Oh. You mean your drug dependency-slash-addiction messy life business?" Carla said, the tone of her voice cutting through his irritable self-pity. Without waiting for a response, she grabbed the car keys from the corner of Mike's desk. "I'm driving."

He followed her out the back doors, a few steps behind. As they walked to the car, he discreetly popped the last of the Percs the hospital had given him. The bitterness hit his tongue, an unpleasant reminder of the price he was paying, but Mike welcomed the numbness that would follow.

* * *

By the time Carla parked the car, Mike's eyelids were heavy, his gaze unfocused as the pills started to pull him under.

"Shall we get a coffee first, Michael?" Carla suggested loudly, despite knowing that natural fatigue wasn't the issue.

"Sure," Mike said, shaking himself awake.

"And how about I take the lead on this one?"

"Great," Mike said, his mind and body enveloped by the soothing numbness he craved.

"Great," Carla said, holding back a flood of things she wanted to say.

Should have said.

"How's the shoulder?" the doctor from the other night asked as they both walked through the emergency room.

"So far, so good," Mike said. "But I'm out of the pills you gave me, and I was wondering if—"

"This way, Michael," Carla said, gently pushing him in the direction of the elevators.

"Sure, but first—"

"Amanda wants that interview done sooner than later," Carla said, watching the numbers above the elevator doors count down. "And look. The elevator's here."

Carla practically shoved Mike in as soon as it emptied out.

"I thought we were going to get a coffee first," Mike said.

"Plans change," Carla said sharply, the door sliding shut behind them. Rather than face him, she watched the numbers go up.

"Is something wrong?" Mike asked.

"Yes," Carla stated.

"Okay," Mike said slowly. "Want to talk about it?"

"Yes," Carla said as the doors opened. "When we're finished the interview."

She strode out of the elevator, leaving Mike almost having to jog to keep up with her.

"Knock knock," she called as she pushed the door to Seth's room open. "Are you decent in there?"

The young man glanced up from his bed as the two detectives stepped into the room. Though he remained tethered to the monitors, the tubes that had once poked into his arms were gone. As were the four-point restraints.

"I'm Detective Hageneur and this is my partner, Detective O'Shea," she said, pulling a couple of chairs around. "I don't know if you remember us, but—"

"Yeah," he said. "I remember you."

"Lovely," Carla said, pulling a steno pad and a tape recorder out of her purse as she settled into the chair closest to the bed. She noticed that Mike was still standing in the doorway, appearing adrift. "Michael, why don't you sit over there?"

"Right," he said.

"And have you got a steno pad?"

"Uh…"

"Never mind. Okay, so," Carla said, focusing her attention on Seth. "I'm going to start the tape recorder, and we're going to ask you a few questions."

"Sure," Seth replied, taking a deep breath.

Carla pressed the record button on the tape recorder, her gaze unwavering as she informed him that he was expected to give a truthful account of events or face the possibility of criminal charges. Then, with a deliberate calm, she waited.

"I don't even know where to start," Seth said at last, his voice trembling as tears welled up in his eyes.

"Why don't we start with the last thing you remember?" Carla prompted, her voice steady despite the nagging distraction of Mike's peculiar behavior and her growing concern that he might be sliding into serious addiction.

"Ugh," Seth said with a sigh. "So, yeah. I remember going out with this friend of mine. Maybe it was the night before…? I don't know. But it's the last thing I remember."

"Great," Carla said, noticing out of the corner of her eye that Mike's head was starting to bob. "Let's talk about that, then, shall we?"

"Sure," Seth said. "Me and her, we get together once in a while. Not, like, you know, boyfriend and girlfriend but, like, you know…."

Carla waited.

"So yeah. I made sure Mom was okay. Gave her all her meds, made sure she had the remote for the TV. You know, like that, and then I went out."

Carla nodded slowly at Seth while noticing that Mike's eyes were now shut and his head continued to bob with a disconcerting rhythm.

"And then we came back to my place. Mom was asleep and we kind of, you know, started fooling around, and then I noticed that Mom was kind of having a hard time breathing, so I went over and made sure there was nothing blocking her breathing apparatus or anything like that, but she was still kind of gasping, you know?"

Seth paused.

"Did this happen regularly?" Carla asked.

"No, not really," he replied and then was silent.

"When you say 'gasping'…?"

"You know, gasping," Seth said, and then began to gasp.

"And did you call for an ambulance?"

"No."

"Why not?"

"Um, mostly because we were pretty, you know, fucked up."

"What do you mean, 'fucked up'?" Carla said, shooting a glance over at Mike, who was now slumped in the chair, either unflatteringly asleep or, even worse, completely passed out.

"You know. We'd taken some shit, right, so, you know…."

"Do you know what kind of…shit?"

"Not totally, no."

"Okay, so your mother is gasping," Carla said. "Then what?"

"Then, well, she calls this guy who comes over."

"So you're too—fucked up—to call an ambulance, but not to call some guy over?" Carla asked, her voice tight as she wrestled with her conflicting emotions towards Mike—part anger, part pity—while trying to push aside the troubling image of Seth as a grim projection of her partner's potential future.

"Yeah. I know. It sounds really fucked up, doesn't it, but that's what drugs'll do to you, you know?"

"I do know," Carla said, not looking at Mike. "And so…?"

"And so this guy comes over and he says it sounds like my mom is having an asthma attack."

"And he would know this because…?"

"He said he had asthma."

"Of course," Carla said. "And then what?"

"And then he says that he's got an old inhaler, and that maybe it would help if my mom could just inhale some of it, you know

"And did she?"

"Not exactly," Seth said.

"Meaning…?"

"Well, she was kind of passed out, you know? So we kind of figured that if we kind of got some of that shit from the inhaler into her machine…."

Seth let his sentence hang, as if the conclusion was obvious.

"What does that mean?" Carla asked.

"Well, he, the guy, kind of opened up his inhaler and tore off a piece of his t-shirt. He covered it with the medicine stuff inside the inhaler, you know, and then figured that putting the cloth inside the breathing apparatus would get it into her."

"And did it?"

"I guess," Seth said with a shrug.

"You guess?"

"Yeah. Well, I mean, after that, she stopped gasping."

"And did you check in on her to see if…?"

"Naw," Seth said. "Like I said, we were pretty fucked up, and that was before that guy came over. He must have brought more shit or something because I remember taking something from him, and the next thing I know, I'm here."

"I see," Carla said. She looked at Mike, wondering how she was going to wake him up without appearing obvious.

"Do you know who this guy that came over is?"

"Nope. Never saw him before in my life."

"Okay. But you do know who the woman you brought home is, I'm assuming."

"Yeah. Of course I do. I already told you I knew her."

"And…? A name…?"

"Madison. Her name is Madison."

Carla looked at Seth and then, realizing that he wasn't going to say anything more, asked, "Madison, who?"

"Dunno."

"But you said you've been seeing her for a while…?"

"Not seeing but, you know….yeah."

"So how did you…see her that evening?"

"Met her at the coffee shop where she works," Seth said plainly.

Carla got a description of the woman, along with a general location for the coffee shop where she worked and an estimate of her working hours. She then asked Seth if there was anything else he wanted to add.

"Naw," he said with a yawn. "Not really, except how did I end up lying there for so long?"

"I'm sure the doctors here can explain that to you better than I," Carla said, stashing the tape recorder and the steno pad in her purse, "but I'm thinking you probably overdosed and would have died if the dog groomer hadn't called the police."

"Wow," Seth said, nodding slowly. "So we both could have died?"

"I'd say so, wouldn't you, Michael?"

"Hmm?" Mike said, rousing himself. "Yes. Absolutely."

"Well, thanks for…finding me, I guess," Seth said.

"You're welcome," Carla said, passing him her card. "I'm sure they have our number at the desk, but if you think of anything else, please give me a call. Ready, Michael?"

* * *

Later that evening, Carla popped the cork off the prosecco bottle she'd had chilling in the fridge, her present self silently thanked her past self for remembering to stash the bottle in the fridge as soon as she'd taken possession of the apartment that afternoon.

Not quite midnight, and I'm moved in. Not bad. Not bad at all.

With a flourish, she poured the bubbly into the solitary champagne flute she'd meticulously packed for this occasion, then sank onto her new IKEA couch, propping her feet on a box still waiting to be unpacked.

"To me," she said aloud, raising the glass. "To me."

She savoured the tickling fizz of the bubbly wine, even taking a moment to swish it around her mouth before swallowing. While this wasn't where she'd thought she'd be at this juncture, Carla had to admit that, given a little time, she could fall in love with this apartment. Instead of settling for a bland, cookie-cutter condo with no soul, she had splurged on something with character: a two-bedroom, two-bathroom find, complete with a den, a good-sized living room with a decommissioned fireplace, and a dining room that flowed into a large-ish kitchen. The only box that wasn't checked on her wish list was a balcony, but, given the four-story walk-up's age, it was to be expected. And the charm of the place far outweighed her need for a balcony.

The move went as expected—better than expected, actually—proving that there was something to be said about being able to pack all of your worldly belongings into a few boxes.

Thank you, Linda, Carla thought, raising her glass to the ex-wife who had destroyed everything she held dear from her previous life.

All of the other things—the furniture, the pots and pans, the bed, sheets, and towels—arrived from the stores without a hitch. Aside from a few curious glances from the deliverymen, the process went smoothly. Admittedly, those looks might not have meant anything, but Carla assumed they did, having learned over the past few months that part of her new life involved accepting that not everyone would immediately see her for who she had become.

If they could see me now, that little gang of mine, Carla sang softly to herself as she looked at the empty walls, wishing she'd had the time to paint before moving in.

Probably could have waited a few days, she thought, pouring herself another splash. *Actually could have. I'm sure Mary-Margaret wouldn't have minded. Michael would have, but....*

As she sipped the second glass, actively trying not to think of him, Carla was struck by the silence of her new home. The sort of silence that invited the voices in one's head to start weaving their deceptions.

Not tonight, Carla said out loud, taking the box her feet had been resting on into the main bedroom to begin to unpack.

Ping

Carla checked her iPhone.

Hope you're settled in. Mom misses you already. LMK if you need anything. Sorry about today. Tomorrow will be better.

She looked at the message for several minutes, feeling the anger rise inside of her. And the judgement. And the sadness. She now knew, beyond a shadow of a doubt, that Mike was in trouble. She also knew that she couldn't save him, especially after the talk she'd had with him that afternoon and the silence that had followed. But she also knew that she couldn't stand by and watch him destroy himself.

Thank you, Michael. Enjoying some prosecco at the moment. And unpacking. Still. CU in the am.

She hit SEND, then quickly turned to her Spotify app, opening her Happy Songs playlist before her emotions could overwhelm her. She pressed play, turned up the volume, and proceeded to retrieve a sweater from the box, placing it neatly in her freshly assembled dresser.

Chapter Twenty-Four

2:17 p.m., Tuesday, April 16, 2019

"Where's Mike?" Amanda Black asked.

"He didn't come in today," Carla said.

"Oh. That's surprising."

"Is it?" Carla responded with a sad smile, fully aware that they both knew about Mike's declining situation but preferred to talk around it.

"I guess everyone's entitled to a sick day now and again," Amanda said, her attention returning to the closed door, behind which a woman sat on the metal table that was screwed to the floor rather than the metal chair, also screwed to the floor. "Good job on that report yesterday, by the way. We found her."

"Who?"

"Madison Olsen, Seth Samuels' girlfriend."

"Oh," Carla said, wondering how long either of them could keep away from the elephant in the room.

"She was just brought in, and we need to get a statement from her. Are you coming or going?"

"I'm not sure these days," Carla said.

"I could use the help, if you're able to stay. Ralph's in court and—"

"I'm supposed to be off in an hour, but—"

"I'll talk to the Staff. Can you go downstairs and get the interview room ready, please? Her lawyer is on the way."

"Boss?" A uniformed officer from the front desk poked his head in the door. "Guess Who is at the front desk."

"Shit," Amanda muttered.

"Do you want me to—"

"No. Tell her the investigation is in its infancy, we're dedicating all of our available resources, blah blah blah. You know the routine. I don't have time for this right now. Especially when it comes to Janelle Austin."

"Do you want me to tell her that last bit, too?" the uniformed officer said with a laugh.

"Jesus," Amanda said with a smile. "That's all I need."

"Especially if they promote you into Corp Comm."

"Don't ever let those words leave your mouth again, do you hear me?" she said with a shudder. Having to spew corporate jargon was enough to make her stomach churn. Hopefully, The Powers That Be would have enough sense not to send her there.

"I'll get rid of her," the uniformed officer said, heading back to the front.

"And let me know when Olsen's lawyer gets here," Amanda called after him.

"Who is it?" he called back.

"Rejeanne Carr."

"Speaking of pains in the asses," he called as he strolled back to his post.

"Is her name written on the interview room walls or something?" Carla said. "This is the fourth time she's represented one of our accused."

"Probably ticking off her pro bono hours," Amanda said, knowing that most of the defendants from Six District didn't have the means to afford a defense lawyer of Carr's caliber.

"I gotta pee!" Madison Olsen called out from behind the interview room door.

"Just a minute," Amanda said. "I'll get someone to take you to the bathroom."

"I'll do it," Carla offered.

"No," Amanda said. "I need you to get the interview room ready."

As Carla exited the detective office, she couldn't shake the thought that

Amanda's choice might hint at some underlying bias against her being transgender.

"Grace, Carla. Give them grace," she murmured to herself as she walked down into the dingy basement where the DVD equipment was set up. "And try not to jump to the worst conclusions."

One of the phones in the detective office began to ring. Amanda ignored it. Shortly after it stopped ringing, another started to ring. Amanda ignored that one, too. When a third phone began to ring, Amanda picked it up.

"Detective Sergeant Black speaking," she said.

"Christ, Boss," the uniformed officer said. "Do you need an invitation?"

"What do you mean?"

"I've been trying to call you to let you know that Carr's here. I would have just come back and got you, but Austin's still hovering."

"Damn it. Get someone from the front to escort Carr downstairs before Austin can get to her," Amanda snapped, slamming the receiver into its cradle. The unsettling image of Rejeanne Carr giving a stand-up with Janelle Austin on the six o'clock news nearly made her gag.

"Hello?" Madison called out.

"Hang on," Amanda said. "I've got someone coming."

"Can't wait," Madison replied.

"Ugh," Amanda said, turning to the interview room and opening the door. "Okay. Here's the deal: I'll take you, but, if you run, I'll throw my shoe at you and it'll probably kill you."

Madison looked down at Amanda's stilettos, clearly unimpressed.

"I'm not kidding," Amanda said, standing on the toe of one shoe to display the slender three-inch heel. "And then we're going to go downstairs to talk."

"But I want my lawyer—"

"She's here," Amanda said, grasping Madison's arm and guiding her down the narrow hallway to the solitary cell at the end of the row, the only one without a camera fixed on it. Once they reached the cell, Amanda let go of Madison's arm. "Go."

"I can't go here," Madison groaned.

"I'll turn away," Amanda said.

"But—"

"This is your only choice," Amanda said, taking a deep breath.

"Fine," Madison said. "But…yeah. Look away."

"Don't worry," Amanda said as she turned her back to the young woman. She held the cell door slightly ajar.

"Everything okay, Detective Sergeant?" the booking hall officer bellowed from the top of the row of cells.

"We're fine," Amanda called back.

"I can't go now," Madison whined.

"Oh, sorry," the booker said, suddenly understanding why Amanda had brought her prisoner to that particular cell. "I should have figured as much. Never mind. It's okay, Madison. You can pee now."

"Thanks," she called back. "Nothing like making it a public event."

Despite her objections, Madison was able to urinate in the metal toilet.

"The water doesn't work," she said, twisting the faucet on the tiny metal sink.

"Sorry," Amanda said, taking her by the arm. "I can give you a wet wipe when we get downstairs."

* * *

"Oh, here you are," Carla said as Amanda led Madison Olsen into the room. "I was just about to comment on the lovely suit Ms. Carr's wearing."

"Thank you," Rejeanne Carr said with a hint of condescension, peering into her attaché case in a manner that suggested there were actual files relating to her current client's matter inside.

"Rejeanne," Amanda said, thrusting her hand out—not so much as a greeting, but more as a signal that the game had begun. The two women were very familiar with each other, having crossed swords in countless homicide trials. In many ways, they were quite similar: both clever, intense, and fiercely competitive. They also shared a love of fashion, though Carr, with her life in private practice, had far more freedom to indulge her personal style—something Amanda, bound by the protocols of her profession and the limits of a police-officer salary, could only dream of.

"Amanda," the lawyer said, not making eye contact as she limply shook Amanda's hand.

"Those wipes?" Madison said as she sat down beside her lawyer.

"Oh," Amanda said. "Right. Carla, would you mind...?"

"I've got some in my purse," the lawyer said, pulling out a package of sanitized wipes and passing them to her client.

"All set?" Amanda asked, looking at the antiquated recording equipment that faced Madison and her lawyer.

"Rolling," Carla said, leaning back to press the PLAY button on the DVD player.

Both Amanda and Rejeanne Carr put their iPhones on the table and activated the audio record feature on their devices. Given that it was not unheard of for the audio portion of a video recording to fail—whether due to human error or equipment glitches—they knew all too well that the audio could fail. This was not the first rodeo for either of these women.

"What I'm looking for is the name of the male you called from Seth Samuels' home on or about April 6th, 2024," Amanda said after having confirmed Madison's identity, relationship to Seth Samuels, and presence at the murder scene at the time of Eureka Samuels' death.

Madison looked at her lawyer, who nodded.

"Boots."

Everyone in the room looked at Madison.

"What?" Madison said. "That's his name."

"What's his given name?" Amanda asked.

"I don't know."

"Phff," Amanda said and then sat back. "Okay. What's his phone number?"

"I don't know," Madison said. "I mean, it's in my phone, and I lost it."

"You lost it. Okay. So, how would you get hold of this...Boots?"

"I don't know," Madison said. "He's around, I guess."

"Around where?"

"You know. Just...around."

"Okay," Amanda said. "Could you help us find him?"

148

"I doubt it."

"Why?"

"I haven't seen him for a few days."

"But you just said that he was around."

"He usually is, but he's not now."

"Okay," Amanda said. "Have you got a picture of him?"

"Sure," Madison said. "On my phone. That I don't have."

"How about a description?"

"I don't know. Average? White guy. Always has good shit?"

"Hair?"

"Depends. Sometimes it's long. Sometimes it's short, you know?"

"Age?"

"Hard to tell. Maybe around thirty-ish, maybe forty-five."

Carla could feel Amanda's frustration.

"What was he wearing the time you saw him?"

"I don't know. I mean, I was pretty, you know, fucked up."

"Tattoos?"

"Lots."

"Where?"

"I don't know. All over, I guess?"

"Perhaps," her lawyer said, picking up on the interview's lack of progression, "if you could provide my client with an incentive, her memory might improve."

"You're kidding me, right?" Amanda exclaimed.

"I'm really hungry," Madison said.

"Perhaps some food might—" the lawyer began.

"Perhaps they call that inducement once we get to court," Amanda said. "No. No food. No coffee. No cigarettes. Now, if I were to show you some pictures, do you think—"

"What about—" Madison cut in.

"Madison," Amanda said, "right now, you're being charged with murder."

"Are you saying that, if she assists you in identifying this unknown male who actually administered the noxious substance that killed the deceased, then she could—"

"I'm not saying anything, Rejeanne," Amanda said, her tone deliberate and measured. "I'm simply reminding your client that she's facing a very serious charge. It might be in her best interest—"

"If you're not willing to offer her anything," the lawyer said, her voice crisp as she began gathering her steno pad, "then I believe we've reached the end of this conversation." She glanced at the camera with a look of finality. "Please turn off the camera."

Rejeanne Carr's tone clearly indicated that there would be no further discussion. Carla looked at Amanda, who nodded. Carla turned off the DVD recorder while both Amanda and Rejeanne took their iPhones off the table.

"I look forward to receiving the disclosure at your earliest convenience," Rejeanne said as she got up. She then turned to her client. "And I'll see you tomorrow in Show Cause court. Detective, could you direct me out, please?"

Chapter Twenty-Five

3:30 p.m., Tuesday, April 16, 2019

"Well, I'm sure that didn't go as well as you'd hoped," Carla said when she and Amanda got back to the detective office.

"No, although I wasn't expecting much, to be honest." Amanda looked at the stained chair shoved under the desk beside Mike's— the one she was going to sit at—and swapped it out with a marginally less soiled one from the desk behind her. "I know this new station is going to be a panacea for all the ills of Six District, but do you think they'd at least spring for a couple of new chairs before the move?"

"I don't know anyone named 'Boots,'" Carla said, ignoring Amanda's comments as she put the DVD into a property envelope. "But in fairness, it's been a few months since I've been on the road."

"I'm sure the MCU guys will know him," Amanda said, logging into the computer. "Speaking of which, did you put your name in?"

"For what?"

"The MCU spot."

"I don't think—"

"Have you forgotten everything I've taught you?" Amanda said with a smile. "Let *them* tell you that you're not what they're looking for. Don't disqualify yourself from—"

"Ah, my favourite detective sergeant." Paul Langdon, the lanky unit commander of Six District poked his head in the detective office. "And what's this I hear about disqualifying anyone?"

"I was just telling Carla here that she should put in for the MCU spot," Amanda said. Carla's face flushed slightly. "You know she can run a squad."

"Uh, I hardly think running the Foot Patrol is the same as—" Carla stammered.

"You mean you haven't?" he said, his eyes widening.

"I really don't think I—"

"Let me tell you something," he said, sauntering over to the desk next to Carla's. "Do you mind if I pull up a seat? Didn't think so. Here's something you probably already know, but I'm going to tell you again: I've never been in a purely investigative role—not ever. And yet, here I am as a unit commander in charge of several investigators, including you. Now, you'd think a desk-bound type like me wouldn't make the cut, but apparently, I did. So if you want the MCU spot, apply."

"But what if I only get the job because I'm the only one who applied?"

"I'll leave the spot empty before I'll put an unqualified person in that chair," he said. "It's more than a detective that I'm looking for this time around. You've seen those guys. Without the proper leadership, who knows what they'll get themselves into. And I, for one, would prefer not to have to deal with the fallout from their actions."

"Hmm," Carla said, fidgeting with her wristwatch.

"Apply," he stated. "Now, as much as I love talking career development with one of my most capable detectives, that's not why I came down here. Where's Mike O'Shea?"

"Sick day," Amanda said.

"He's in trouble," Carla blurted.

"Is he sick or is he in trouble?" Paul asked, looking from one to the other. "And if he's in trouble, how can we help?"

"You're his partner," Amanda said, deferring to Carla.

Carla took a deep breath before speaking.

"He's been...well, his drinking has gotten out of hand, and he's been abusing prescription drugs." The words tumbled out in a rush. "I'm really worried that he might overdose or something."

"He's seeing Rachel Shimner-Lewis, isn't he?" Paul asked. "Does she know?"

"He is, but I have no idea whether she knows or not. I doubt it, though."

"Well, at least he's seeing her, which is a good thing because I sent him, and I don't recall rescinding that order. Whether he's telling her about the pills or not is another thing. That's between the two of them." Paul looked at Amanda. "Did you know about all of this? No, don't answer that. You're on the promotion list. How long has he been off the rails? Don't answer that, either. Doesn't matter. Where is he now?"

"At home, I'm assuming," Carla said.

"He lives with his mother, doesn't he?"

"Don't let him hear you say that," Amanda said under her breath.

"His mother lives with him," Carla corrected.

"And you live with him?" Paul asked.

"Not like that, no. And I just moved out yesterday."

"Not that it's any of my business, but because...?"

"I found a place I liked. We were never romantically involved, if that's what you're thinking. It's just that I was living in my car and Mike offered—"

"You were living in your car?" Paul exclaimed, his body jolting upright in the chair.

"For a short time, yes, but—"

"What else don't I know about my people?" He looked at Amanda. "Never mind. So Mike's likely at home now. When is he supposed to be back in?"

"Tomorrow, unless he calls in sick again."

"We can't have him doing that," Paul said. "No. We need to get him in here. Keep an eye on him. In the meantime, I'll give Rachel a call and see what she can do. Oh, and how's our murder investigation going? You see? I told you I wasn't an investigator."

"I'm working on it," Amanda said.

"Excellent." Paul got up from his chair with newfound purpose. "Be sure to keep me in the loop. And you, Detective Hageneur, be sure to put your application in."

"Yes, Sir," Carla said, forcing a smile as he walked out of the office.

"I knew he was struggling, but I had no idea...." Amanda began.

"That's how those middle-class addicts do it, isn't it?" Carla said, her mind going back to yesterday. "Nobody suspects a thing until their friend is found passed out in his car. Or starts passing out at work...."

By the look on Carla's face, Amanda knew that Mike had already crossed at least one of those lines.

"Are you going to give him a call later or drop by the house or...?" Amanda began, her mind darting from Mike to the urgent paperwork for the woman in the cells, then to her planned run with her older daughter after work, and finally back to Mike. "And do you want me to come with you?"

"About that food...?" Madison Olsen shouted from the tiny interview room.

"No," Carla said. "You've got enough on your plate right now. If it's all the same to you, I'm going to sign out and go home. I'll give Mike a call and see if he wants to see my new place."

"Keep me posted," Amanda said, realizing that as much as he was a friend, he might become her liability.

* * *

Amanda knocked on the locked MCU door, her annoyance at having to do so mounting. Every Major Crime office in the city had a door like this—locked with a code that only a select few knew. Even the OIC of the station didn't know it. She could hear the shuffling of footsteps on the other side, but there was no response. This cloak-and-dagger secrecy was part of the mystique of the unit, a given in a world where investigations were still often done in silos. She pounded on the door this time, and still—no answer.

"It's Detective Sergeant Black. I need to talk to you guys," she bellowed at the metal door. Then lowering her voice, she added, "And I'm just in the mood to try to kick this goddamned door down."

"Oh," Billy-Bob said, opening the door just enough to peer out at her.

"What? You got a meth lab going in here? Let me in," she demanded, looking past the detective constable, vaguely aware that he might have been holding a can of beer in his hand and might not have been wearing pants.

"Uh," he said. "Give me a minute?"

Amanda could feel the blood rushing to her head but stifled the impulse to push her way in. The thought of having to see something she would never be able to unsee, never mind having to start a disciplinary investigation on top of everything else she was juggling, was just too much.

"Five minutes," she stated. "I'll be back in five minutes."

Exactly three hundred seconds later, she was back standing in front of that same door. Billy-Bob opened it before she could knock. She didn't spot any beer cans, and she noticed, much to her relief, that he was fully dressed.

"Sorry about that, Boss—"

"I don't even want to know," she said as she barged in. The stench of booze and stale body odor nearly knocked her over. "My god, do none of you have homes? Or access to running water? What the hell were you—forget it. Don't want to know. Where is everybody?"

"Court."

"Doubtful." Amanda made a valiant effort to ignore the sweat-stained white shirt, the gleaming black dress shoes, a pile of something on the floor that she assumed was a dark suit, and a pair of enormous boxer briefs she could only assume belonged to Billy-Bob, all crumpled under a desk she hoped was his. "I need you guys to find someone named Boots. What time does the afternoon team come in? I'm assuming about now?"

"Boots," Billy-Bob said, ignoring her question. "Doesn't sound familiar. When do you need him by?"

"I don't need him, just his particulars. I'm waiting for the tox report before I get a warrant for him.

"Well, we can try—"

"Hey, Amanda," another MCU officer said, sliding past her as he came into the office. "I just need to get something from my desk. Where are we all going for dinner tonight, big man?"

"Dunno," Billy-Bob said. "We had Korean last night and burritos the night before. Man, those didn't sit well with me. Still have gas. How about we go over to see Vince at—"

"Excuse me?" Amanda said, gesturing to herself. "Not a social call."

"Oh. Sorry, Amanda," the other officer said. "I didn't think—"

"Maybe Carla shouldn't put in her name," Amanda muttered under her breath.

"Huh?" Billy-Bob said. "Do you mean Carla as in Hageneur? For the D spot?"

"Yes, I do," Amanda said, preparing to do battle. "And yes, for the D spot. Is that a problem?"

"Not really," the other officer said. "It's just that we've never had a...you know...girl boss before."

"Well, it's never too late to drag yourselves into the twenty-first century," Amanda said acidly.

"What we mean is that, well, Lucy's the first chick we've had in here, and she's been on mat leave pretty much since she got here, so she doesn't really count. It would be kinda pushing things to have to jam another chick in here so soon, don't you think?" Billy-Bob asked.

"Really?" Amanda said. "So it's not about—"

"About what?"

"You guys never cease to amaze me." Amanda shook her head. "Anyway, I need you knuckle-draggers to find this Boots character. All I've got on him is that he hangs out down in the south end of the district and deals drugs. And he has asthma."

"Asthma?" the other officer repeated.

"He's my number one suspect for the Samuels murder."

"What does that have to do with—"

"Just get me a name and an address for him. Please." She reached for the vibrating phone attached to her skirt.

"Is there a jug in it?" Billy-Bob asked, referring to the age-old policing tradition of providing whoever came up with a name or arrested a body first with a bottle of his favourite liquor.

"No, but I also won't tell anyone about what you may or may not have been doing in here about," Amanda looked at her watch, "eleven minutes ago. Sound good?"

"Sounds good," Billy-Bob said.

"And remember, I don't want him arrested," she repeated. "We do *not* want another Ricky Jergensen incident."

"Gotcha."

"While I'd bet my promotion on promethazine being her cause of death, I don't have the tox report yet. Given her physical state, the pathologist is just as likely to say that she died of a massive heart attack, so we're going to wait."

"What the hell is prometha…?" the other officer asked.

"The shit in those inhales," Billy-Bob replied. "My kid has asthma. We'll get your intel for you before the night's over, Boss."

"I knew you would," Amanda said, breathing in a gulp of fresher air as she stepped out of the MCU office. "And stop calling me Boss."

"That's what you say now," Billy-Bob grumbled. "Wait until you've had the lobotomy course and they give you a white shirt."

Chapter Twenty-Six

8:00 p.m., Tuesday, April 16, 2019

"Welcome to my humble abode," Carla said, opening the door to Mike. "What are these?"

"Housewarming gifts," he said, handing Carla a basket and a bottle of prosecco as he looked past her into the apartment. "Well, one is. I thought we could christen your new place with the other. Prosecco is your drink of choice, isn't it?"

"It's like you know me," Carla said with a laugh. "Come in."

Mike stepped into her apartment, glanced around, and nodded. "Well done."

"It needs paint, and I've got to get something on the walls, but it'll do for now," she said with a hint of self-deprecation. "Here. Let me take your coat and the basket. It's lovely, by the way. I'm sure you can handle the bubbly. I mean, you're good with that, right?"

Mike paused, catching the subtle layer of concern beneath her words, but he just gave a tight smile. "Yeah. I'm good with it."

"Is it raining yet?"

"No. Just overcast." He swapped his coat for the bottle, casting one more glance at the apartment. "Glasses in the kitchen?"

"Yes, but I've only got one flute unpacked. Let me get another from the box just—"

"I'll get it," he said, waving her off. "You sit down and relax. Where is it?"

"In the box teetering precariously on top of those Amazon boxes." She unwrapped the plastic from the basket, placing it on the coffee table before sitting down on the couch. "Oh, Michael. This is lovely!"

Pop!

"Sorry," he called out. "Have you got a cloth?"

"Just use the tea towel. Everything has to be washed anyway," she gently lifted out the contents of the basket, her face lighting up as she held up the candle. "Oh, my goodness. This candle smells divine! I can't wait to light it. And the bath bomb...how did you know?"

"I wasn't always a troglodyte, you know," he said, coming back into the living room to pass her a glass of prosecco before raising his own. "And my mother suggested it. 'May your home always be too small to hold all of your friends.'"

"Thank you." She raised her glass to him and then took a sip of the wine. "Oh my goodness, Michael. This is so lovely. Please. Sit."

He sat on the chair positioned at a sharp angle from the couch that looked too expensive to be as comfortable as it was.

"Sorry about today," he mumbled. "And yesterday."

"Oh, Michael." Carla glanced down at her glass, then at his, as if uncertain how to respond. She swallowed, unsure of how to bridge the distance between them.

"What?" he asked, voice flat.

"Oh, Michael," she repeated. She inhaled deeply, as if bracing herself. "I don't even know where to begin."

Mike stiffened, already anticipating the conversation he knew was coming. He opened his mouth to speak, then shut it.

"I could say you're too good for this. Or I could say that you're ruining your life. There are a lot of things I suppose I could say. But what I really want to say is you're my...me...Carla's...first best friend and I...I don't want to lose you."

Mike leaned forward and placed his glass on the coffee table. For a split second, he considered just getting up and walking out, not because he didn't appreciate what she had said, but because he couldn't deal with her emotions.

Or another chance at connection. Or opportunity for loss.

But he didn't. Instead, Mike settled back into his chair. He could almost feel the lines in his face deepen, as if carved by the weight of having to possibly confront what it meant to be truly alive. He realized, in that second, that he missed that feeling. Any feeling.

Carla sat and waited for him to say something. A minute passed. Two minutes.

"Let me take these into the kitchen," she said awkwardly, reaching for his glass. "It's getting late. I'll just clean up—"

"No," he said. "It's okay. I'm…okay."

Carla froze for a moment, her outstretched hand still hovering near his glass. She looked down at her own drink, then back at him.

"I'm still new enough at this girl thing to remember how uncomfortable emo—"

"I'm okay," he repeated.

"I-I don't think you are, Michael," she said as she dropped back onto the couch. "And neither does anyone else who cares about you. I'm not a psychologist, but I'd say you're drowning."

Mike's gaze hardened, then softened. His voice came out quieter, almost raw.

"I'm hurting, Carla."

"We're all hurting, Michael," she said gently, leaning forward, eyes steady. "We're all hurting."

"Yes, but—"

"We're all hurting," she repeated.

Mike looked away.

"But we're the lucky ones, Michael."

He looked over at her.

"We have jobs. Good jobs. Money. Friends."

He looked down at his lap.

"Sorry," he said with a bitter laugh. "I sure know how to bring a party down, eh?"

"You're a good man, Michael," she said softly, reaching out to place her hand on his knee but then withdrawing it. "You're a loved man. You've just gotten a little...lost."

Carla might have said more, but, if she did, Mike didn't hear it. His mind was inundated by a flood of memories: the sight of his father's coffin being lowered into the ground as he stood alone while his mother held the younger ones close; the smell of garlic from the untouched dinner simmering on the stove while he held baby Max, Angie frantically stuffing her suitcase and walking out on them both; the sound of metal on metal as the fire door was flung open, followed by the jarring crack of the gunshot that blew Sal's head off; the almost imperceptible squeak of Robby Williams' shoe just as he let go and plummeted to his death; the—

"Michael?" Carla's voice broke through.

"Hmm?" he said slowly, giving his head a shake as if to erase it all.

"You know, last night was the first night I'd ever spent alone—actually living alone, by myself. When I was unpacking, I kept looking for things I knew I had before but don't now."

"I bet."

"And this is the first time in my entire life that I haven't had to ask anyone where the plates should go. Not that I've unpacked them all, mind you, but still. And as liberating and exciting as it's supposed to be, I kept telling myself it... I... will be alright. Well, actually, I hope I'll be more than just alright. I didn't go through all this," she added with a grin, rubbing her hands down her body, "just for life to be 'okay.' I had 'okay' before. No. I'm sure... I hope... well, maybe..."

Mike didn't respond.

"Well," Carla said, Mike's awkwardness filling the room. "I guess you might as well get on your way then."

"No, I—"

"I..." She hesitated, "I didn't mean to dump on you."

"You didn't. I just...."

"I guess we both have...matters to resolve," she said with a smile that didn't quite reach her eyes.

"I guess," Mike mumbled, afraid that she might start crying and unsure of what to say next.

"This," she said as if she were perusing a police procedure, "is the part where you're supposed to tell me that everything's going to be alright. That everything's going to fall into place. For both of us. That we're going to get through this and be better people for it. Come on, Michael. We've both had the same training. Been given the same script."

"Funny how things don't go according to script, eh?"

"You can say that again," Carla said with a chuckle. She looked down at her hands before looking back at Mike, who was now sitting up a bit straighter. "Promise me something, will you, Michael?"

"Maybe."

Carla gave him a mock glare.

"Sure."

"Will you promise to come to work tomorrow?" she said, her tone serious.

"Sure."

"And will you promise to tell Shimner-Lewis everything? Sooner rather than later?"

"That's two promises."

She arched her eyebrow.

"Yeah. Okay, although I think she already knows," Mike muttered, a little embarrassed.

"Well, you make sure she really knows. Okay?"

"Sure."

"And about those pills," she said, her voice softening.

Mike's eyes flickered down, and he fought the urge to look away. He swallowed hard.

"The pain isn't physical anymore, is it, Michael?" she said gently, this time placing her hand on his knee. "Those pills aren't really doing you any good."

"I know," he quietly admitted.

They both stared at the naked walls, the silence thick between them.

"If we're making promises," Mike said at last, clearing his throat, "will you promise me something?"

"I'll tr—yes. Yes, I will. What is it?" she replied, pulling her hand back.

162

"Don't let the bastards win," he said, his voice quieter now.

"Meaning…?"

"Like you said, you've come too far to be just okay. So go live the life you imagined when you became…you."

Carla bit her lip and looked down.

"And promise me you won't cry as much as Julia Vendramini does."

"That's two promises," she said, wiping a tear from her cheek. She took a deep breath. "Do you want a house tour before you go, or…?"

"Ha! I thought you'd never ask," Mike said with a smile.

"Bring your glass, then. And how about you give us a little top-up before we begin?"

Chapter Twenty-Seven

9:45 p.m., Tuesday, April 16, 2019

"Are you about finished?" Billy-Bob said, looking over Nerdster's shoulder at the report the two of them had been working on for the past three hours.

"Give me a minute," the younger officer replied, formatting the document they'd put together. "This guy should buy himself a calendar."

"About ten years too late for that," Billy-Bob commented, his eyes scanning the rows of Fail to Appear convictions on an otherwise minor criminal record. "If he gets picked up for anything now, he'll probably be kept in custody until his trial's over."

"Surprised that there are no drug convictions here."

"Maybe he just never got caught," Billy-Bob said, sauntering back to his own desk. "When you're done, do you want to go for a drive?"

"Where to?" Nerdster asked.

"Dunno. Just out and about," Billy-Bob replied, grabbing the keys from his desk drawer.

"Sure. And...I'm done. Were we supposed to call the D/S when we were finished this or just send her an email?"

"Email will do," Billy-Bob said, gathering up the clothing from under his desk. "She's attached to that iPhone anyway. I'm just going to run out and throw this shit in the back of my car. See you in the back lot?"

"Okay," Nerdster said, pressing the SEND button. "Can we hit an

Instabank while we're out?"

"We can do whatever you want, Sunshine," Billy-Bob said, opening the MCU door. He paused as the air from the hallway wafted in. "Maybe we should get some of those windows open one of these days."

* * *

No one but members of the MCU used either of the unmarked cars designated to the unit. No one but members of the MCU had keys to either of the unmarked cars. While there was a duplicate set of all of the keys to every other car in the district—including the unit commanders'—in a locked cabinet in the sergeants' office, no such set existed for either of the MCU cars. Unlike the other police vehicles, these cars also did not have any sort of GPS attached to them. Not that they may or may not have when they originally arrived at Six District, but they did not now. And, surprisingly, considering the state of the MCU office, the interior of both cars was pristine.

"Where are we off to?" Nerdster said, pulling his seatbelt across himself.

"You said you wanted to go to a bank machine," Billy-Bob said, putting the car in gear, not putting on his seatbelt. While he was too young to recall the days when wearing a seatbelt was optional, he ascribed to the oft-debunked theory that a good cop had to be able to jump out of the car at any time, and a seatbelt was just an encumbrance. Nerdster was clearly of a different generation.

"Yes, no rush."

"Still living with Mommy and Daddy, huh?"

"What does that have to do with anything?"

"Nothing," Billy-Bob said, maneuvering the car out of the crowded back parking lot. "Man, I can only look at a computer screen for so long. I don't know how those data-entry girls at HQ do it."

As soon as they were on the main street, Billy-Bob leaned forward, his eyes scanning the empty sidewalks.

"Who are you looking for?"

"Nobody in particular," he said, settling back in his seat. "It's a bit late for an arrest anyway. I told the wife I'd take the kid to school tomorrow morning before heading to court. You putting in for the promotionals?"

"I didn't know they were having them this year."

"They have to. Got no choice. Everyone who can's retiring, and we're already down twenty or so supervisors city-wide." Billy-Bob instinctively drove the car towards the bottom of the district where they did most of their business.

"I don't know if I'm ready—"

"Ready for what? To drive around in square circles ten hours a day?"

"Well, no. I mean, I'm not sure I want to—"

"That's why I'm not putting in. I'm still having fun chasing down these shitrats. Look over there," Billy-Bob said, pointing to four scrawny men huddled together just outside the 7-Eleven. "If I wanted the overtime, I'd arrest them. Probably all carrying."

"We could call over—"

"No point. They'll be gone in a minute. Pffff," Billy-Bob said, looking away. "Want a coffee or something?"

"I need to get some cash."

"Right. Okay," Billy-Bob said, doing a U-turn in front of the 7-Eleven. "Let's get you to a bank machine."

"Do you think Detective Hageneur'll—"

"I doubt it. Not qualified. Just got into the D office and probably has enough shit on his…her…plate as it is. I heard she and O'Shea broke up."

"I heard—"

"I heard her talk about moving into a condo a while back. Gotta say: never saw those two getting together. But love is love, right?" Billy-Bob said, scanning the streets again, picking up on any movement, unable to turn off his cop instincts.

"I guess," Nerdster replied, not wishing to engage further.

"But they'll push her to apply," his partner continued. "And they'll give her the spot. Even though she's not qualified."

"Why?"

"Optics. Make Landon look good. Show his bosses how," Billy-Bob said,

166

lifting his hand from the steering wheel to gesture air quotes, "'open-minded and liberal' he is."

"But he is."

"Whatever. Her coming into the unit will make everyone look good. Except us."

"What do you mean?"

"She'll be a disaster."

"Maybe not."

"Have you met us?" Billy-Bob said with a chuckle. He pulled alongside a bank machine. "Now, get out. Grab some cash. I want a coffee."

While Nerdster began tapping in his PIN, a man approached from the side. Nerdster glanced quickly over at him, then focused again on the screen. The man stood a reasonable distance away as Nerdster continued with his banking. When he was done, Nerdster took the five twenties from the machine and turned to take a good look at the man. He then glanced nervously over at the car and saw Billy-Bob looking down, his face lit up by the light from his phone.

"You done?" the man asked as Nerdster stepped away from the machine.

"Uh, yes," Nerdster mumbled, stuffing the bills in his pocket before walking over to the car.

"That's him," Nerdster exclaimed as he opened the passenger side door.

"Who?" Billy-Bob replied absently, smiling as he scrolled on his phone.

"Boots," he said, sliding into his seat.

"You sure?" Billy-Bob said, looking past his partner to the bank machine while clicking off his phone.

"Pretty sure. What do we do?" Nerdster asked, closing his door.

"Shit," Billy-Bob said, looking at his watch.

"Should we give the D/S a call?"

"Fuck that. Let's just grab him," Billy-Bob said, opening his door.

"But didn't you say that the D/S said—" Nerdster began. It was too late. Billy-Bob was already around the car, rushing towards the man.

"Hey!" Billy-Bob called out.

The man looked over his shoulder and, seeing a burly man run towards him, took off.

"But didn't you say…" Nerdster repeated as he threw open his door and leaped out of the car to chase after his partner.

Despite his considerable size and the presumption of unremarkable physical ability that went with it, Billy-Bob moved with surprising agility. In just a few steps, he had tackled the scrawny man to the ground. Caught completely off guard and unaware of Billy-Bob's identity as a police officer, the man struggled wildly, using every ounce of his insubstantial strength to resist. Billy-Bob, however, easily overpowered him, subduing the man and then pinning him face-down on the ground. As the man continued to flail, Nerdster came in and cuffed him, bringing the one-sided struggle to an end.

"Stop. Police," Billy-Bob said sarcastically, tearing his own shit as he gave Nerdster a wink. "You're under arrest for resisting arrest."

* * *

"What. The. Absolute. FUCK!" Amanda Black screamed as she came into the detective office. "Is Mike O'Shea here because I need someone to punch you in the head."

"Why? He's under arrest for resisting arrest," Billy-Bob replied with a smirk. "Look at my shirt."

"I don't believe you."

"Why would I lie?"

"Where's your partner?"

"He booked off."

"So he doesn't believe you, either?"

"No, the Staff said only one of us could stay. Overtime. Budget."

"I still don't believe you."

"Believe what you want," Billy-Bob said, gesturing to the paperwork on his desk. "But he's going to court tomorrow for a Show Cause hearing."

"His sheet's that bad?" Amanda said, picking up his criminal record.

"Nerdster sent it to you, so you should know."

Amanda gave him the side-eye before squinting to look at the paper listing all of the accused's Fail to Appear Court convictions.

"I still don't believe your story, but I'll give the lab a call and see if they can put another rush on Samuels' tox report."

"You gonna go in there and talk to him?"

"Absolutely not," she said, turning on her heels before marching out of the office.

"You're welcome," Billy-Bob called after her.

Chapter Twenty-Eight

9:20 a.m., Wednesday, April 17, 2019

Mike turned off the engine and sat there, staring across at the car parked on the other side of the aisle in the underground parking lot at the courts. His ears were ringing. He first noticed the ringing after Sal got shot. Over the years, it seemed to come and go. At one point, he thought it might be tinnitus, but his doctor assured him it wasn't. Likely some damage from the gun being fired at close range, the doctor had said. Likely something that would go away on its own.

It never did.

He watched a couple of cars drive by, probably fellow cops like himself, heading to court for their 10:00 a.m. cases. Most of them would be witness officers—cops who had arrested the accused, seized evidence, or taken statements. Mike was the detective. The officer in charge of the case. The Crown Prosecutor's right hand. He had been Bridget Calloway's right hand. Until she got shot. In the parking lot he was now sitting in. By Malcolm Oakes—or one of his henchmen.

Mike leaned to his left, shoving his hand into his pants pocket. He felt a small envelope, some loose change, and his personal car keys.

"Thank Christ," he mumbled as he got out of the car.

He opened the envelope, popped the two pills into his mouth, and swallowed hard, crushing the empty envelope in his fist before pocketing it. As soon as he got them down, he regretted taking them both, leaving himself with nothing for later.

"Detective O'Shea!"

Mike turned and saw a uniformed officer walking quickly toward him. It took a moment for Mike to recognize him as Preston McAfee, a constable he'd known since the younger man joined a few years ago.

"You going to court, Detective?" Preston asked, quickening his pace to catch up with him.

"Yeah. You?"

"Unfortunately, yes."

"Aren't you still one of the guys who steps in to stabilize people before they go too far offside?" Mike said, referring to the Critical Incident Team. "Keep them out of jail—or from getting shot by us?"

"Yes, sir! And loving it," Preston said as the two men approached the stairwell. "Our guy's the victim this time. How about you? What have you got up?"

"Just some case of Ron's. It's pretty straightforward and Carla's doing something for Detective Sergeant Black."

"I'm assuming it's about the DOA in the back of the dog place?"

"Murder more like it," Mike said, hoping the drugs would kick in soon.

"How is Detective Roberts? Have you seen him lately?" the young officer asked as they walked up the flight of stairs to the street.

"He's—the same," Mike said with a slight smile, the smell of urine permeating his nostrils.

"I know I saw you at the funeral, but I don't think I ever said how sorry I was. I know you and Bridget Calloway were pretty close," Preston said. "Any updates?"

"No," Mike said dismissively as they approached the front of the court-house.

"That's surprising," Preston said, pulling one of the heavy doors open for Mike. "I would have thought, given that she was a Crown and all, that they'd—"

"Yeah, well," Mike said, checking his watch, "life is full of surprises. Listen, take care of yourself, eh? I have to run."

Mike strode ahead of Preston, flashing his badge at the court officer to skip the line at the secure entrance, then disappearing into the crowd of lawyers, cops, witnesses, victims, and reporters.

"Detective Sergeant O'Shea!" A familiar voice cut through the din of the crowd.

Shit.

"Detective Sergeant," Janelle Austin said, pushing her way towards him. "Have you got a minute?"

"No. Sorry. And it's still Detective. You know better," Mike said without slowing or turning around.

"I want to talk to you about the Samuels case," she persisted, still trailing behind him. Her tattooed camerawoman struggled to keep up with them both.

"I'm busy."

"Black says it's related to Bridget Calloway's murder."

"What?" Mike said, stopping abruptly.

"I was told—" Janelle said, catching up to him and signaling for the camerawoman to get the camera ready.

"You were told nothing," he spat, eyes locked on the seasoned reporter. "The Samuels case has nothing to do with the Calloway case, and you know it."

"But the Calloway case does have something to do with your partner getting shot, doesn't it? And when was he shot again? Your partner, Detective O'Shea…?" Janelle said, turning to face the camera.

Mike paused, feeling the painkillers start to kick in. He noticed a crowd gathering around them—and the camera focused squarely on him. He took a deep breath.

"My partner, Detective Constable Brian Salvatore, was shot at pointblank in an underground parking lot on October 31st, 2005, by Malcolm Oakes. You know that."

"Yes. I covered that story, remember?"

"No. I don't. I was a little busy at the time."

"And they've been trying to find his killer ever—"

"Oh, they've found him. We've all found him."

"But nobody's arrested him yet, not even you. Is that correct, Detective?"

"Excuse me, ma'am," a court officer said, pushing through the circle that had formed around them. "You can't have your camera operating inside the courthouse."

"What does that have to do with the Samuels investigation?" Mike asked, feeling increasingly light-headed. *I shouldn't have taken both of them. Shit shit shit.*

"Ma'am?"

"Oh, did I say Samuels?" Janelle said with a flirtatious smile. "I meant Calloway. Those two murders are related, aren't they? The one with the Crown Prosecutor and your partner?"

"Ma'am, I've asked you once, now—" the court officer said as another officer appeared behind him.

"Sorry, gentlemen," Janelle said with a wink. "Didn't realize...."

The seasoned reporter turned away from Mike and motioned for her camerawoman to turn the camera off before the two gently nudged their way through the crowd that had gathered around them.

The court officers stood staring at Mike. One of them sucked his teeth.

"Sir?" the court officer who did not suck his teeth asked, as if this was something Mike was responsible for.

Preston McAfee made his way towards them.

"Everything okay, gentlemen?" he asked. "I believe you're wanted upstairs in the Crown's office, Detective," he added, nodding at Mike before glancing from one officer to the other.

"Yes. Thank you. I am," Mike said, nodding imperceptibly at Preston before turning and stepping into the crowd. Without pausing, he rushed up the marble staircase and disappeared into the men's room.

"Well, if it isn't Mike O'Shea," an old clothes detective Mike only knew as Griffiths said slowly, stepping away from the urinal and pulling up the fly on the pants of his cheap black suit. Griffiths glanced around the washroom. "Everywhere you go, there's a camera. I hope there isn't one in here."

"Detective Griffiths," Mike said, standing over the sink, looking at the other man's reflection in the bathroom mirror. "Nice to see you, too."

"Still banging that trans detective partner of yours?" he said with a sneer as he approached the sink beside Mike's and began to wash his hands.

"No, she dumped me," Mike said with a smile, a mellow numbness beginning to wash over him. *Maybe it's just as well I took both. Otherwise, this fucker'd be splayed out on the floor by now.*

"She get tired of your conspiracy bullshit, or did she just not want to get tangled up with a washed-up pillhead?"

Mike slowly turned to face Griffiths.

"Word travels, man," Griffiths said with a shrug. "You can only blame your partner for getting capped for so long. Good luck in court." He looked at the paper towel dispenser and, seeing that it was empty, shook his hands before wiping them on his pants. As he started for the door, he paused. "I'm assuming, of course, you're the OIC and not the accused…yet."

Mike didn't say a word as he watched Griffiths leave the washroom. He turned to the mirror above the sink, staring at his own reflection. A young guy wearing sagging pants that hung down below his ass bounced in and headed for one of the urinals.

"What you lookin' at, you fuckin' old perv," the kid said before unzipping his pants.

Mike took a deep breath and walked back into the hallway, down the marble staircase, through one of the heavy front doors, past the urine-smelling stairwell, and into the unmarked police car.

Fuck fuck fuck!

He slammed the steering wheel a few times with the palms of his hands, then sat in silence. Tires squealed as a car sped past. He could smell gunpowder, then the subtle aroma of Armani perfume. He shook his head, eyes locking on the car across from him—an Audi, just like Bridget's. He stared at it until he saw her by the driver's side, purse tucked under one arm, fumbling with the handle with her free hand. Then he heard a shot. After that, she was gone.

"Hey! You coming or going?"

Mike glanced to his right and saw a car with the driver's window open.

He heard it again—the sound he thought was a gunshot. But it wasn't. It was a car horn.

"Buddy," the driver called out from his open window. "You coming or going?"

"Uh," Mike began, fumbling for the button to lower the passenger window.

"Never mind," the driver said before speeding across the front of Mike's car in search of another parking spot.

Mike turned off the engine and stared at the Audi across from him. He closed his eyes. When he opened them, he checked his watch. It was 3:47. The Audi was gone, along with most of the other cars in the underground.

He started the engine and drove back to the station.

Chapter Twenty-Nine

6:30 p.m., Wednesday, April 17, 2019

"Surprised to see ye home, my son," Mary-Margaret said when Mike walked in the front door. "Let me put the kettle on and make ye a cuppa. Unless, of course, a wee dram is more to your liking?"

The image of his brother slumped in the cells the other day flashed in front of Mike.

"A cuppa would be perfect, Mom."

"Grand. And shall I get ye a plate—"

"I'm good. Just a cup of tea."

"Well, go on upstairs and get that suit off. Yer da, God rest his soul, always used to say, 'Never trust a man in a suit'. If he could see ye now," she said as she went into the kitchen.

"If he could see me now," Mike repeated as he went upstairs to his bedroom, took off his jacket and tie, undid the top button of his shirt, and changed from his dress pants into a pair of jeans. For a split second, he could smell his father's aftershave. He could feel his father's big hand on his back. He could feel his father's lips next to his ear.

Smarten yourself up, Michael. Let's see a bit of effort, ya?

"I'll do better, Da," Mike sputtered. "I promise."

I know ye will. I'm proud of ye, son. Always have been and always will be.

And then, just as quickly as they had presented themselves, the touch, smell, and the sound of his father's voice were gone. Mike straightened up, gave himself a shake, and wiped the tears from his eyes.

"I've a plate of McVitie's as well for ye," Mary-Margaret said when he came back downstairs. "Now, how was yer day, Michael?"

"Just the usual," he said as he settled into one of the wingback chairs.

His mother looked at him and smiled.

"What?"

"Ach, Michael. Ye might be able to lie to the lads at work, but ye can't lie to your mam," she said. "And, since ye aren't comin' in with yer head bashed in or yer arm shot off, I hardly think today was a usual day for ye."

Mike smiled back at her and took a sip of tea.

"And yer not having a wee dram. That's the mark, lad."

"Well, if that's the case—"

"Which 'tis."

"Then let's just say it was a long day."

The two sat quietly and sipped their tea until there was a knock at the front door.

"Who in the name of God could that be?" Mary-Margaret asked.

"One way to find out," Mike said as he got to his feet.

"I hope I'm not interfering," Carla said, "but I was just in the neighborhood and…."

"Ach, come in. Yer out!" Mary-Margaret exclaimed. "And I've just now had the kettle on. Michael, make Carla a cuppa. Shall we sit at the dining room table, then? And don't worry about yer shoes. Arthur, my cleaner, will be in tomorrow."

Mike smirked as he went into the kitchen, recalling that Arthur—the person from the service he'd contacted to clean his mother's home several years ago after her surgery—was more of a build-a-bear project for his mother than a house cleaner.

"So what brings ye here?" Mary-Margaret asked as the two of them sat at the dining room table.

"Well, like I said," Carla began. "I was—"

"A mother knows," Mary-Margaret said, patting Carla's hand. "Feelin' a bit wobbly this evenin', bein' alone in yer new place?"

"Guilty," Carla said.

"If it's any consolation, luv, had it not been for the smallies, I'd have packed up and gone back home after—"

There was another knock on the front door. This one was the crisp, tell-tale knock of a police officer.

"Like Kingsbridge Station around here. Michael, get the door."

"Well, if it isn't Amanda Black," Mike said, swinging the door open, his voice flat, edged with irritation.

"Ach, Mandy!" Mary-Margaret exclaimed. "Michael. Make another cuppa. If I'd known ye were all comin', luv, I'd have had Michael make us a pot. Never mind. Michael?"

"I'm sorry," Amanda said. "I was just around the corner—"

"No need to explain," Mary-Margaret said, clearly enjoying the surge of activity in the house. "Come on in."

"I can't stay. I was just hoping to speak to Mike," Amanda said. "In private."

"Oh, well, we girls can just step into the kitchen, can't we, Carla?"

"How about we step outside?" Mike suggested. "I don't think it's going to rain."

"Suit yourself," Mary-Margaret said, turning back to Carla. "We've got enough to say to keep us busy, don't we, luv?"

"What's up?" Mike said, stepping out onto the doorstep, closing the door behind him.

"I'm not supposed to know this, and neither are you," she said, her voice dropping to just above a whisper, "but the bullet that killed Bridget likely came from a discarded gun found in a dumpster in Niagara Falls earlier this morning."

Mike's mind momentarily went blank before he started to piece together the implications of this news.

"My intel is solid," Amanda stated.

"Any prints?"

"Wiped clean."

"No cams on the dumpster or…?"

"None."

"Shit," Mike said with a sigh. "Who has the gun now?"

"Niagara Regional."

"Any way we can get it?"

"Billy Gill is sending someone to get it in the morning," Amanda said.

"What about you?"

"What about me?"

"Can't you have someone go now, or…?"

"Not my investigation, and I'm as good as gone from Homicide now," Amanda said.

"Shit."

"If they can tie that gun in with the bullet that grazed you—"

"Meant to kill you," Mike corrected.

"Grazed you," Amanda stated, "then, well, I hate to say it, Crumply Pants, but you might be right about this whole conspir—"

"I am right," Mike interrupted. He shifted his weight and rubbed his temples. "You taking your gun home now?"

"Yes. Although a fat lot of good that's going to do me. Can you imagine me running down to the basement to try to unlock my gun box while my house is getting shot up?"

"Do your slippers have high heels, too?"

"Fuck you!" Amanda laughed.

"Have you told anyone else?"

"What, and joined your Crazy Train?" Amanda said, giving Mike a playful poke. "No. I haven't told anyone. And no one knows I…we know about this gun from the Falls."

"Right," Mike said with a wry smile. "So what do we do now, Boss?"

"I really hate it when you call me Boss," Amanda said, a touch of exasperation in her voice.

"I really hate it when you don't listen to me," Mike retorted.

"Touché. In the meantime, we've got Billy looking after Bridget's mur—"

"Calloway," Mike corrected. "He's looking after the *Calloway* murder."

Amanda gave Mike a questioning glance.

"It's too close when you call her by her first name."

"I get that," Amanda said. "So, Billy's responsible for getting the gun, and they'll be seeing if it links up to any other shootings."

"It will," Mike said flatly.

"We don't know—"

"Yes, we do," Mike stated. "And we know that this all goes back to Sal's murder, which would have been solved about twelve minutes after he was shot if there weren't a lot of crooked cops—"

"I know," Amanda said with a sigh. She looked at the brightly lit house across the street. "You know, it must cost them a small fortune to—"

"In the meantime," Mike redirected.

"In the meantime," Amanda echoed, her voice now steady and deliberate, "I think it's fair to say that anyone from our side who may have been involved is either dead or close to it, so I'd really like us to focus our investigation—"

"So we've got an investigation now, do we?" Mike said with a smile. "With you just, what is it…? Hours away from a promotion? Helluva time to go rogue."

"I think catching that cop-killing fucker is more important than a promotion, don't you?" Amanda said sweetly.

"Just watch your back, okay?"

"Once they bring Malcolm Oakes in for Bri—the Calloway murder, they'll have him for Sal's murder. And then we can start peeling back the onion."

"One would hope," Mike said with a sigh. "In the meantime, be careful."

"Mike, if they wanted to kill anyone, it would be you with all of your conspiracy theories."

"Which is why they haven't. I'm the crazy one. You and Bridget were the credible ones. And she's gone. Now it's you they need to silence."

"All we have is a gun for analysis. We still don't know whether or not it was the one used to kill Bri—Calloway or that shot you—"

"Was meant to kill you," Mike said with absolute clarity. "Otherwise, you wouldn't be standing here, staring across at my neighbour's house, telling me about a gun the boys found in a dumpster in the Falls."

"Just don't tell my husband," Amanda said, reaching into her purse for her car keys. "Speaking of which, I'd like to see him sometime before I get cranked—"

"Have they told you when yet?"

"Next Tuesday. Going to be the 2-IC at Four District. Anyway, I'm heading home now. By the way, good job on the interview with the sister. Are you two in tomorrow?"

"As if we have anywhere else to be," Mike said as Amanda walked towards her car.

She waved without turning back to him.

"And be careful," he added softly. "I don't want to lose another part of me."

Chapter Thirty

6:27 a.m., Thursday, April 18, 2019

Mike jumped.

"And this is why ye need to get a desk job, me son," Mary-Margaret said as she entered the kitchen.

"And this is why you need to...I don't know...sleep in?" Mike said, pouring coffee into his travel mug.

"A moment before you head off," she said, motioning towards the dining room.

"I don't have—"

"Sit. Ye. Doon," she commanded.

Mike went into the dining room and sat down.

"While ye were out having a chinwag with Mandy, Carla told me a few things that I didn't enjoy hearin'. I've already lost one son to the drugs. Don't look at me like that, Michael. Do ye not think I don't know what's goin' on out there? So. I've stood by while ye tried to save the world, and I've stood by and watched ye make a right dog's breakfast of yer personal life, but, as God is me witness, I'll not stand by while ye toss away yer health and me grandson's future."

"I know."

"Ye do, do ye? And what are ye doing about it, then? Ye know, yer da, God rest his soul, was always so proud of ye. It would break his heart if he knew—"

"I'll get myself sorted out, Mom. I promise."

"It's that easy, then, is it? Just a promise and yer away? I don't think so, Michael."

Not raising his eyes, Mike saw that her hands were beginning to shake.

"I'm sorry, Mom."

"It's as if ye've shut yerself off, luv. Buried yerself in yer work, which was bad enough. And now these bloody tablets, or so Carla was tellin' me."

Mike felt his face redden thinking of how Carla had told his mother something that was not hers to tell. And to what end?

"When yer da died, God rest his—"

"Enough with dad, okay?" Mike stated, looking up at his mother. By the look on her face, he knew his lashing out had hurt her deeply.

"Well," she replied, getting up from the table. "I'll just let ye be on yer way, then."

"Mom—"

"Michael, I know we don't always see eye to eye. Nor should we. And I know ye view my bein' here all these months as an imposition. I get that. Max'll be away soon enough, and I'll be followin' behind, if that's what ye want."

"Mom—"

Mary-Margaret walked into the kitchen and stood over the sink for a moment before turning back towards the dining room. Mike was still seated, his elbows on the table, his face in his hands. She walked over to him.

"Me son," she said softly, rubbing his shoulder. "I have loved ye since before ye were born. I shall love ye long after I'm dead and gone from this world. In the meantime, yer stuck with me. For better or for worse. And this is one of those times when the woman sayin' it actually means it. Come on, luv. Tell yer old mam what's got ye tyin' yerself up in knots."

"I miss her, Mom," Mike said, his eyes welling up.

"She was a lovely girl."

"And I miss him. I miss them both."

"Yer Da—"

"I was talking about Sal," Mike said more aggressively than he had intended.

"Right," Mary-Margaret said, taking a breath. "Of course ye were."

"Sorry," Mike said. "I'm just…tired. Tired of fighting a losing battle."

"Ach, me son," Mary-Margaret began, "it may seem like that some days, but think of all the good ye've—"

"Good? Good? What good? That fu—that guy who killed Bridget and Sal and stole so many girls' lives is still out there, and I'm—"

"Yer doin' yer bit, luv."

"You don't get it, do you, Mom? You float around in your world, just like everyone else, and you have no idea what's really going on out there."

Mary-Margaret paused before speaking.

"I know yer hurtin', Michael. As ye should be. I'd be worried about ye if ye weren't. But lashin' out at—"

"I have to go," Mike said, starting to get up.

"Go where? To the job that ye've spend most of yer life doin' that ye all but told me just this minute is suckin' the livin' daylights out of ye? Is that it?"

"To work. Where they pay me."

"They couldn't pay ye enough to do what it is ye do, Michael. 'Tis a callin', this kind of work, not a job," she said. "Now sit back down. I'll make us a cuppa and we'll have a wee biscuit. But just this once. Don't go on thinkin' we'll be havin' biscuits for breakfast every mornin'."

Mike settled back in his chair.

"Before all of that, though, and I'm only goin' to say this once, so listen closely. When yer Da died—and yes, I'm goin' to say it again and keep sayin' it every time I mention him—God rest his soul, a piece of me died."

Mike began to shuffle in his chair.

"Give me another moment before ye shut me out. When he died, everythin' changed. Not only was me husband, lover, and best friend gone, but everythin' we'd planned went with him. He was the whole package for me, was yer da. God rest his soul. I know ye and Sal weren't quite like that, but yiz were like two peas in a pod. And I was so angry with God—had a right old row, we did. And more than a few. Ye see, I wanted justice, not just for what had been ripped away from me, but for what had been snatched from ye smallies. Now, I know yer da wasn't murdered, so I don't have the luxury of havin' anyone to blame. Except God, of course, and we're still wrestlin' with that one, aren't we?" she said, looking up, curling her lip, and then looking back at her son. "Point bein', it's horrible that Sal got shot. And now, all these years later, 'tis a sin that the same thing has happened to Bridget. And, while ye weren't married to either of them—although I think ye missed the boat with Bridget, if truth be told—ye thought ye had a kind of future together with both of yer mates. And, while Bridget's passin' is still fresh in yer mind, I'm sure ye'll agree that 'tis not so much the death of the person that keeps us down. 'Tis the constant reminder of the breaths they never took that haunts us. Am I right or am I right?"

"You're...probably right."

"No, Michael. I am right. Now, about those tablets—"

"I'll get it sorted out."

Mary-Margaret looked him in the eye.

"I will."

"I believe ye. Now, and this will be the end of it: where were ye Sunday afternoon that was so important that ye were late for dinner?"

"I don't know."

"Michael...." she said, the word left dangling as she gave him a look he knew very well.

"I was driving around thinking about how I could kill Malcolm Oakes without anyone knowing he'd been murdered," he blurted out. *Shit shit shit!*

"And who is this lad that's turnin' yer world inside out?"

"The fu-the guy who killed Sal. And Bridget. And—"

"I see. And did ye come up with a plan, then?"

"No."

"Just as well. The last thing we need is a murderer in this family. Allan would have a field day with that. I can just hear him next Sunday, goin' on about how the Big City Police Detec—"

"I really have to go to work now, Mom."

"Well, don't let me hold ye back. And always remember, Michael. No deed goes unpunished, but it's not our place to do the punishin.'"

"Tell that to the judge."

"There's only one judge, and He's got things well in hand, whether we know it or not."

* * *

Mike circled the block looking for a parking spot before finally parallel parking his truck two blocks from the station. His mother's words were still echoing in his head—*breaths they never took.* She was right, but more than that, there were the "what ifs." What if Sal had stuck to the plan and hadn't bolted down that stairwell? What if Mike had been able to keep up? What if Malcolm Oakes' gun hadn't jammed? What if—

"I'm less than two minutes from the station," he said after seeing Amanda Black's name on the call display of his phone.

"Good, because I'm waiting for you," she replied before ending the call.

For fuck's sakes.

Mike saw Carla already at her desk when he walked into the office.

"Mike, I'm really sorr—" she began.

"It's fine," he snapped.

"Sit down," Amanda said before he had a chance to get his coat off.

"Can I at least get in the door?"

He felt his phone vibrate in his coat pocket.

"I gotta get this," he said. "What?"

"Dad?"

Mike froze for a second.

"Oh. Sorry, Max. I thought it was your grandmother, not that I should talk to her like that. Never mind. What's up?"

"I need you to transfer some money into my bank account."

"Why? Are you in jail and need bail? Really?" Mike said, his voice dripping with exaggerated sympathy, annoyed that someone could think that he could fall for this all-too-familiar phone scam. Mike had seen it all before— the frantic voice on the other end, claiming to be a distressed loved one trapped behind bars, pleading for money to secure their release. It was a script as old as the telephone itself, and just as tiresome. *And to think....*

"No. It's me, Dad. And I'm not going to stay in res next year, so I need—"

"What the hell are you talking about?"

"I'm going away to uni, remember?"

"And we need to talk about this at," he looked at his watch, "8:03 am? I don't think so. Let's talk about it later. I have to go."

Mike ended the call without waiting for a response.

"I didn't mean to make your life any more challenging than it already is," Carla began.

"It's fine," he snapped. "Maybe he'll take my mother and that bloody dog with him when he goes."

"Over here?" Amanda said. "Homicide investigation? At work? Anyone?"

"Sorry. It's just been…a morning," Mike muttered.

"Well, Grumpy Pants, it's about to get a whole lot more interesting. Seth Samuels is dead."

"What?"

"Yeah. His heart stopped at 3:02 am. Nobody notified me until 7:08 am, which is a whole other issue."

"What happened?"

"Don't know, but it wasn't suicide."

"But he was under some pretty strict supervision, wasn't he?"

"Yep."

"So are we talking murder?"

"We'll have to wait for the autopsy, which should be later this afternoon. Want to go? Sounds like you could use a break."

"Sure. Let me make a couple of phone calls," Mike said.

"Big date?"

"Appointment with Shimner-Lewis."

"Then disregard. Carla, you go."

"I've got a judicial pretrial," she replied.

"Never mind," Amanda said. "I'll find someone else."

"If it was murder," Mike said, logging into his computer, "the only one who could have done it was his sister. Or someone from within the hospital.

They were the only ones who really had access to him."

"Let's wait until after the autopsy," Amanda said. "Have you done up your statement for the shooting the other night?"

"Shit. No."

"I didn't think so. Why don't you take some time now and get that done? I'm surprised no one has asked you for it yet."

"Have they confirmed you were the target?" Mike asked.

"Give it a rest, okay?" Amanda's tone was sharp.

"And have you given any thought as to how anyone knew we were there?" Mike pressed.

"Mike, nobody's saying either of us was targeted. Right now, we're just the victims, so let's let the D's do their job, okay?"

"What if someone from inside the pub tipped off the shooter?"

"Why don't you just go find an empty room and start writing up your statement before you head off to see Rachel," Amanda said. "If anything comes in, they can call you."

Mike grabbed a pad of paper and his coffee before heading downstairs to the interview room. As he began writing down the events of the night, his mind wandered back to the moments before the shooting. Who had been in the pub? Upstairs? Downstairs? Anything different that night? Different crowd? New servers?

Though Mike wasn't a regular at The Blind Pig, he was no stranger to pubs. The more he thought about it, the more something bothered him: From where he was sitting, he'd never actually seen the bartender's face. Every time he glanced over, the bartender would turn away.

No. It was probably nothing. I happened to look up when he was drying a glass or restocking.

But the nagging feeling didn't go away. He kept writing, but each word brought him closer to a troubling thought. The timing of the drive-by was too precise. Someone had to know exactly when he and Amanda would be out on the street.

What if the bartender had called someone right as we were leaving? He'd have to know exactly who we were. And he'd need a shooter on standby. Or at least know someone who could be nearby.

Before he could finish that thought, Amanda walked in.

"Okay," Amanda said as she came into the interview room. "Remember how I said this day was going to get a whole lot more interesting? Well, I just got a text. The bullet from Brid—the Calloway murder, and the one that grazed you? Same gun."

"That was quick," Mike replied.

"Billy Gill's a good man. And, get this—the analysis suggests that the bullet the other night was likely the only bullet fired after the one that killed—"

"So whoever killed Calloway held onto the gun until after they shot at you—"

"Grazed you, yes."

"You were the target."

"You don't like to think of it as Bridget, who was murdered. I don't like to think that it was me who was the target. Fair enough?"

"Sure," Mike said. "So whoever it was didn't get rid of the gun until after—"

"Sounds like it."

"Not a lot of people drive to Niagara Falls just to dump a gun, do they?" Mike mused. "Unless they were already there when they decided to get rid of it."

"You're Crazy Train is starting to look a lot less cra-cra, Mike," Amanda said. "Oh, and you and Carla are back on my investigation. Or did I ever have to give you back?"

Mike's phone began to vibrate.

"Jesus," he mumbled after he pulled it out of his pocket. It was an unknown number. "I better get this. The way this day is going, it's probably the hospital saying my mother has—"

"Don't even—" Amanda began as she turned and walked out of the room.

Chapter Thirty-One

10:15 a.m., Thursday, April 18, 2019

"Thanks for being able to come in early," Dr. Shimner-Lewis said as she led Mike into her office.

"Well," he said as he sat down, "this frees me up to go to an autopsy this afternoon."

"You do realize how messed up that is, right?" she said with a smile.

"Yep," Mike said as he sat down across from her.

"Okay," she said, flipping open her notebook. "How's the drinking going?"

"You're not cutting me any slack, are you?"

"Should I?"

"You've got your job, I've got mine," he said with a smile.

"Seriously, Mike," she pressed. "Any changes in your drinking patterns?"

"I had tea with my mother last night, if that's worth noting."

"It is," she said, looking at him approvingly.

"And that was before my father told me to get my shit together."

"I thought—" she began, cocking her head.

"He is, but he came to me last night. While I was getting changed. But that was after I'd said I'd have a cuppa with my mother, so I figure I should get some credit for not having a drink."

"Okay," she said, nodding slowly.

"It's an Irish thing," Mike said.

"Well, that's not how we interpret it in psychological circles, but, if it works for you…. And the painkillers?"

"I saw my brother yesterday afternoon," Mike said.

The psychologist turned her head sharply.

"In the cells," Mike replied. His voice took on a hard edge. "At the station."

"Did you…talk to him?"

"Hurmph. Hardly," Mike said. "He was really fucked up."

"Do you know what he was arrested for?"

"No. And I didn't check."

"How did that make you feel?"

"Feel?" Mike said, rubbing his temples. "I didn't feel anything."

"Did you tell your mother?"

"No."

"Why not?"

"Because she still thinks he's the same kid who ran away thirty years ago."

"Do you really think she does?"

"No," Mike said after a short pause. "She knows he's fucked up."

"So why didn't you tell her? At least that you saw him."

"I don't know."

"Do you think that's fair?"

"What's fair?"

Neither of them spoke for a few minutes.

"Do you want to tell me about getting shot, Mike?"

He shifted in his seat, uncomfortable.

"It was all over the news. And I work at Police Headquarters. Kinda hard not to hear about it," she said.

"Well," he said, clearing his throat as he adjusted himself in the chair, "there's that, too."

"Tell me more."

"Aman—Detective Sergeant Amanda—"

"Yes, I'm familiar with her."

"Yeah. Well, she was the target. I just pushed her out of the way."

"You saved her life by taking a bullet for her," Rachel corrected. "That's a very courageous thing to do, Mike."

"Sure. Anyway, it seems the bullet meant for Amanda came from the same gun used in the Calloway case."

Mike paused, waiting for a response.

"I'm sorry, Mike," Rachel said with a slight shrug. "I'm not a cop. What does that all mean?"

"It means that I was right about the shooter."

"Start again."

Mike sighed.

"Same gun that shot Calloway was used to take a shot at Amanda, which means it was likely the same shooter."

"I may not be a cop, Mike, but I would think that more than one person could use the same gun."

"But they didn't," Mike announced.

"You seem awfully sure."

"Because I'm right."

"Okay," Rachel said as she took a deep breath and leaned back. "Let's start again. Have you ever heard of something called 'moral injury', Mike?"

"No. Is that a TV show?"

"No," Rachel replied. "It refers to the psychological or emotional distress a person experiences when their own moral beliefs have been violated."

"Okay. So...?"

"Or when someone witnesses or participates in events that conflict with their moral values," she continued.

"Great," Mike said, distracted by a hangnail.

"The thing with moral injury," Rachel went on, "is that it's more of an inside job than PTSD."

"Meaning?"

"Meaning it's about an internal conflict—because of the actions, or inactions, of others. Things that don't match up with what we believe is right."

"Cool," he said with a shrug, picking at his finger.

"Not really, Mike. The fall-out here is a deep sense of guilt, shame, and inner turmoil. Makes it hard to have healthy personal relationships because the person feels alienated. They lose track of their purpose."

"Hmmm. Is this from a textbook or just spitballing?"

"Does any of this sound familiar, Mike?" Rachel said, ignoring his comment.

"Not really. Should it?"

"Well, consider your issues with personal relationsh—"

"So it's my fault they keep getting shot? That's great. Thanks for that, Doc."

"I was thinking more of your romantic re—"

"You mean my fucked-up marriages? I was talking about Amanda being shot at and you want to talk—"

"We were talking about you getting shot, actually. Because you jumped in front of your colleague."

"That's what cops do, Doc. We run towards danger when everyone else is running away."

Rachel was silent.

"What else was I supposed to do? Stand there and let her get shot? Like I did with Sal?"

Rachel watched Mike closely. He sat there, not moving.

"Do you honestly believe that Sal died because you did nothing?"

"Yeah," Mike said softly. "I do."

"But you also know that that's not true, right?"

Mike didn't respond.

"Mike," Rachel continued, "our brains can struggle to distinguish between what's actually real and what we believe is real. We often internalize what happens to us and make it fit our worldview. You see yourself as a rescuer."

"No, I don't."

"Mike, it's what you do. You're a cop. You've said it yourself: you rescued girls from those prostitution rings. Your biggest regrets are when you can't save people."

"Isn't that a normal response?"

"It is to a point. But it's also a heavy burden. You take it on too much."

"So you're saying," Mike said slowly, considering what she had said, "my being treated like I'm paranoid by those assholes at work has something to do with this moral injury thing?"

"What do you think?"

"Lots of guys have seen worse."

"It doesn't have to be about work, Mike. Can you think of times in your life when—"

"I don't know," Mike said, rotating his neck, concentrating on the tiny cracking noises it made.

"Okay. Let's go back to Sal," Rachel said.

Mike stiffened.

"Or is this really about the man you think killed him?"

"Malcolm Oakes. That's who killed my partner. And a lot of innocent girls. And I don't think it. I know it. And so does everyone else involved in the case. He killed Bridget Calloway. And tried to kill Amanda Black. What else do you want to know?"

"Do you think they know he killed Bridget Calloway and tried to shoot Amanda Black as well?"

"Who the hell knows?" Mike said. He looked squarely at Rachel and added, "Yes. They know."

"What I'm hearing you say is—"

"They're letting a killer—an active killer—walk free," Mike said with a grimace, shaking his head slowly.

"And that bothers you."

"You think?" Mike snapped.

"And this all began...?"

"October 31, 2005."

"And how's your life been ever since, Mike?"

"Fucked."

"So does this idea of having a moral injury sound..."

"Great. Sounds just great, Doc."

Rachel stopped to take a breath while Mike shot daggers at her.

"And you're making strides to get clean and sober?" she continued.

"I was never—" Mike began, thinking of Petey in the cells.

"Really, Mike?" she said softly. "You know that there's drinking and there's *drinking,* right? And there's pain relief and there's…addiction? Which side of those coins are you on?"

Mike didn't respond. He looked down at his watch. She waited and then looked over at the clock on the wall.

"I'll see you next time," she said, standing up before opening her office door.

Chapter Thirty-Two

11:30 a.m., Thursday, April 18, 2019

"Where are you off to, Crumply Pants?" Amanda Black asked as Mike stepped into the elevator.

"Are you stalking me?"

"You wish. Come with me to the South. I'm going to talk to Aldridge. You have a car?"

"Yes. And who's Aldridge??"

"Trevor Aldridge. Our asthmatic. Car gassed up?"

Mike gave her the side-eye as the elevator doors opened to the main floor of headquarters.

"What? Like you've never gotten into a car that was left on empty before?" she teased.

"We're good," he said, pressing the button that would take them to the third level of the underground parking lot.

"How was Shimner-Lewis?" Amanda asked, picking a piece of lint off her jacket.

"Lovely."

"She really is good, you know."

"I'm sure she is."

Mike's stride stuttered slightly as Amanda pushed the crash bar on the door before stepping into the parking lot.

"Where'd you park?"

Tires squealed as an SUV sped around the corner up towards the exit. Mike made a note of the driver and the license plate.

"McFly?" Amanda raised an eyebrow.

"Huh?"

"The car, Mike. Where'd you park it?"

"Just...just over there," he said, blinking as he pressed the fob. The car chirped as its doors unlocked a few feet away.

"Do you realize that there's a whole generation of people out there who have no idea what it's like to lose their cars in an underground?" Amanda said as she got in the passenger's side.

"There's a whole generation of coppers who couldn't find a car fourteen years ago," he muttered, starting the engine.

He put the car in gear and drove out of the underground. Neither of them spoke for most of the drive.

"So," Amanda said, breaking the silence. "Trevor Aldridge, aka Boots, twenty-seven years old. No significant criminal record, but doesn't like to show up in court. More than a dozen Fail to Appear charges."

"So bail is unlikely?"

"Very."

"Even on Billy-Bob's trumped-up charge?"

"I don't even want to talk about that," Amanda said, rolling her eyes.

"Don't blame you."

"We'll charge him with Murder One, but he'll likely get convicted of Manslaughter."

"Is that a bad thing? A conviction's a conviction, isn't it? You want to leave on a high note, don't you?"

Amanda didn't respond. Instead, she looked down into the footwell and admired her shoes. This pair was one of her favourites—she'd bought them after the successful conviction of Sibby Mac's killer. She had so many shoes now, each one a reminder of a victory, each one purchased after putting another murderer behind bars.

"I don't know if I'll have much use for all of them when they put me back in uniform," she said wistfully.

"Does he know you're coming to see him?" Mike asked as they turned the corner into the parking lot of the jail.

"Yes."

"So he's lawyered up?"

"I have no idea. If he has, I hope it's not that damn Rejeanne Carr."

The two of them exited the car and headed toward the jail. Amanda flashed her badge at the bulletproof glass. The guard slid a clipboard and two plastic containers through the slot. Mike emptied his pockets into one, while Amanda placed her attaché case into the other. They were buzzed through, and Mike unloaded his gun at the loading station, securing it and the clip in the designated locker.

"No gun?" the guard asked Amanda.

"No gun," she replied.

"Walk through, please," he said, nodding towards the metal detector.

When nothing activated the machine, the guard called for another guard, who led them to an unremarkable interview room. Amanda and Mike sat on one side of the metal table and waited for Aldridge to be brought in.

"Are you going to charge him here?" Mike asked.

"Yes. And then, if he wants to give a state—"

A loud clang echoed through the room as the metal door opened. Neither Amanda nor Mike stood up.

"Sit," the guard barked, shoving Aldridge into the chair across from them. Once he had complied, the guard took the handcuffs off. "I'll just be outside."

"Thank you," Amanda said. She waited for the guard to leave. "Mr. Aldridge, I'm Detective Sergeant Amanda Black from Homicide, and this is Detective Mike O'Shea."

Aldridge nodded.

"Do you have a lawyer, Mr. Aldridge?"

"No."

"Right." Amanda opened a binder and pulled out a page, reading from it. "Mr. Aldridge, I am charging you with the murder of Eureka Samuels. It is my duty to inform you that you have the right to retain and instruct Counsel in private, without delay. You may call any lawyer you want. In the event that you do not have a lawyer—"

"I know," he interrupted.

"So, do you want to speak to a lawyer?"

"Will it make a difference?"

"Not to you being charged, no. But—"

"Then no. Can I leave now?"

"What—have you got some other appointment or," Mike quipped, looking at his watch, "is the food that good in here?"

"Neither," Aldridge said flatly. "I just don't have anything to say."

"Fair enough," Amanda said, making a note. "And the time is—"

"1:06 by my watch," Mike said.

"The time is 1:06," Amanda repeated. She wrote it down, then closed the binder and put it back in her attaché case. "Guard?"

"Well, that was anticlimactic," Mike said as they headed back to the station.

"I wasn't expecting much from him," Amanda said. "Eureka Samuels' funeral is tomorrow."

"And?"

"And I'm going. Do you want to come along?"

"Are there sandwiches afterwards?"

Amanda rolled her eyes.

"Detective Sergeant Black," she said, her cell phone at her ear. "Oh. Great. Thank you. So…? Really? Do you think…I see. Okay, well, thanks for letting me know. How soon will the rep…oh, great. I'll take a look at it when I get back to Six District."

"So?" Mike asked.

"That was Polermo. God, I love that man."

"You're the only person I know of who fangirls over a chief pathologist," Mike said with a smile.

"What can I say—the man's a genius," Amanda said with a smile. "Anyway, Seth Samuels died of a myocardial infarction."

"Don't we all?" Mike joked. When Amanda didn't respond, he added, "I bet you hear that all the time. Sorry."

"Point being, he wasn't murdered."

"I'm sure having all of those drugs in his body didn't help, though."

"Given that they all consumed the same or similar drugs, I think I'd be hard-pressed to show intent to harm."

"So...?"

"And, given that he was clearly suicidal beforehand...."

"So he died of a broken heart," Mike said. "A boy's love of his mother knows no bounds."

"Can I tell your mother you said that?"

"I'd prefer you not."

Chapter Thirty-Three

9:45 p.m., Friday, April 19, 2019

The last funeral Mike had been to was Bridget Calloway's. His mother had organized it, so it was at St. Francis of Assisi Catholic Church. The rows of wooden pews had all been freshly polished for the occasion and were packed in equal parts with suits and uniforms, with more people spilling out into the main hallway of the church. The casket—her casket—had a huge bouquet of white roses and lilies draped over it. The service itself was full of music, prayers, and eulogies made by her boss, a neighbour, and some of her old law school friends. Mike had been asked to say a few words, but declined. Afterwards, O'Leary's was packed to the rafters for the reception, with top-shelf whiskey flowing freely and glasses frequently raised in tribute, where, or so he was told the next day, Mike's oratory talents had shone.

This funeral was very different. Mike signalled before turning the unmarked police car into the industrial mall lot. Had he not googled the address beforehand, he would likely have driven by.

"Down near the dumpster, I'm thinking," Carla said, noticing the plastic planters out in front of the end unit.

Mike had no trouble finding a parking spot near the front doors.

"Careful when you step out," Mike said, noting the cracked asphalt as he got out of the car.

Aside from the drawn blinds on the large windows and the sign indicating that it was a funeral facility, this unit could have been used for anything. Mike suspected the flower shop next door had sprung up to cater to unprepared mourners, or perhaps it thrived on online orders. Or was a front for some criminal activity. It was definitely not in a location where someone would find himself casually shopping for flowers.

"Thank you for coming," Ruth Samuels said, holding out her hand to Mike and then Carla as they came into the small viewing room.

Mike smiled weakly as he glanced at the closed coffin in the corner.

"Is your brother here as well?" Mike asked, looking around the room, empty except for themselves and the casket.

Carla gave him a very sharp jab in the side.

"Simon…couldn't get away on such short notice," Ruth said apologetically.

"I see," Mike said, looking over at a table with photos of a much healthier woman with her children at various stages of their lives.

"Hey! Mike," Susan Strang said as she and her assistant walked into the room. "It's so kind of you to come. Menga and I were just in the ladies. We closed the shop for the morning." She thrust out her hand as she noticed Carla. "I'm Susan Strang. And you must be…?"

"Oh, I'm Carla," she said. "Carla Hageneur. I work with Michael."

"Detective Sergeant Black is just over there," Susan said. She pointed to Amanda, who was outside in the hall on her phone.

"Yes, we saw her on our way in," Mike said. "And this is *Detective* Carla Hageneur, my partner."

"Excuse me," a slender woman dressed in a somber black skirt suit and black flats asked Ruth. "Are we expecting anyone else?"

"I…I don't think so," she replied, nodding her head slowly.

"In that case, may I direct everyone into the chapel," the woman said, motioning towards the doorway before turning to Ruth. "I'm assuming you'd like a few moments alone with your mother?"

"No. I'm…good," Ruth said, leading the way out of the room.

"Excellent," the woman said, motioning for her colleagues to enter the room to prepare to move the coffin.

Much to Mike's surprise, the tiny chapel at the back of the unit was bright and airy. Its crisp white walls seemed to open the room up, and, if the skies had been clear, sunlight would probably have streamed through the window near the ceiling. The front of the chapel offered ample room for floral displays, such that the funeral home's attempts to make the three modest arrangements appear more plentiful were obvious.

Mike paused and crossed himself before sitting down on one of the dozen or so folding chairs that had been set up for this morning. Carla sat beside him.

Amanda, who had walked in after them, leaned forward from her seat behind them and whispered, "I'm surprised your mother isn't here."

"She would be if she knew about it," Mike whispered back over his shoulder.

"I'm not seeing Simon Samuels," she commented, looking around the sparse gathering.

"He was too busy," Mike said with a smirk, his eyes returning to the cross hanging at the front of the chapel.

"Really? And I'm surprised that they wouldn't wait for Seth's body to be cremated and include him."

"I wouldn't be surprised if they dump his ashes by the side of the road," Mike mumbled.

"Michael!" Carla chided, rapping his knee.

The five people in the chapel all stood up as the opening bars of a poorly recorded version of "Amazing Grace" began to play through a small speaker concealed behind the floral arrangements. Ruth Samuels walked to the front of the room alone and took her seat, followed by the coffin containing her mother's body, which was wheeled in with the solemnity of a royal funeral by four funeral home attendants. The woman who had spoken to Ruth in the viewing room brought up the rear of the small procession.

Once the coffin was in place, an older woman wearing a vividly neon green scarf walked up the aisle carrying a Bible and a plastic bottle of water. The volume of the music was turned down until it was inaudible by one of the attendants.

"You may all be seated," the woman said before identifying herself as a humanist celebrant.

"Just as well Mom's not here," Mike whispered to Carla.

The funeral unfolded as the detectives thought it would, given the small turnout: brief and to the point. Lasting no more than twenty minutes, the service covered all the logistical aspects of a funeral and little else. There was no eulogy.

The woman in the neon green scarf led the coffin as it was rolled out of the chapel, followed by Ruth, Susan Strang, Menga, Mike, Carla, and Amanda while "Ave Maria" played through the speaker. They followed it back to the viewing room before briefly offering Ruth their condolences. In less than five minutes, Ruth was standing alone beside the coffin containing the remains of Eureka Samuels.

* * *

"Mind if we pop in here for a few minutes?" Mike asked Carla as he pulled up in front of The Blind Pig.

"The sun isn't over the yardarm yet, is it?" Carla asked with a smile.

"I'm not going in for a drink," Mike said with a sigh. "I just want to talk to the bartender."

"If you say so," Carla said, following him inside.

"Excuse me," Mike said to the bartender. "Is upstairs open?"

"You see the sign?" the bartender said, pointing to the sign on the chain that ran from one side of the stairwell to the other, clearly marked CLOSED.

Mike nodded.

"Then why you askin' me?"

Carla could feel Mike's anger rising.

"What my friend, here, is trying to say," she began, "is, well…he's…we're looking for the bartender who was working last Friday night. Do you happen to know him?"

"Nope."

"Could you, perhaps, find out who he is for us?" Carla said, pulling her badge out of her purse.

"Oh," he said. "Sorry about that. We get a lot of hounds in here at this hour of the day."

"And we look like hounds?" Mike said, looking down at his suit.

"Hounds and creditors," the bartender corrected.

"Be that as it may," Carla said. "Do you know who this bartender fellow is or how we can find out? Oh, and I'm Detective Hageneur. This is my partner, Detective O'Shea."

"Sid," the man said, wiping his hand on the bar cloth he had over his shoulder before extending his hand out to her. "I'm the owner. One of them."

"Pleased to meet you, Sid," Carla said. "Now, about that—"

"Yeah. Last-minute call-up when my usual guy called in. I wasn't working that night so I never saw him."

"What do you mean, you never saw him?" Mike snapped. "You must have enough staff to cover—"

"We usually do, but it was just one of those nights, you know? Everyone I called either didn't pick up or couldn't come in. The guy was recommended to me by one of my staff, and I was desperate, so I figured, what the hell? He worked out well enough. Paid him cash at the end. Said he was usually available and to call him if I was ever short-staffed again. Here," Sid said, reaching into his pocket, "let me check my phone."

Mike and Carla waited.

"Look," the bartender said, passing his phone to Carla, who motioned it away to Mike. "Not the greatest bartender, but you know how it is. When you're on the short end, you take what you can get. Don't know that I'd call him again, but you never know, right?"

Mike stood motionless, his hand getting tighter around the phone.

Malcolm O.

P: 647 555 2323

"Can I, uh, have my phone back, buddy?" the bartender asked.

"Sure," Mike replied. "Just let me jot this number down."

"Here. I'll write it down," Carla said, practically prying Mike's fingers off the phone.

"Did he say anything else?" Mike asked. "Like where he lived or…?"

"I never asked. I just needed someone to cover this shift, you know?"

"And the server. Was she one of your usual staff?"

"Uh, what night was that again? Friday? Oh, that would have been Stef. Yeah. She's upstairs five nights a week."

"Is she in tonight?"

"Yeah."

"What time? I can come back. I'd like to talk to her."

"Perhaps leaving your card would suffice, Michael," Carla said, sensing Mike's desperation. "It's already been a…long day."

"Right," Mike said, pulling one of his business cards out. "Here. Let me write my cell number on the back. Get her to give me a call, okay?"

* * *

"What's going on?" Carla asked when they got back in the car.

"What do you mean? I'm fine," Mike said as he pulled out into traffic, the car behind him screeching to a stop.

"You know that would have been your fault, right?"

"Once a traffic man, always a traffic ma—officer, eh?"

"What are you going to do with that phone number?"

"I'm going to see if I can trace it, and then I'm going to talk to Stef or whatever her name is, and I'm going to find Malcolm myself."

"And then what?"

"I'm going to kill him."

"You do know how crazy you sound, right?" Carla asked. "And how someone who didn't know you as well as I do would think that they ought to either have you formed or arrested?"

"Good thing you know me so well, then," Mike said as the car squealed into the back lot of the station.

"Seriously, Michael. You can't get invol—"

"A bit late for that, don't you think?"

"Isn't there someone else who can look into this for you?"

"Like who? The bastards who've been letting this asshole run wild all these years?"

"Like Amanda," Carla suggested.

"She's going to Four District on Tuesday."

"So?"

"So she's gone. They've pulled her out."

"So we no longer believe she's a part of the conspiracy?"

Mike looked over at Carla.

"Are you fucking with me?" he asked.

"No. I'm serious."

Mike's cell phone vibrated in his jacket pocket.

"Did you take the scenic route home, Crumply Pants?"

"I'm in the backlog, Boss," he replied.

"Well, get in the back door and into your office. I need to talk to you. Or, better yet, wait there for me and we'll go for a little drive."

Being close enough to Mike to have heard the other side of the call, Carla let herself out of the car.

"Where are you going?" Mike asked.

"I think she wants to talk to you, not us, Michael," she said before closing the door. "I've got paperwork to do. Oh, and you might want to consider passing that intel over to her to take care of."

Chapter Thirty-Four

12:07 p.m., Friday, April 19, 2019

"Anywhere in particular?" Mike asked as Amanda fastened her seatbelt.

"Why don't we go park down by the lake?" she said. "I always find it so…calming."

"Wasn't too calming when Lisa Clayton got murdered there," Mike said dryly.

"You have a remarkable ability to ruin everything, don't you, Crumply Pants?"

"Sorry. Just…never mind."

"Before we get there, can we just drop by this little coffee shop I know and pick up a coffee and something to nosh on? My treat."

"Can't say no to that, can I?" Mike said with a smile. "Especially when you'll be outranking me by a couple of bumps soon."

"Oh, about that," Amanda said, looking casually out her side window. "I'm not going to Four District."

"Oh?"

"No. I'm staying in Homicide. Turn here. Sorry. I should have told you sooner."

Mike made a hard right onto the little side street.

"Anyway, they decided that I should stay. Here. Park anywhere here. It's just up the street there."

Mike pulled the car up along the curb as Amanda looked at her watch.

"You know what? You might as well come in with me and we'll talk there."

Mike followed Amanda into a place that was about the size of a walk-in closet.

"I know," Amanda said, anticipating Mike's remark, "but the pastries here are out of this world. And they've got a place to sit in the back."

"Hey, Amanda," the barista, who looked no more than seventeen, exclaimed. Standing behind a counter just big enough for an espresso machine, Mike figured that this guy could likely reach every corner of the shop without taking a step.

"Oooh," Amanda said with a sigh. She stepped back and almost touched the wall behind her as she eyed the small shelf of pastries beneath the counter.

"I know, right?" the barista said. "They've been selling like hotcakes these days. This is the fourth batch I've put out. Is Julia working this afternoon? She's been coming in every day and cleaning us out, so, if she is, I'll—"

"I think she's on days off now, isn't she, Mike?" Amanda said, not taking her eyes off the pastries. "I'll have that one. And an Americano. You?"

"I'll just have—"

"Oh. Sorry," Amanda said. "Jordy, this is Mike. Mike, Jordy."

"Yeah, yeah. I thought I recognized you," Jordy said, looking Mike up and down. "You were that cop who almost got his head bashed in last year by Cockeye Johnston. Man, he was one tough son-of-a....can't say he's missed. Here. Let me get you a pastry. On the house."

"No, I'm good," Mike said, raising his hand in refusal.

"Jordy is one of Julia's kids," Amanda said as he handed her the pastry she had chosen.

"She's one in a million, that woman," he said with a grin. "Sure I can't get you anything?"

"No," Mike said, shaking his head. "Just the coffee."

"She saved my life, you know," Jordy continued as he made the two coffees. "You're from Six District, aren't you?"

"Yes."

"Surprised you don't remember me. I'm Jordy Ashton," he said, handing

Amanda her coffee.

Mike took a closer look at the young man.

"I guess I clean up pretty good, eh?" he said, handing Mike his coffee. "Used to be a real punk in the south end. Theft from auto, mostly. I was there when you and Cockeye got into it. Thought for sure you were dead. We all did. You sure you don't want a pastry?"

"Positive," Mike said.

"Yeah, it's all fun and games until you become an adult," Jordy continued. "That's when Julia stepped in. She was the OIC on one of my first...my only charge as an adult. Sat me down for a couple of heart-to-hearts. Enough for me to figure things out. And here I am."

Amanda handed Jordy a twenty-dollar bill.

"It's on me, Amanda," he said.

"Suit yourself," she said, stuffing it in the tips jar before turning to Mike. "Follow me."

Mike trailed after her towards the back and through a yellow door that led out into a small courtyard. They pulled out a couple of folding chairs and sat down at one of the two IKEA tables.

"A little cool for sitting outside, but it's private. Sit."

Amanda placed her coffee on the table, took a bite of her pastry, and let out a satisfied murmur.

"Oh my god, this is good. You don't know what you're missing, Mike."

"I'm not hungry," he replied bluntly, settling into the chair across from her. "So, what do you want to talk about?"

"Where did you go after the funeral?"

"For a drive."

"Really?"

"Really."

"And where did that drive take you, then?" Amanda asked, raising an eyebrow.

"Nowhere in particular," Mike said, staring past her, unfocused.

"You are aware, of course, that all our vehicles are equipped with tracking devices, right?"

"So you've been keeping tabs on me?" he asked with a smirk.

"I noticed you made a stop at The Blind Pig. Why?"

"The bartender that night was Malcolm Oakes."

"Really?"

"Really," Mike replied, pulling a scrap of paper from his jacket pocket. "And here's his number."

Amanda glanced at the paper, then met Mike's gaze.

"Okay."

"So now we trace the number and go get him," he prompted.

"Do you honestly believe that number will come back to anything but a burner phone?"

Mike's shoulders slumped.

"Come on, Mike. You know better than this. You're too close to this. You've lost your objectivity."

"You think?" he muttered.

"But I'll take that," she said, putting out her hand.

Mike hesitated but handed her the paper.

"And, while we're at it," she added, "let's talk about the box."

"The box?" Mike asked, narrowing his eyes.

"The box of evidence that you have stashed at Ron Roberts' house."

Mike looked squarely at Amanda as he took a sip of coffee. He slowly put the cup down and took a deep breath.

"We're the last ones standing, Mike," Amanda said. "And whatever's in the box might—"

"What about Julia?" he cut in.

"Do you really want them chasing her down, too?"

"No," Mike said softly, shaking his head.

"Tell me what you know, then."

The two investigators spent nearly an hour discussing the various documents, newspaper clippings, and the scribbled notes that Robby Williams had jotted down on scraps of paper, all of which had been crammed into that single box. He had records of everything. There were no gaps, and he had gathered enough evidence for what appeared to be an air-tight case. All the evidence corroborated Mike's claims: that a handful of senior officers, a few well-known philanthropists, and several municipal politicians were deeply enmeshed in a sophisticated criminal network, which included a highly profitable prostitution ring that exploited underage girls.

"The question I have now is: what do we do with it?" Amanda asked, wiping a couple of crumbs off the table.

"We arrest Malcolm Oakes," Mike said. "It all comes back to him."

"Obviously," she replied dryly.

Mike glared at her.

"He's good for Sal's murder and Bri—Calloway's murder. I get that. But what do we do with all of this other information?" Amanda asked.

"What do you mean?"

"Come on, Mike. That was a long time ago. Everyone named in those files is either dead or close to it. So where do we go from here?"

Mike thought for a moment.

"Are we sure that there aren't some people still actively involved. People who might have stepped in after Robby...?"

Amanda looked away, not wanting to see the desperation in his face.

"Ralph Crowley is taking over the Samuels' case," she said abruptly, changing the subject.

"Seems like a cakewalk for him," Mike remarked, a touch of irony in his tone. "Congrats on his first slam dunk."

"It's not a win until the key turns in that cell door."

They both glanced at their empty mugs.

"Amanda," Mike said softly. "If the rot that's tied to Malcolm Oakes is really dead, he wouldn't still be out here trying to kill anyone who could connect the dots."

"I know," Amanda said, her voice barely above a whisper.

"Enjoy the promotion," Mike said as he rose from his seat. "I need to get back to the station. Want me to drop you back at Headquarters?"

Chapter Thirty-Five

2:07 p.m., Friday, April 19, 2019

"Michael," Carla said as he walked into the office. "We've been relieved."

"What?"

"Well, Ralph Crowley—"

"Yes, I know. He's taken over."

"And he's told me that we're—"

"Hey Mike!" Ralph said as he ducked into the office. "Just the man I want to see. I've taken over the Samuels investigation, and you and your partner are no longer required."

"And so...?"

"And so," Ralph said, flashing a wincing smile, "I guess you and Carla'll go back to your platoon."

"You know there's still a lot of work to be done on this file, right?" Mike said, recalling Amanda's words.

"Are you telling me how to do my job?" Ralph shot back, his voice tinged with the defensive edge every insecure investigator falls back on when their decisions are being called into question.

"No, not at all," Mike replied with a knowing smile. He was well-acquainted with that tone from his own days of wrestling with it.

"Good. So thanks for all of your help, and I guess I'll, uh, see you around. Like whenever someone else gets killed in this district," Ralph said, his words tumbling out as he hurriedly made his exit, practically sprinting toward the front desk.

"And I thought I had a shitty bedside manner," Mike muttered. "So? What now?"

"Well, as you know, we'd be starting on afternoons if we were still on the platoon," Carla explained, shrugging slightly. "I spoke to the Staff, and he said we can just...start whenever we like." She paused, as if unsure how to finish. "So, I guess...?"

"I don't have any plans this evening, do you?" Mike asked.

"Not when there's a wrong to be righted," she replied with a grin.

"Well then," Mike said with a sigh.

"Well. Then." Carla replied.

* * *

"Hey!" the front desk uniformed officer said as she toddled into the D office.

"Are you...?" Mike began, but stopped after Carla gave him a deadly look.

"No, I'm not pregnant, if that's what you were going to ask. It's the new meds I'm on. Bloat me like a stuffed pig, but thanks for pointing it out."

"Sorry," Mike said.

"Staff wanted me to come back here to tell you there's been a shooting."

"Gangbangers?" Mike asked after the uniformed officer had given him the occurrence number.

"More than likely," she said. "I don't actually know, though. Anyway, the Staff wants you two to go have a look."

Before either of them could answer, the officer was waddling back to her post at the front.

"I'm just going to the ladies," Carla said, grabbing her purse from the bottom drawer of her desk. "Don't know how long we're going to be there. You know, if there's one thing I miss, it's the ease of toileting as a ma—"

"Jesus Christ!" Mike exclaimed, his eyes widening as the occurrence popped up on his screen. "This is Amanda Black's address!"

"I'll drive," Carla said, turning left instead of right at the doorway.

Minutes later, the two detectives were standing on the street in front of Amanda Black's house, surrounded by flashing red lights and uniformed officers darting about like headless chickens. Mike walked over to one of the senior constables.

"Where is—" he began.

"Ambulance has come and gone," she replied breathlessly.

"Is she—"

"Detective Sergeant Black went in the ambulance with her daughter. Her husband followed behind in their car."

"What do you mean 'with her daughter'?"

"The daughter was shot. She went in the ambulance—"

"I know what that means," Mike snapped. "Okay. Who's the uniform sergeant?"

"There isn't one. I've been—"

"For fuck's sake!" Mike muttered, his frustration mounting.

"I can help. Officers!" Carla said, her tone commanding, reminiscent of her time as a foot patrol sergeant. Mike was half-expecting them to snap to a salute.

With impressive efficiency, Carla quickly directed the constables to establish and secure the perimeter and to canvass the area. Meanwhile, she informed the dispatcher that neighboring divisions would need to handle the radio calls until further notice and updated the Staff at the station.

To his surprise, Mike felt as if everything was happening in slow motion. His arms and legs felt heavy, and the hum of voices from the crowd became indistinct. Even the blaring sirens, still activated, seemed muted.

"Michael!" Carla boomed.

The sound of the sirens suddenly became almost unbearably loud.

"Michael," she repeated, her voice dropping to a softer tone. "Why don't you go to the hospital and see how everyone is?"

"Right," he replied.

Unaware of how he had gotten back into the car, Mike found himself pulling into the designated police parking area at the hospital. Without hesitation, he ran into the emergency room.

"Detective Mike O'Shea," he said, holding his badge up, his voice edged with a frantic desperation. "Where is she?"

"We're here, Mike," Tony said, his voice calm but strained. Mike recognized it as the kind of calm that comes with shock.

"Where's Amanda?" he demanded.

"She's gone with Kristie," Tony replied. "They're going to try to get the bullet out."

"Did anybody see anything? The shooter?"

"I...don't know. I didn't ask."

"Fuck fuck fuck," Mike said, running a hand through his hair. "Where did she get shot? How serious—"

"I don't know, Mike. In the leg? I-I'm not a cop," Tony stammered.

"Right," Mike said, taking a slow, steadying breath. "Sorry. Are you okay?"

"I-I-I don't know. Amanda's...my...our kid just got shot. She got shot, Mike. *Amanda* got shot at a couple of days ago. I...I just don't know."

"Fair enough. Any idea—?"

"I really...I just don't know," Tony said, starting to shake. "All I really know is that our daughter's been shot."

A young woman in combat boots and a black t-shirt featuring The Pretenders approached with a couple of coffees from the vending machine.

"Here, Tony," Nicolle said, passing her stepfather a coffee. "Hey Mike."

"Nice boots," Mike said, and then noticed the t-shirt. "Have you ever heard their music?"

"Thanks," she replied and then looked down at her t-shirt. "And no. I picked it up in Kensington."

"Chrissie Hynde. You don't know what you're missing," he replied. "Listen, why don't we go find a more private room for you two to wait in, okay?"

"I'm not going anywhere," Nicolle said, defying the suggestion with predictable Goth resistance.

"Yeah," Tony said more appreciatively. "I...I'd rather just wait here. But thanks, eh?"

"Can I at least get you another chair?"

"Excuse me," a voice that clearly belonged to a nurse began. "Only one pers—oh, it's you."

"Yep. And it's a cop's kid who's been shot," Mike stated without even looking in her direction.

"Right," the nurse said. "Let's go into this room over here."

She pointed to a closed door. The sign on it read 'Contamination Room'.

"Don't worry," she assured them. "It's been cleaned."

"But what if they can't find us when they bring her back?" Tony asked, looking at the bloodied t-shirt on the floor where the gurney had been.

"I'll make sure they find you," the nurse said.

"And I'll take that," Mike said. He pulled a latex glove out of his pants pocket before turning to the nurse. "Do you have anywhere I can put this to dry?"

"Uhh…" she began.

"Never mind," Mike said, plucking the shirt up from the floor. "I'll just hold on to it."

They all stared at him.

"Evidence. This is a criminal investigation."

"In here," the nurse said, opening the door to the Contamination Room. "I'll bring in another chair. Do you need anything else?"

"I…don't know," Tony said, shaking his head.

"Come on, Tony," Nicolle said, taking her stepfather by the arm and leading him into the private room.

Mike watched them for a moment before turning to the nurse.

"Any updates?" he asked.

"No."

"Is she going to be…?"

"I haven't seen her chart," the nurse said, clipping her words, "so I can't say. Sorry."

***

"Michael," Carla said as she rushed towards him. "Any—"

"Not yet. Tony and the younger daughter are in there," Mike replied, holding Kristie's blood-soaked t-shirt, now bundled into a makeshift bag made from a wad of brown paper towels.

"Okay," she said. "We're going to need to seize all of her clothing. Do you have any idea what she still has on and where the rest of it is?"

"I've got her shirt here," he said, holding up the makeshift bag, "and I'm thinking they cut the rest off in the O.R.. I don't know. I didn't see her go in—"

"So she's not out yet?"

"Do you see her?" he snapped.

"Right," Carla responded. "Good thing you seized the shirt. Hopefully, we can get the rest of the clothes without too much commotion. Anyway, the good news is that one of the neighbours' cameras caught the plate number of the shooter's car, and Video Services thinks they can enhance the image to get a good picture of the occupants."

"Big fucking deal," Mike said.

"And," she continued after taking a deep breath, "even if they can't get a good picture of the shooter from those pictures, the suspect vehicle ran through a red light that has a camera on it, so we'll be able to get a good shot of—"

"We know who the fucking shooter is," Mike said, cutting her off.

"No," Carla corrected, "we *think* we know."

"No. We *fucking* know. And, if we don't, we *fucking* know who ordered it."

"Michael," Carla said, then paused. "*Fucking* knowing and actually knowing—like, what the courts would consider beyond a reasonable doubt—are two different things. Now, are you able to continue with this investigation, or should we let our relief take it over?"

Mike sucked his teeth. Carla glanced at her watch.

"Judging by the time, I'd say our relief is going to be taking it over anyway," Carla said.

"Hrmph," he muttered. "How did you even get here, anyway? I've got the car."

"On my broom, what do you think?" Carla said. "Seriously, though, I had one of the uniforms drop me off. I'm surprised you made it here without having an accident. Speaking of which, the car is up on the sidewalk. Is that the look you were going for, or—?"

"Excuse us, please," an orderly said as he pushed a gurney towards them, then stopping as he noticed that the room was occupied.

"They're over there now," Mike said, pointing to the Contamination Room.

"My own room," Kristie said slowly, her voice slurring, the effects of the anesthesia having not yet worn off. "That's pretty cool."

"Yes, well…" her mother said, walking alongside the gurney, her voice trailing off. If Mike hadn't known better, he might not have recognized Amanda Black in that moment. The usual sharpness of her eyes was now replaced by a foggy stare, and her nose was raw from continuous wiping. In the few hours since the shooting, lines seemed to have been etched onto her face. She appeared so much older. And smaller. Mike soon realized the change stemmed not just from grief but from the running shoes she wore, a stark contrast to the stiletto heels that he was used to seeing her in. No longer the fierce 'Pitbull in Stilettos' they had all called her at the office, Amanda Black now looked like every other mother whose life is now forever changed because her kid got shot.

"How—?" Carla began, but Amanda cut her off.

"She's going to be fine," she stated, the words meant as much for her own sake as for anyone else's reassurance.

"And you?" Mike asked quietly.

"Give me a minute," she said, following the gurney into the private room. "I just need to be with my family now."

"Sure," he said, his chest tightening as the door closed behind her. As a cop, he understood. As her friend, it stung.

"Mikey?" Julia Vendramini called out as she rushed into the emergency room.

"Julia," Mike replied flatly, not realizing how emotionally flooded he was.

"Are you okay?" she asked, enveloping him in a tight hug.

"Yeah, I'm not the one who was shot," he replied, a flicker of annoyance in his tone. He expected to catch the scent of Armani perfume on her jacket, just like he had when Sal had been shot.

"Great job at the scene, Carla," Julia said as Mike shrugged off her hug.

"You've made my job easy…as easy as investigating your friend's daughter having been shot can be. *Che cazzo!* When did we become this? Used to be the bad guys shot the bad guys. Now…? How's Amanda? Is she in here?"

"Yeah, but," Mike said, holding up his hand, "give her a minute. They just got back from the O.R."

"Is Kristie…?"

"Awake," Mike answered.

"So I should—"

"Just give her a minute," he snapped, and then softened his tone. "Tony and the younger girl are in there as well."

"Of course," Julia said. *"Che insensibile da parte mia!"*

"We're all just doing the best we can," Carla said, rubbing Julia's arm.

"Is that our car parked out front?" Julia asked. When Mike didn't respond, Carla nodded. "What? Were you going for that '80s *Miami Vice* parking job look, Mikey?"

"I—"

"I'm kidding," Julia said with a soft laugh. "I'm just glad Kristie's going to be okay." She leaned in a little closer to Mike, her voice dropping. "She *is* going to be okay, isn't she?"

"I assume so," Mike said.

"Good," Julia said, crossing herself. "Every day I pray to you, and every day you test me. Why? I know. Mine is not to reason why…." She turned her attention back to Mike and Carla. "Do we know where the bullet hit her?"

"No," Mike said.

"Well," Julia said slowly, as if coaxing a child, "when she came back, was her head wrapped up or…? Come on, throw me a bone, here, Mikey."

"No. It wasn't," Mike answered, giving Julia a look that unintentionally wounded her.

"I don't imagine we'll be leaving any time soon," Carla said, her voice laced with the sort of false cheer she'd learned to adopt in difficult situations, "so why don't you give me the keys, Michael, and I'll go out and get us all a nice coffee and then park the car properly?"

As Carla was walking away, the sliding door of the private room opened just enough to let Amanda, looking so frail now, step out into the hallway.

"They're going to be releasing her shortly," Amanda said with a sharp inhale.

"*Mia cara Vecchia amica,*" Julia said, giving Amanda a heartfelt embrace that was eagerly returned, tears beginning to spill from both of them. Meanwhile, Mike stood by, looking anywhere but at them, his chest tightening again.

"You'd think, after all of these years, I'd have a clue about what you're saying," Amanda blubbered and laughed at the same time from within Julia's embrace.

"You'd think, after all of these years, *I'd* have a clue about what I was saying," Julia said with a smile, wiping the tears from her own eyes as she stepped back from Amanda.

"Thanks, guys," Amanda said, inhaling quickly as she tried to regain her composure.

"We haven't done anything yet," Mike mumbled, fidgeting with some loose change in his pants pocket.

"No. Thanks for being here," her voice catching. "With me. And my girls. And my husband. Just...thank you."

"Mom?" Kristie's voice called from within the room, still groggy but clearer. "If you're just standing around out there doing nothing, can you see if there's a machine or something and get me some food?"

"My baby," Amanda said, glancing at the cubicle behind her as she wiped her eyes, "is going to be fine. A little sore, but...fine."

"If you're getting something for her, can I have something, too?" Nicolle asked.

"Girls, your mother is talking to the—" Tony could be heard saying.

"We'll be going home soon," Amanda said as she stepped back into the cubicle. "Nobody's getting anything until we get home, and then you can all have whatever you want."

"Still don't know where she got shot, do you?" Mike said to Julia.

Chapter Thirty-Six

2:00 p.m., Saturday, April 20, 2019

"Is it just me, or does it feel like we were just here?" Carla asked as she dumped her purse into the bottom drawer of her desk.

"At least the cells are empty," Mike said, typing his password in.

"Did Julia leave any notes on the shooting?"

Mike opened the case file and saw the number of completed actionable items.

"Not that I'm seeing," he said as he scrolled down the page. "Good job at the scene, by the way."

"Well, somebody had to step up," Carla said. "You don't happen to have any coffee hidden around here, do you? I'm starting to feel like I need an IV drip at this point."

"Shit. I didn't think—"

"No worries. Since it's all...in order here," Carla said, stopping herself from uttering the cursed 'q word' that, once spoken, would undoubtedly unleash a shitstorm that would keep them busy until the end of their shift, "why don't we go pick something up, and maybe drop by Amanda's place to see how they're doing?"

"Hopefully, they've got a car sitting out front."

"A bit late, wouldn't you say?" Carla said, retrieving her purse. "How did they know where she lived? She must be in the Address Suppression Program, wouldn't you think?"

"Dunno. Wouldn't be too hard to follow her home. Or I *could* say they have someone on the inside, but—"

"So I'm assuming they know where you live?" Carla asked, raising an eyebrow.

"Sure," Mike replied casually as he logged off the computer.

"Doesn't that bother you?"

"If they wanted to kill me—"

"Or intimidate you or your family," Carla added.

"Yeah. If they wanted to do any of that, they'd have done it by now. Clearly," he said, pulling the keys to the unmarked car out of his desk drawer, "I'm just not worth the effort. And could you imagine anyone trying to intimidate my mother?"

"Do you think they'll go after me?" Carla said with a sudden gasp.

"Your guess is as good as mine. I mean, if you want to go down that path, we're all targets in this game, aren't we? Anyway," he said, stretching as he stood up, "are we going for coffee or are we going to sit around discussing worst-case scenarios?"

"No. You're right. I'm just being...I don't know. I swear it's the estrogen. Karl would never have—"

"Sure," Mike interrupted, not wanting to hear the rest. "And, if we're going to Amanda's, we might as well drop by this little place she took me to yesterday and pick up some coffee and pastries for everyone."

* * *

Mike pulled up beside the curb in front of Amanda's house. Carla looked up and down the street.

"What?" Mike said, sensing her unease.

"Unless they're *really* undercover, I'm not seeing any police presence here, are you?"

"No," Mike said as he turned the engine off and reached for the tray of coffees. "You take the pastries?"

"Before we go in," Carla said, reaching out to him, "can I ask you something?"

"Sure," Mike said, hoping it wasn't anything too personal.

"I'm just wondering why they shot Kristie and not Amanda. She's their target, isn't she?"

"I don't know. Maybe, like you said, intimidation?"

"Maybe," Carla began, her brow furrowing. "Or what if they *meant* to shoot Amanda and accidentally shot Kristie?"

"Now who's sounding crazy?" Mike said, getting out of the car.

"I don't know," Carla continued, grabbing her purse and the pastries as she followed him, "but hear me out. They're both similar builds. They both run. Maybe—"

"They have lots of opportunity to take out Amanda, it's what they want to do," Mike said, ringing the doorbell. "She's pretty accessible. They wouldn't need to take a chance and—"

"Unless they're getting impatient?" Carla suggested. "Or sloppy?"

After what felt like more than enough time for Mike to respond, the door opened.

"Here," Mike said, grabbing the bag of pastries from Carla before pushing it and the tray of coffee at Tony. "We were just out and about and thought you'd like a coffee. And some pastries."

"Amanda?" he called over his shoulder without taking either from Mike. "It's for you."

Mike and Carla exchanged glances as they stood in the doorway, the tray and the bag still outstretched. Tony turned and walked back into the house.

"Hey, Crumply Pants. And Carla. Come on in," Amanda said, rushing past her husband to meet them.

"Is this a bad...I mean, a worse...?" Mike began.

"No. It's fine. He's just...upset. Come in," she said reassuringly, gesturing for them to enter.

Mike and Carla stepped inside while Amanda poked her head out of the doorway, looked up and down the street before closing the door firmly behind her, and then double-checked to make sure it was locked.

"The house is a bit of a mess," she said, pointing towards the living room.

"Didn't get to clean up after work last night. Just sit anywhere. I'll get us some plates."

"How's Kristie?" Mike called after her.

"Sleeping. Well, she's upstairs, anyway. She'll probably be sore for a while. Lucky for her, the bullet didn't hit anything important. Dishwasher didn't get put through last night, so will a napkin do?" Amanda asked, a stack of them in one hand.

"How are you doing?" Mike asked.

"Fair to middling. Wow, these are good," she said, taking a bite of one of the pastries.

"Tony doesn't seem too well," Mike said.

"He's just tired. Long night. He'll be fine."

"How's Nichole?" Mike asked.

"She's the one I'm worried about. I've got a call in to Shimner-Lewis for a referral for her. I don't want to let it sit too long with her, and I know I'm not the right person for her to talk to."

"Well, if there's anything we—" Carla began.

"Where's the goddamned can opener?" Tony hollered from the kitchen.

"It's in the drawer," Amanda countered, taking a deep breath to steady herself.

"No, it's not!" he shouted back.

"Yes, it is," Amanda replied with a feigned sweetness that did little to mask her exasperation.

"If it was in the goddamned drawer," he yelled back, his voice breaking, "I would have found it, so where the hell is the goddamned can opener?"

The next thing they heard was the crash of the cutlery smashing down on the kitchen floor.

Amanda sighed and looked apologetically at her friends.

"I've got this," Mike said, walking towards the kitchen. "Give us a minute."

"It just, uh," Tony mumbled, looking at Mike and then down at the broken drawer and the numerous knives, forks, and spoons scattered about.

"Let's sit over here," Mike said, motioning towards a couple of kitchen chairs.

"Yeah," Tony said, sitting down. "And, uh, sorry about earlier. At the front door. It was, uh, good of you and, uh—"

"It's okay. I get it," Mike said, sitting in a chair beside him.

"Yeah."

"Been a tough couple of days, huh?"

"Yeah."

Both men sat silently, nodding their heads.

"We've been married a long time, me and Amanda, and she's locked up a lot of assholes, but this is the first time—"

"Yeah."

They nodded their heads in silence again.

"You ever seen something like this before, Mike?"

"No," he said, pursing his lips.

"So why now? She's so close to being off the front line."

Mike looked at Tony, wondering what Amanda had told her husband and, more importantly, what she had chosen not to.

"Dunno," he said.

"I don't know if I thanked you for saving her life the other night, but, if not, thanks, eh?"

"Yeah. No problem, although I'm not sure—"

"I thought I knew what I was signing up for. But this? This is something else. We can't even protect our own kid."

"I get that."

"They tried to kill an innocent child. Her...our little girl. What are we supposed to do with that, Mike?"

"I-I don't know," Mike stammered.

"I mean, do we just hope they catch whoever did this, or do we keep looking over our shoulders, or do we hide? What do we do?"

"We'll...we'll catch him," Mike said.

"When? And what do I do until then? How do I keep my family safe, Mike? What do I do?"

Tony slouched forward and buried his face in his hands, his shoulders shaking as he let out a ragged sob.

"We'll catch him," Mike repeated. He took a deep breath and patted Tony's shoulder.

"Sure," Tony said, inhaling quickly before wiping his eyes and straightening himself up.

"I'm uh…sorry about…that."

"Yeah."

They both looked at the mess on the floor.

"Well," Tony said, taking a deep breath. "I guess we better pick this shit up. I think I've got a bracket or something downstairs that I can use to fix the drawer. If not, she's going to be pissed."

"Yeah. Can't be that hard," Mike said, crouched down beside Tony as they gathered the scattered utensils. "Nothing a little duct tape can't fix."

Tony shot him a perplexed look.

"What?" Mike asked. "I'm a mangiacake."

"No, you're not," Tony said, giving Mike a playful slap on the back as he tossed a handful of cutlery into the broken drawer. "You're Irish. Some of the finest craftsmen in the world are Irish."

"Well, I'm certainly not," Mike replied, picking up some spoons.

"Pfff. Can't be good at everything. Here. Leave it. Let's get out there and grab a pastry before they're all gone."

Chapter Thirty-Seven

6:30 p.m., Saturday, April 20, 2019

"Here," Carla said, passing one of two glass Tupperware containers she had fished out of the station's upstairs fridge to Mike.

"What's this?" he asked, eyeing it suspiciously.

"Dinner. Pop it in the microwave for about two minutes, and then I'll pop mine in."

"Hmm," Mike said, lifting the lid and giving its contents a sniff.

"It's not quite your mother's Sunday dinner," she admitted, "but it tastes pretty good and it's a lot cheaper than picking something up."

"Counting our pennies, are we?" he asked as he got up from his desk and walked over to the ancient microwave. He chucked the container in before pounding a couple of the faded buttons.

"Not really. I just made a big batch of lasagna and realized that I would grow sick of it before I ate it all."

"You could always freeze some of it, you know."

"My fridge has a pretty small freezer and, besides, it's reserved for eclairs and vodka."

The phone on Mike's desk rang.

"I'll get it," Carla said. "Six District. Detective Hageneur."

Mike's attention drifted back to the microwave. The more he watched the glass plate begrudgingly rotate, the more he thought that pitching the whole thing and getting a new one might not be a bad idea. He should mention it to Julia. She was good at getting the guys to cough up some money.

"I'll let him know. Thanks," Carla said, hanging up Mike's phone.

"So?" he asked, as he carefully pulled the hot container out of the microwave. "Shit, that's hot!"

"Ralph Crowley. They got the tox report back for Eureka Samuels."

"And?" he continued, gingerly carrying the container to his desk and then quickly dropping it down. "Shit shit shit!"

"Promethazine poisoning."

"From the inhaler?"

"Yes. I'd say Mr. Aldridge's life just got a lot worse."

"What about the son? Do they have anything on him yet?"

"Crowley's going to stick with heart attack as COD."

"That's bullshit. If Amanda were here, she'd—"

"She'd what?" Amanda Black said as she came into the detective office wearing jogging pants, a sweatshirt, and running shoes rather than her usual attire.

"You look...short...er," Mike commented.

"I just came to thank you for your little talk with Tony," she said. "And yes. Those heels are high. So, what would I be doing if I were here, which I'm not?"

"Your job," Mike grumbled.

"Michael," Carla cautioned, looking inside the microwave, her own Tupperware container still in hand. "This is disgusting. Hasn't anyone ever cleaned—"

"Is there a problem?" Amanda asked.

"Not if you think it's normal for a guy in his early twenties to die of a heart attack, no," Mike said, pulling a plastic fork from his drawer.

"Michael," Carla said again, going back to her desk to get something to clean the microwave with. "Michael, Michael, Michael."

"What? It's true," he said, stabbing at the food in the container. "Listing his cause of death as—"

"No. I meant about the plastic fork. Here," she said, pulling a metal one out of the top drawer of her desk and tossing it across to him. "Use this."

"It's Crowley's investigation now," Amanda said.

"I know," Mike said, picking up the metal fork from his desk before loading it up with lasagna and shoving it into his mouth.

"So, were you just out for a run and thought you'd pop in or...?" Carla asked. She'd found the spray bottle and paper towels they used to wipe down the desks and began spraying the inside of the microwave.

"Not exactly," Amanda said, sitting down at what had become her usual spot at the desk beside Mike's. "I mean, yes. I was out for a run, but then I got to thinking."

"That sounds dangerous," Mike said between bites. "Hmm. Not bad."

"Which is to say: I got to realizing," Amanda said, correcting herself.

"Should I go check for something at the front desk or go powder my nose or...?" Carla asked.

Amanda looked from Carla to Mike and then back again.

"Yes," Carla said, tossing the soggy paper towel in the trash bin by the office door. "I think I should. Will you two excuse me for a minute?"

Mike and Amanda glanced over at the container still on her desk as Carla strode out of the office.

"What's up?" Mike said between bites. "This is actually very good. Who knew?"

"Someone really did try to shoot me outside of The Blind Pig on Friday, didn't they?"

"Yes. And I've got the flesh wound to prove it," Mike said, wiping the sides of the container with his finger.

"And someone just shot my daughter. Outside of my house."

"Yep. Carla thinks they might have mistaken Kristie for you," Mike said, licking his fingers while looking Amanda up and down. "You do kind of look the same in your running gear."

"They're after me."

"I'd say so, yes."

"Someone. Wants. To. Kill. Me."

"No," Mike said, getting up, leaning over his desk, and then putting the empty container on Carla's desk. "Malcolm Oakes *is trying to* kill you."

"Why?"

"Because he thinks you know whatever it was he thought Bri—Calloway knew."

"He *is* going to kill me, isn't he?"

"Likely," Mike said, sitting back down. "Unless we kill him first."

"I didn't just hear you say that, did I?"

"Safe to come back in?" Carla called from the hallway. "I hope so, because I'm famished!"

"All clear," Mike said, deliberately sidestepping Amanda's question.

Amanda sat silently at the desk, lost in thought.

"Oh my," Carla said. "How rude of me. Would you like some?"

"Pardon?" Amanda asked.

"Some lasagna. I'm sure I've got more than I can eat here. Would you like some?"

"No. I'm...I'm—"

"I'll have it if you don't want it all," Mike offered.

"I'm sure I can finish it," Carla said. "How are we feeling, Amanda?"

"I was just thinking about my parents."

"And?" Carla said, putting her container into the microwave.

"How they must have felt when they found out my sister had been shot."

Carla pressed a few buttons, and the microwave began groaning again.

"And they didn't find out until she was at the hospital. I can't even begin to imagine how scared they must have felt."

"I didn't know...never mind," Carla said.

"Are they going to give your address special attention now?" Mike asked.

"I think so," Amanda said. "There were two u/c cars parked down the street from me when I left."

"What about you? Are you going to get—"

"Not very good u/cs if you could spot them," Carla commented as she delicately pulled her container out of the microwave. "My goodness, Michael—you were right...this really *is* hot."

"I live on a small street and we all know each other. And our cars. It's either a couple of u/c cars or whoever shot my daughter is getting pretty

231

ballsy."

"And what about you and your family?" Carla asked, her voice dropping in volume. "Are they assigning a team—"

"We're just a cop's family."

"Yeah, but—" Mike began.

"No," Amanda stated bluntly. "They're not assigning a team."

"Well, that's fucked," Mike said. "So what's the plan, then?"

"I have no idea," Amanda said, getting up from her chair. "Keep running and hope to hell they can't hit a moving target? I have no idea. But one thing's clear: this has just become *very* personal."

Chapter Thirty-Eight

11:55 p.m., Saturday, April 20, 2019

"I can't believe you talked me into coming here," Carla muttered, taking a sip of her prosecco. She glanced around The Blind Pig, noting that, once again, they were the only patrons upstairs.

"What? Like I had to twist your rubber arm? Sláinte," Mike said, raising his pint of Guinness.

"One of the reasons I got my own place was so that we wouldn't be on top of each other, and I think I'm seeing more of you now than when we lived in the same house."

"I'm like glitter," Mike said with a wink. "Once you get me in your life, you can't shake me off. So, you still putting in for the D spot?"

She took another sip of her drink, her smile faltering.

"I was never putting in for it, so, no. I'm not."

"You should."

"What, and deal with Billy-Bob and his rogue colleagues every day?" she said, giving him an incredulous look. "No thanks."

"You'd be a good influence on them," Mike said.

"Pfff," Carla said, taking another sip of her drink. "Just like I'm a good influence on you?"

"Hey, I'm not taking any more of those pills, and I'm only going to have one, maybe two pints tonight. That's a big step."

"I'm glad to hear it," Carla said with a mix of skepticism and concern. "You do know you're—"

"Yeah, yeah, better than that. I've got too much to lose. Blah, blah, blah," Mike interrupted, waving her concern away.

"Is Amanda going to be okay, do you think?" Carla asked, changing the subject to something they both took seriously.

"What do you mean? Is she eventually going to get capped? Likely," he replied, casually taking a sip of beer.

"You seem awfully blasé about it," Carla said, her mouth slightly agape.

Mike rolled his neck from side to side.

"How are things going with Shimner-Lewis?" she asked.

"Peachy," Mike said, the word dripping with sarcasm as he leaned back in his chair. "But we weren't talking about me. Or Amanda. We were talking about you. Put in for the MCU spot."

"Why? Do you want to get rid of me?" she asked with a grin.

"No, it's just that I think it would be a great opportunity—"

"And then what, Michael? Put in for promotion? Pu-lease," Carla said, taking a sip of prosecco.

"No. Stay there. You'd be great at it. And," he said, leaning forward, "you'd likely keep them from getting themselves into serious shit."

"Do you think that's what I want to do with my life?" Carla said with a guffaw. "Babysit a group of manboys?"

"What about the work? They do some great stuff. Provided all of their arrests stick."

"Name one societal problem their enforcement has resolved, Michael," she shot back, settling into her seat and crossing her arms in front of her.

"Wow. Aren't we snippy tonight?"

Carla made a face and then sat up in her chair.

"I'm sorry, Michael. I truly am, but the more I think about it, the less I think that what we're doing here—any of us—is making any difference at all."

"Should I pull out a lighter and start singing 'We Are The World'?"

"Stop it," she said, and then smiled. "I don't know. Maybe it's me. Maybe I'm just seeing things…differently now."

"So what are you going to do? Quit?"

"Absolutely," she replied with a chuckle. "Just as soon as my inheritance clears the Caymans. Unless that European prince gets his visa sorted out first and can come and rescue me. No. I'll stay. For now."

"You'll be okay," he said, finishing his beer off in one guzzle. "It'll all sort itself out. You ready for another?"

"I wish I could turn it on and off like you, Michael," she said. She stared at her glass, tracing the rim with her finger.

"Yeah. Me. The guy who gets ordered to see the company shrink. Sure," he said with a laugh. "I'm a real poster child for managing stress."

"I'm sorry. That was…idiotic of me. What I meant was, it doesn't seem to bother you that we arrest the same people, over and over again, and—"

"No. It doesn't. Because I don't give a damned about them," Mike said, his voice dropping as he leaned in closer to her. "All I want to do is get that fucker who killed Sal. And that's all I've wanted to do for the past fourteen years."

"I don't believe you," Carla replied without missing a beat.

"What? You think I'm lying to you?"

"No. I think you're lying to yourself."

"Sure," Mike said, looking at his empty glass. He raised his hand for the server. "I don't give a shit about—"

"So why haven't you caught him already?" Carla's question hung in the air, sharp and quiet.

"It's not like I haven't been trying," Mike said menacingly. "If those—"

"Michael, your work in the Juvenile Prostitution Task Force is practically legendary," she interrupted, leaning forward, eyes locked on his.

"So? That was before."

"And your work at Six District is—"

"Thanks," Mike said as the server set the pint down in front of him with one hand while removing the empty glass with the other. "Sure you don't want another?"

"No, I'm still nursing this one, thanks," Carla answered, waving the young woman off.

Neither Mike nor Carla spoke for a few minutes.

"I like my new place," Carla said with a smile.

"That's good," he said, raising his glass. "Sláinte."

"I think what I really like about it, Michael, is that I feel that I can finally be myself. And that's a wonderful feeling."

"I'm sure it is," he said, taking a swig of beer.

"Do you have any idea what that feels like, Michael?"

"What?"

"Being yourself."

"Apparently, it makes you not want to be a cop anymore," he said with a smile.

"Michael…?"

"Well, what did you want me to say? Of course, I know what it feels like to be myself."

"Really?" Carla said, pausing to take a sip of her drink. "When was the last time you were yourself?"

"Huh?"

"You heard me. When was the last time you weren't *The Partner Of The Cop That Got Shot*? When were you just…you?"

"You just finished telling me I've done a lot of good work."

"And you just finished telling me that the only reason you get up in the morning is to find the guy who killed your partner. Which is it, Michael?"

"Jesus," Mike said, taking another gulp of Guinness. "If you keep this up, Shimner-Lewis'll be out of a job."

"You and I both know it's not just about the job," Carla said softly. "We will catch Malcolm Oakes. We will send him away for a long time." She leaned in, her voice firm. "But then what, Michael? What happens after?"

"They should throw away the key on that piece of shit," Mike muttered.

"And what if they do? Which they won't. But still. Then what? What about you?"

"What about me?"

"What will you do?" Carla asked.

"I don't know. I retire?"

"Really?" Carla said with a smirk. "And do what?"

"I don't know. I've got…stuff. And since when did this become about me again?"

"Said no man ever," Carla quipped.

"What?"

"Never mind. You were saying…?"

"Are you going to have another, or are we done here?" Mike said, noticing Carla's empty glass.

"You're not an easy man to work with, you know," Carla said. "But I think I've made a difference in your life."

"What are you talking about, and what the hell was in that glass?"

"Estrogen, Michael. It's all about the estrogen. At least it is for me."

"I'm not following."

"It doesn't matter. Just know that I'll always have your back. And yes, I think I will submit my application for the Major Crime spot. And now, if you'll excuse me, it's getting close to my bedtime and I don't want to turn into a pumpkin."

She got up and walked to the bar. Mike followed, reaching into his back pocket for his wallet.

"I've got this," she said, handing the server her credit card.

"Thanks," he said quietly.

She took her card back and turned towards the door.

"Safe home, Michael," she said over her shoulder.

Chapter Thirty-Nine

3:07 a.m., Sunday, April 21, 2019

F*uck, I'm getting too old for this.*
Even while it's unfolding, Mike knows he's stuck in the same recurring dream. It's so predictable that he feels like a spectator in his own nightmare. He's running, getting closer, chest pounding, mouth dry. He's at the door again, yanking it open. Always the same click—not the bang of a gun, just the click of it malfunctioning. And then Sal's head is blown off, his body collapsing against Mike, blood everywhere. Every damned time. The only difference is, sometimes there's a blur as the car squeals away, and sometimes he wakes up before the car comes by. Either way, Mike is always overcome by that familiar wave of helplessness. And then he wakes up.

Mike opened his eyes and reached for his iPhone. 3:10 am.

Shit.

As per usual, following one of these nightmares, he found himself drenched in sweat. His t-shirt and boxers clung to him like a second skin, the sheets thoroughly soaked with his blanket wrapped around his legs in a tight, unwelcome embrace.

After disentangling himself and removing his soaked clothing, Mike pulled his bathrobe on and headed downstairs.

"Ach, me son," Mary-Margaret said, turning from the stove, her own bathrobe tightly wrapped around her.

"Jesus!" he said, almost tripping over the Jack Russell terrier that was now running around his feet.

"What are ye doin' up at this hour of the night, Michael?"

"The same could be said of you," he said, stepping around the tiny dog.

"I'm makin' meself a cuppa," she replied indignantly. "Any ejit could see that. But ye...?"

"Have you got enough water to make two?"

Mary-Margaret looked at her son, taking in the state of him.

"I've an ocean of joy and a sea of tears to fill the kettle with," she said with a sad smile. "Which would ye prefer?"

"I think water from the tap would suffice," he said, reaching for the McVittie's.

"Are we makin' a show of it, then?"

Mike did not respond.

"Ach, me son," she said. "Ye've not had an easy go of it lately, have ye?"

"Lately?" Mike grunted as he took a biscuit from the box.

"Are ye plannin' on gobblin' them all up yerself, or might ye spare one or two for yer aged mam?"

"Sorry," Mike said, dumping a handful of cookies onto a plate that had been left on the counter just a few hours earlier.

"Let's take it into the other room, shall we?" Mary-Margaret said, passing by him with two mugs of tea in her hands.

The mother and son sat at the dining room table.

"Now," Mary-Margaret said. "What's troublin' ye, lad?"

"You might be right," he said with a heavy sigh.

"Of course I'm right," Mary-Margaret said, taking a sip of tea. "About what?"

"About packing it in."

Mary-Margaret froze, the mug still at her lips.

"Ye are jokin' me, aren't ye?" she said.

"No. Why would you think that?" Mike asked.

"Mister Big City Detective packin' it in? What in the name of all that's holy would ye do with yerself, or would ye be one of those silly buggers who drops dead a month or two after retirin'?"

"I don't know, but I don't want to do this anymore. And I thought you wanted me to—"

"Well, ye thought wrong, didn't ye? I mean, yes, I want ye to stop gettin' yerself beat up and shot at and all of that nonsense. And yes, I want ye to stop workin' around the clock. And yes, I want ye to get more rest and eat better and stop drinkin' so much and the like, but I never said I wanted ye to pack it in now, did I?"

"Well, yes," Mike stammered. "You did. At dinner the other—"

"Ye heard wrong," she exclaimed and then, her voice softening, asked, "What is it, exactly, that yer doin' that's not suitin' ye?"

"Sitting here at three in the morning drinking tea and having cookies with you, for starters," he said with a slight smile.

"Well, if it's about me livin' here, I was just beginnin' to think that maybe—"

"No, it's not that," Mike said.

"Oh. Well then. This must be serious. So what is it, Michael? What's got ye up at this ungodly hour, sittin' across from yer mam, havin' a cuppa?"

"I don't know."

"Michael," she said, placing her hand on his arm. "Whatever 'tis that's tearin' ye apart

isn't goin' to go away when ye hand in yer badge. Ye do know that, don't ye? We don't just turn off those kinds of things. When I left St. Francis, for example, I didn't just let it all go, now, did I? I'm still—"

"I know," Mike said, looking down at his tea.

"Ach, if yer Auntie Brid was here, she'd be able to sort out yer troubles just from lookin' at the money on yer tea."

"Very scientific, Mom. I'm glad Rachel Shimner-Lewis hasn't heard of—"

"Don't ye be temptin' the Fates, me son. In any event, I've got to get meself back to bed.

Big day tomorrow, bein' Sunday and all," she said, pushing herself up from the table. "The New Girl has yet to put out a proper Order of Service, and that daft Laura-Jean McQueen would have us all drinkin' hot water at the afterwards if I didn't...ye see, it never leaves ye, does it. Now, be sure to bring Carla by for dinner. And maybe see if Mandy and her lot want to come over as well. I'm sure a nice plate of corned beef and cabbage would do them a world of good. Right. I'm off, then. Be a luv and take the mugs and the plate into the kitchen before ye go up. No need to have the place lookin' like a pigsty."

Mike watched his mother gripping the rail as she went up the stairs, her step careful and almost laboured. He never recalled her looking that old before. He took the last biscuit off the plate, dunked it into his tea, and sighed. Surprisingly, the dog remained downstairs with him.

That last-minute bartender. Was he really Malcolm Oakes, or just a last-minute bartender who happened to be named Malcolm? And that night. Was Amanda really the target of the drive-by, or was it just a case of wrong place, wrong time? Had the intended target actually been someone else who was standing in front of the pub at the same time as...? And the other drive-by. Was it meant for Amanda, or could there be something going on with Kristie that hasn't come to light yet? Or have I imagined it all?

Mike winced as he rubbed his shoulder.

No. It all happened.

And what about the gun that killed Callo—Bridget? It was Bridget who was killed. My Bridget. My...friend, Bridget. That was the same gun they used to try to shoot Amanda. And it was found in a dumpster in Niagara Falls. Lots of criminals go to Niagara Falls. What if her murder had nothing to do with Malcolm Oakes? And what if that particular gun had just been handed off to someone else who was intending to kill someone in front of the pub that night? And what if...?

"Are ye comin' up to bed, luv, or are ye startin' the day early?" Mary-Margaret called down.

"I'm on my way up," he called back.

"Don't forget to put the dishes—"

"I won't."

"And Wee Phil. Wherever he may be. Let him out for a piddle or he'll have me up at half five."

Mike opened the back door to let the tiny dog dash out before gathering up the dishes and putting them into the dishwasher. He whistled softly at the door, and the dog ran back in before charging upstairs into the bedroom that had become his mother's. Mike closed the back door and went up the stairs. He lay on his bed, not bothering to take his bathrobe off, and looked up at the ceiling, the glow of the streetlights making shadows on the walls.

* * *

"Are you okay, Michael?" Carla asked, looking across her desk at her partner.

Mike looked up from his keyboard with an equal mix of exhaustion and mild annoyance. "Peachy. Why?"

"Are you...?"

"No, I'm not," he stated, knowing what she was thinking. "I just didn't sleep much last night."

"Just checking. I wouldn't want—"

"I'm fine. Want to grab a coffee while it's—" he cut in, eager to redirect the conversation.

"Don't use the 'q word'," Carla cautioned in a sing-song voice. "Let me just finish this and we'll go."

"Sure," he said.

"Aren't you curious?" she asked.

"About what?"

"About what I'm doing. I'll give you a clue. The cells are empty, so I'm definitely not processing a body."

"I have no idea. What are you doing?"

"I'm putting in for the D spot in the MCU," she said with a huge smile.

"Well done," he said approvingly. "I guess this means no more Coco Chanel suits for you."

"Right?" she said with a laugh. "Although I don't think I have to look completely homeless to be a part of the unit, either. Honestly, Michael. And to think they get a clothing allowance to dress like that."

The unmistakable click-clack of Detective Sergeant Amanda Black's stiletto heels echoed on the tile floor in the hallway.

"Ah, my favourite detective team," she said as she poked her head into the office.

"I bet you say that to all the detectives," Mike said with a smile. "What are you really doing here?"

"I work for this organization, remember?"

"Yeah, but aren't you getting cranked on Tuesday?"

"Yes. And this is Sunday."

"And didn't—"

"How's Kristie?" Carla asked, sensing that her partner was likely going to say something anyone else would have kept to themselves.

"She's doing great. It's amazing, really. I get a paper cut, and it takes three weeks to heal. The mark from where the bullet entered already looks like a scab from an ingrown hair."

"And how is Nichole handling everything?" Carla asked.

"Seems to be okay, surprisingly. Her friends, as dorky as they may be, are really rallying."

"How's Tony?" Mike asked.

"He's good," Amanda said. "Thanks again for that."

"So," Carla said, "I took your advice."

"Which bit?" Amanda asked.

"About putting in for the spot. Although Michael is just reminding me that it'll mean another wardrobe adjustment, but it's not like I haven't already made a few adjustments over the past few months."

"I think you'll have a huge impact in that office," Amanda said.

"I'm sure I will," Carla replied, pressing SEND.

"I'll get my notes in for the Samuels case today," Mike said.

"And the shooting last Wednesday?" Amanda asked.

"Oh, right."

"Classic denial, Michael. Not healthy," Carla said under her breath.

"They're waiting for them," Amanda said.

"Sure," Mike replied. "We were just going out for a coffee. Want us to pick you up one?"

"No. I actually came in here to talk to you, Mike," Amanda said. "Do you mind, Carla?"

"Oh, no," Carla said politely. "I was just going to pop up to the front to see if we could pick up anything for anyone else."

"I'm not picking up for the whole station," Mike grumbled.

"Then I will," Carla said, pushing her chair away from the desk. "Enjoy your chat."

Amanda waited until Carla had left the office.

"What's up, Boss?" Mike asked.

"Please don't—"

"Get used to it. As of Tuesday...."

"I know."

"You nervous?"

"Have you met me?" Amanda asked, her eyes bulging.

"Still...."

"I'm ready," she said with a nod.

"I'm sure you are," he said, his eyes skimming through a lengthy list of outstanding cases the auto-generator had just assigned him. As he scanned the page, he couldn't help thinking that each item seemed as insignificantly depressing as the one before it: theft from auto, assault, shoplifting. If an arrest hadn't been made at the time, solving the case was pretty unlikely now. Unless there was a pattern, in which case, it would probably be reassigned to the MCU. Maybe to Carla.

"Remember that talk we had yesterday?" Amanda asked.

"Which one?" he said, frowning at the screen.

"About Malcolm Oakes."

"And...?" Mike did not look up.

"And about how you think he's going to kill me?" she said, struggling to ignore what she had actually just said.

"Uh-huh," he said, pulling a pad of paper out of his desk drawer and jotting something down on it.

"Unless you—"

"Yep."

"You know you can't do that, right?"

"If you say so," he said, tearing off the piece of paper and setting it aside.

"Mike," Amanda said with a sigh. "Are you even listening to me?"

"Sure," he said, opening up one occurrence after another and clicking the box that read: No Further Action Taken At This Time. "I'm thinking about putting in my papers," he said, without looking away from the screen.

"What?" she said, her knees almost buckling under her.

"Yeah," he said, finally looking over at her. "I'm done."

"But—" she began, stepping closer to Mike's desk.

He looked back at the screen, leaning in, his eyes squinting. "Are they making the fonts smaller or am I going blind?"

"I don't want you to go," she said, her voice barely above a whisper.

"You know," he said, looking over at her with a chuckle, "I think you may be the first woman to have ever said that to me."

"I'm serious, Crumply Pants. I need you to stay."

"Really? And do what? Clear dip-shit occurrences? Process Fail to Appears?" he said, returning to the monitor. He opened up another one of the cases he'd just been assigned and skimmed the synopsis. "Spend every night and day in this hamster wheel?"

"I need you," she stated, leaning against his desk, "to find Malcolm Oakes."

"Already did," he said, unmoved. "More than once. You want me to deliver him on a platter, too?"

"No. I need you to bring him to justice."

Mike stopped what he was doing and looked up at Amanda.

"Okay. Maybe that was a bit much," she conceded with a shrug. "But I do need you to put him before the courts so that we can lock him away forever."

"That ship has sailed. Many times," Mike said, his focus returning to the monitor in front of him.

Amanda sighed. She saw Carla standing outside the office door, waiting to come in. Amanda shook her head. Carla disappeared towards the front desk again.

"I need you to promise me two things, Mike," Amanda said once Carla was gone.

"Why? You're not the boss of me," he said, opening another case.

"For god's sake, Mike. You sound like my kids...ten years ago. Come on. Promise."

"Sure," he said, taking a deep breath as he pushed his chair away from his desk to look at her.

"First, you won't retire."

"Ever?" he said with a smile.

"Well, not soon."

"And...?"

"Promise that you'll help me arrest Malcolm Oakes."

"As of Tuesday, you won't be arresting anyone."

"I know. So I guess it's up to you to arrest him. Not kill him. Arrest him. Promise?"

Mike didn't answer, running his hand through his hair, sighing again before turning back to the monitor instead.

"Mike," Amanda said, straightening up, "you're not a killer. And you don't golf. Neither solitude nor retirement would work for you. Stay here for another couple of years and do your job. Please."

"I do have a life, you know."

"Really?" Amanda chortled as she stepped back from his desk.

"Well, Max is going away next year," Mike said, still opening and closing occurrences, "so I guess that'll change things. And, if Carla gets that MCU spot...."

"Julia Vendramini will be your partner when Carla...*if* Carla—"

"How do you know?" Mike said, looking over at Amanda.

"Paul and I talk. A lot."

"So who would get stuck with Russ, not that I care," he said, returning to the monitor.

"Well, that's another thing. Julia's told Paul that she'll retire if she doesn't get a new partner, so, if you go, she'll likely go, too, and then who's left?"

"Lots of people," he said, and then looked a bit closer at the occurrence on the screen in front of him. "This is kind of different. Should go to the Family Violence Unit, but—"

"Not that were there. Hoagy's dead now, and the rest of us aren't getting any younger."

"How did you know he was dead?"

246

"Word travels. And some of us keep in touch."

"Oh."

"Not like some people, who just let things fade away," she added.

Mike stopped what he was doing.

"I want you here," Amanda said, lowering her voice. "On the job, with me, when Malcolm Oakes gets convicted of *everything*."

"You mean...?" he said, his full attention now on her.

"Yes. Every fucking murder we can pin on him. Every fucking child exploitation charge we can find. Every—"

"I don't need to be here for that," Mike said, looking away.

"What about Chelsea Hendricks?" Amanda asked.

Mike froze.

"If she's not dead," Amanda said, "then we need to find her. We owe it to her mother."

Mike said nothing.

"Mike, that asshole tried to kill my kid. I will find him. And I need you there to make sure I don't kill him."

Mike said nothing.

"And neither will you," she added.

"I—"

"If you could have, I'm sure you already would have. And I never understood that. Until I saw my girl—my first born— go into that O.R. with a bullet in her leg. Before that, I believed in due process. I believed in the justice system. I believed in it all."

"And now?"

"I believe in vigilante justice, but I'm smart enough to know that the only one that'll hurt is me. And my family."

"Yeah, I don't think you'd do too well spending the rest of your life in PC, either."

"Mike, stick around a while longer and let's get that fucker into court. And then into jail. Where he'll be the one rotting in protective custody instead of me."

"One under arrest," Ricky Jergensen said as he came into the office from the door leading to the tiny interview rooms. "A really beaut."

"Where is he?" Mike asked.

"In the cells."

"Why isn't he in one of the interview rooms?"

"He shit and pissed himself while he was getting booked."

"Lovely," Mike said, closing one app and then opening up another on his screen. "Arrest number?"

"And to think you'd want to give all of this up," Amanda said. "I've got to get back to my real job, so you boys promise to play nice with each other, okay?"

"Just don't piss me off," Mike muttered under his breath.

"And Mike?" Amanda said as she moved away from his desk.

"Hmm?"

"Thank you."

Once she had left the office and Jergensen was logged onto the computer behind him, Mike took a moment to gather his thoughts. For years, he'd told himself he needed to catch that bastard for murdering Sal. Then, after Bridget... But now he understood—it wasn't for them. It was for him. It was about proving that justice, fairness, and goodness—those things he'd clung to like beacons in the dark—still meant something.

No. I'm not retiring. Not until I've seen this case through, or at least done whatever it takes to make sure Amanda Black doesn't become Malcolm Oakes' next victim.

"You're welcome," he said softly, the words fading before they left his lips.

About the Author

Desmond P. Ryan spent almost thirty years as a detective with the Toronto Police Service, working in some of the city's toughest and most challenging neighborhoods. His experience on the frontlines of law enforcement—dealing with everything from routine investigations to high-risk operations—gives his crime fiction a raw, unflinching authenticity. Whether he's digging into the dark, gritty world of policing in *The Mike O'Shea Series* or spinning a more offbeat mystery in *A Pint of Trouble*, Desmond Ryan's writing pulls no punches. His stories reflect the harsh realities of crime, the toll it takes on those who fight it, and the flawed humanity of everyone involved. Desmond Ryan's characters—complicated, sometimes broken, but always real—are shaped by years spent on the streets, making his books as hard-edged as the world they depict.

AUTHOR WEBSITE:

https://realdesmondryan.com/

SOCIAL MEDIA HANDLES:

Insta: https://www.instagram.com/desmondpryan/

YouTube: https://www.youtube.com/@DesmondPRyan
Facebook: https://www.facebook.com/DesmondPRyan/

Also by Desmond P. Ryan

Mike O'Shea Series:
  10-33 Assist PC
  Death Before Coffee
  Man at the Door
  Blind Spot

A Pint of Trouble Series:
  Mary-Margaret and The Case of The Lapsed Parishioner
  Mary-Margaret and The Case of The Thieving Barmaid

www.ingramcontent.com/pod-product-compliance
Lightning Source LLC
Chambersburg PA
CBHW020616110726

47899CB00002B/524